Maloney's Law by Anne Brooke

MALONEY'S LAW BY ANNE BROOKE

CHAPTER 1

The glow from my ex-lover's cigarette lights up the warm night air, and I catch a faint impression of his hand's shadow before the darkness descends again.

In the silence, I sense rather than see his lips draw on the smoky pleasure, tingling tar and need wafting into his waiting lungs. I don't ask to share it, and he doesn't offer. More than anything, this reminds me of the last time we almost had sex.

He coughs.

"I suppose you're wondering why I asked to see you, Paul," he says, and his voice makes me shut my eyes for a moment. In the deeper blackness, I can see the strong, sensual lines of his face as clear as if it were daylight. "I mean why now? Not the greatest of meeting places for us, is it?"

"You're here, aren't you?" I reply and wait for him to speak.

It's 2:02 A.M. and, when he gave me the choice, I picked this disused chapel in Hackney for our meeting. It's near home, it's private, and it's dark. Inside, it's a good place for sex, if you're desperate and don't mind the broken glass. I thought he wouldn't turn up, but I was wrong.

For a moment, he seems to be trying to choose his words, then he says, "I need your help, you see."

I laugh. There doesn't seem any other way of responding.

"I'm serious. It's a business offer."

I shut up. Money is money, whoever it comes from. And five years, ten months, and five days in my job as the proprietor of Maloney Investigations (anything considered) has taught me never to turn down business.

"Go on," I say, and as I speak, a lone car swings into the street, its headlights illuminating our shapes and outlining the solid lines of the chapel that frames Dominic.

Instinct kicks in, and I propel him back into the safety of the doorway. It smells of cannabis and urine. As the car approaches at a crawl, I shield him with my body, pull the cigarette from his mouth and kiss him. He tastes of nicotine and mint. The blokes in the car shout abuse out of the window, but, thank God, don't stop, and after a tense few seconds, they drive off into the darkness. I don't want to stop either, but when the danger's past, I'm the first to pull away.

When I do so, I wonder who he's screwing now—some young, good-looking bastard, I bet. Yeah, I can just see it, and the look on Dominic's face when he gets what he wants, too. Maybe I can try to mix business with pleasure? As he's the last man I've slept with, it must be three years, four months, and one week since I had sex at all. At least with someone else in the room. I wonder if that makes me unusual.

"Sorry," I say. "Thought they might leave us alone if they didn't recognize you. Cruisers only."

He nods. "You were right. Can I have my cigarette back now?"

I pass it to him, my fingers lingering on his before he eases them away. He doesn't comment. Instead, he wipes the back of his free hand over his mouth, and I blink back tears.

When he speaks, he speaks quickly. "There's a business I want to investigate, buy if the money's right. Information Technology. They deal with Eastern European markets, but there's something not quite right about them, and I want to know what."

"What is it? Drugs? Porn?"

He shakes his head. "No. I'd know if it was. But I want you to look into it anyway…see what you can find. My business has to be clean; there can't be any dirt thrown that might stick. Do you understand?"

"Sure. Sounds simple enough. You say something's not quite right, but you don't think it's serious. So what's got you suspicious?"

"Rumor only. You know what the business world is like. I want to be certain, that's all."

Again his answer is too fast, and I don't believe him.

"Why don't you use some of your own hot-shot investigators? I know you have them. Won't they be able to do your legwork for you?"

"No."

"Why not?"

He drops his cigarette and crushes it underfoot before lighting another. In the flash of fire, I catch the intensity of his gaze.

"Even my own people have been known to talk, and I don't want to give my competitors reasons for suspicion. Not at the stage of negotiations I'm at now. I want someone who, if they go down, won't take me with them."

His reasons are too slick, too unconnected, but his last statement makes me blink again. He was always honest with me…something I never got used to.

"Yes, I know what you'll say," he continues. Even though I have no idea what that might be. "You'll say we used to fuck each other regularly, in spite of my situation, and that would be enough to crucify anyone in my position. But no one knows this, except you and me. And that time-waster assistant of yours. So if it becomes public knowledge, I'll know who to blame, won't I? And when I hold a grudge…"

He doesn't have to complete the sentence. I've read enough in the papers about the boardroom—and backroom—battles fought and won by Mr. Dominic Allen to know the extent of his power. Oh yes, more than anyone

I understand his strength compared to my weakness and I've almost made up my mind to walk away from his problems, and my past, when he speaks again. This time his voice is softer.

"And there's another reason," he says. "You're the only one I can trust. Please, will you help me?"

*   *   *

"You don't have to help him, you know. He'll only screw you over, like last time."

First rule of PI work: if you have to hire a secretary, or any staff, never get someone who knows you. They'll only end up telling you stuff you don't want to hear. And, worse, it might even be the truth.

"No, he won't," I say, wishing again for a way to afford more than my one-room office plus kitchen. "This time, I'm wise to him. Anyway, it's cash. I'd be crazy not to take it."

"You'd be crazy to do it, too." Jade stops staring at her computer screen and throws me one of her accusing looks from behind her blonde lashes. "You'll just go stupid again."

I grimace at Jade's use of the phrase, "go stupid." It covers the time, nearing the end of my eleven-month affair with Dominic Allen, and afterward, when I stopped eating, left hundreds of pleading messages on his mobile, and lurked night after night outside his house in Islington waiting for one glimpse of him. After seven weeks of this, on the morning of Friday, June 1, in the office, I'd smashed every single breakable item I owned in front of Jade's horrified eyes. I'd then collapsed onto the floor and sobbed for an hour and a half without being able to stop.

It was a difficult time for us both, and I can understand her concern. Now, though, I'll make sure it's different. I'm older and calmer for one thing and my dealings, if any, with Dominic will be carried out in the light of this new maturity.

"No, I won't 'go stupid,'" I say with a smile. "He's history. So much so that I was fine when we met last night. Or rather early this morning. It was—"

"Did you snog him?"

"What?"

"You heard."

"No, don't be silly. Of course I didn't. He's a client, or might be. I wouldn't be that unprofessional, would I? What the hell kind of a question is that anyway?"

"So you did then."

"But not in the way you think. I was carrying out my duties, protecting him from the greedy eyes of the public. You know he's better known than Beckham. Almost."

"Enjoy it?"

I pause and feel my face redden. "Is George Michael gay?"

Jade nods, her lips pursed. "And while your tongue was reacquainting itself with his tonsils, did you happen to ask after Mrs. Allen and the two little Allens? Or did Mr. Allen's wife and children not cross your mind?"

This is a dirty move, and I don't stoop to answer it. Second rule of PI work: don't employ someone who's moral. Jade has a Baptist background, though I've never seen her enter a chapel since I've known her, and that's twelve years and ten months. But a religious upbringing can never be wiped away. It certainly hasn't stopped her asking a knife-twist question, which I ignore. Instead, I drop the file I've been clutching onto my desk, fling myself into my chair, and flick through the papers to find the one I want.

It takes me longer than I'd anticipated. At the end of ten minutes, I still haven't located it and, just as I'm wondering if it was one of the items I'd burnt After Dominic, there's a slight cough. When I look up, Jade is standing in front of me, holding out a mug of hot chocolate as if it's about to explode. I don't like hot chocolate, though I've never dared tell her this. It's her usual way of dealing with a crisis; Jade counts gay men as honorary women, so I just smile and take it.

"Sorry," she says.

Still unable to trust myself to speak, I nod, and she returns to her desk. While Jade starts tapping away on her keyboard again, I pretend to be looking at my file. It's hard to concentrate on what Dominic told me last night, when all I can think about is either our past or the way his lips felt under mine seven hours ago. I wonder if he's remembering, too, but it's unlikely. He was never one to look back. All he'd done when I lunged at him was to tolerate my kiss before wiping it away and getting down to business. This was a shame, as at 2:05 A.M. last night—or again is that this morning?—and indeed now, the most compelling thought in my head is the memory of how he and I first met. When—

"Paul? Paul? You okay?"

At the sound of Jade's voice, I jump, startled out of my thoughts, and look up to see her leaning over me, frowning. The scent of Anais Anais mingles with the now congealing hot chocolate.

"Yeah, sure. I'm fine. I just need… I think I'll go home for a while. I'll take the papers with me and get to grips with some of the background. If anyone calls, tell them I'm on a case." I pause in the act of getting up. "In a way, I suppose I am, if only for an initial read-through, so it won't be lying."

"Okay." Jade thrusts a slim pale blue A4 folder into my hand. "You'll be wanting this then, whatever you decide."

I glance at the empty file with a fresh label on the top right hand corner, just where I like them to be. On it is typed: The Dominic Allen Case, 11 August to… Below it is my name in italics.

"Thanks." I can't help smiling. "You're right. I'll be wanting this."

"Thought so. You'll be back later, before the end of the day?"

"Sure, see you at five-thirty."

On the way out, I look back at her, and she gives me a little wave before the solid oak door with the central spy hole clicks shut.

The eleven-minute walk home clears my head. I'm glad I don't have to commute; I hate the sweat and sourness of the bus in the morning, and it was a deliberate decision when I set up Maloney Investigations to base myself as near to home as I could. Not that the office is much: just a one-windowed room big enough for two desks and a large, black filing cabinet, with a narrow promise of a kitchen built along one end. But it's mine, and Jade's light touch with the Constable prints and seasonal flowers means clients, when they turn up, aren't frightened away. Or if they are, it's not because of the office.

Hackney's changed so much in the seven years and five months I've lived here; it's become leaner, darker at the street corners and at night when most of the drug dealing takes place. During the day, it's brighter and more strident, filled with the sound of beggars and the sight of Indian women wrapped in saris the color of desert, sky, or fire. It's poorer, too, but that's never bothered me. I hope it doesn't bother the clients. Now my stride takes me along the familiar pavement lined with small squares of brown grass, leading in their turn up to countless flats carved out of Victorian houses once owned by rich people. The air is heavy with car fumes and the taste of undiscovered dreams.

At home, I drop my jacket on the mahogany hall table, next to the emergency cigarette packet, before heading into the box-shaped kitchen and pouring myself a Highland Park. Whisky is for home, for privacy. It's medicinal. Besides, it's turning out to be one of those days, so I deserve better than the Glenfiddich. Gazing at the golden liquid as it shimmers in the glass, I wonder. One breath, two. The smoky scent of it fills my head, and I breathe out again. Then, leaning against the metal coolness of the sink, I pour the drink away, swilling the drips with tap water. It's too early for this. I promised myself once that I would never drink before six P.M., and it's a rule I've always kept. Almost always.

Still, the space in the day where I should have had a glass of whisky in my hand lies empty now so, clutching Jade's file and my papers to my chest, I wander back through the hall and into the living room. The main room, to be honest. My income isn't great. Even though I've lived here for so many years, today it's as if I'm seeing it from a new perspective: the shabbiness, the old beige sofa with its light blue throw—a present from Jade—and the glass coffee table with its immovable scratches. Not to mention the pine dining table for four with the mismatched chairs, the scattering of crime novels and old newspapers, mainly The Independent, which hide the shortcomings of the carpet. Against all this and at the far end of the room is the magnificent Victorian fireplace and mantelpiece. Upon it stand my only ornaments: two Staffordshire dogs, which were a present from my mother for my eighteenth. God knows why.

What would Dominic see if he were here? The dogs he'd always hated, but what would he see that was different from three years and four months ago?

Answer: nothing. Nothing has changed, nothing at all.

Dumping the papers onto the sofa, I stride into my bedroom, where the deep green duvet still lies crumpled at the foot of the bed where I left it this morning. In the long mirror inside the wardrobe, my face gives nothing away.

I take off my clothes. Slowly, as if peeling the layers could remove the present. When I'm naked, I gaze at my image for a long time, trying to see myself as if I'm someone else. There are many things here that Dominic would remember: my face, thin and narrow, a throwback to my paternal grandfather; green eyes framed by short, almost black hair—a wolf on the hunt so another lover told me once; a long body, dark wavy chest hair leading down to strong, muscular legs; an average cock, not too small, thank God, though I've always wished it larger. Don't we all?

There are things here that he wouldn't remember, too: a touch of grey around the hairline; a slight softening of the belly—must get to the gym again on a regular basis if I can afford it—and the scar on my right arm where two years ago a suspect knifed me. It still hurts a little in winter. My eyes are more cautious, too.

Would he find this attractive? Would he?

Damn it. Damn me. Swinging away from the mirror, I drag my clothes back on, curse myself again, and head back into the living room for the comfort of the sofa and the papers I must read this afternoon.

It will become a thick folder, containing, as it will, the outline of DG Allen Enterprises and all the facts of the company Dominic wants to buy. The Delta Egypt Group, maker and supplier of IT accessories and software games to Egypt and northern Africa. Headquarters in Cairo and four hundred-strong. The name is familiar, though I don't know why. It appears to be doing okay and, in my non-expert opinion, the accounts look to be in order. Why is Dominic suspicious, and why now? I should have asked him this last night. Never mind, I'd be seeing him again—at his request—in five days' time for an initial opinion meeting. In five days, four hours and…

God, I should just stick to the business and stop obsessing over time.

Pushing the memory of Dominic out of my mind—never an easy task—I focus myself in the way suggested by the counselor I'd seen for a while after my breakdown. Breathe slowly and concentrate on one aspect of whatever is in front of you. Let it enter and fill your mind so there's no room for anything else. Live in the papers I see—the dark print, the white smoothness.

All very well, but everything I'm looking at has some connection with my one-time lover. The scent of him is clinging to the pages. The counselor never told me what to do under these circumstances. Frowning at my own cunning weakness, I grab the first set of documents and try to plunge into their murky depths to read again all about Delta Egypt.

After a while, I can see why Dominic would want to buy them. They're not too big and their client base would give him access to a geographical market he's never yet tapped into. In his position, and if I were a cutthroat, well-known businessman, I'd do the same. They can't be doing that well either, not in the current economy, but they aren't large enough to have drawn other enemy takeover bids. Apart from Dominic's. He's done well to find them. So why is he so suspicious?

At last, I come to the end of the papers, and I don't know if I've gained much of use from them. Underneath those is the file I took from the office, the file from my lockable drawer Jade doesn't know about. I began keeping it there three weeks into my breakdown recovery regime, believing if I kept it at home I would read it too much. Now it's only in the flat at weekends, when it's easier to update. In it are all the cuttings about Dominic and everything he's ever done that's been in the newspapers since two months after he and I started our affair.

In front of me now lie pictures and articles about him, his family, his successes, his fortune, his public life. Still it tells me nothing about the man. It's only at the end of my search that I find what I think I'm looking for, what I've only half-remembered. A small news item hidden in the corner of a page torn from The Financial Times, the date scrawled in biro across the top. Wednesday, March 6: "Radical entrepreneur Dominic Allen, pictured here on the left—as if they needed to note that even—greets Blake Kenzie, MD of newly set-up IT games manufacturer, Delta Egypt, at the recent International Business & Marketing Conference held in Cairo. Mr. Allen says…"

I put the cutting down. Of course, Dominic already knows more about Delta than he's let me think. Why? He must realize I'll find out. It's in the public domain, no matter how brief the article. What's he playing at? I'll see if he tells me the truth when I meet him on Monday, but I won't raise the subject first.

For the rest of the morning, I gather information, think, make notes, and form a plan of sorts. By three, Jade's file is no longer empty, but I'm starving. As usual, there's nothing in the flat, so I go and grab a pack of sushi and a bottle of orange juice from Sainsbury's and come home again. It's only when I'm standing in my kitchen arranging the sushi on a side plate and pouring the juice that I clutch the nearest work surface, close my eyes, gulp once, twice, to keep myself steady as the wave, whatever it is, passes. I know it will pass—it always does—and when it does, I wipe my hand across my eyes, blow my nose on a torn-off section of kitchen towel, and carry on preparing my meal.

Food for a single person with no lover. They might as well have branded that onto the packaging. I balance the final arrangement onto a tray and transfer it into the living room, where I sit at the table and pretend to eat. This isn't where I expected to be by now, not here, not alone. Until Dominic, I'd had no regular partner, at least never for any longer than a couple of months, and never in a way that entailed not looking at other blokes, acting on it, too, but it hadn't seemed to matter. I'd wanted to get serious with someone one day, become faithful, but there always seemed to be plenty of time. Then Dominic had punched himself into my existence, like a chord of wild music to a man trapped in silence, and I'd learnt what being serious, being committed, had meant. Along with several other words, too: secretive, careless, cruel. Since then, there's been nobody. I've learnt in the end how to be celibate, and now I wonder whether there'll ever be anyone in my life again.

The scattered remains of sushi, only half-eaten in spite of my hunger, stare up at me from the plate. I drink the juice, throw the sushi away, and, after a while, head back to the office.

Jade looks up when I enter. "Good to see you, Paul. The phone's been hot while you've been out. You okay?

"Uh-huh. Just a memory trip, you know? I'll recover. Who called?"

Flicking through the pad on her desk, she names a couple of my regular clients, just checking up, I imagine, on what I'm doing for them. Right now, I'm doing nothing. There's also one newbie, and I tell myself I'll contact him by the end of the day. Or maybe tomorrow.

PI Rule Number Three: never call straight back or they'll think you've got nothing to do. Make them wait.

It's the last call that interests me most. No name given, no message, just a number to call. A foreign code and not one I recognize.

"What did this one sound like?" I ask, leaning over her shoulder to study the information.

She thinks for a minute. "Male. Terse. Any age. No social graces. When he'd given the number, he put the phone straight down. Didn't even say goodbye. Oh, by the way, have you had time to catch the London paper yet?"

"No. Should I have?"

In answer, Jade unfolds her copy of today's Standard, turns to page five, and points. I pick it up and read.

"Muswell Hill Author Charged with GBH?" I query.

"No, you idiot." She snorts. "The one underneath that."

I turn back to the page and find the article she means. It's only six lines long, so I'm not surprised I missed it. Obeying instructions, I read it out for both of us.

"'Body Found Outside City Pharmacy: The body of a young woman was found abandoned last night outside one of the city's major pharmacies. She is thought to have been stabbed to death, but so far no identification has been made. Police are continuing their enquiries…'" I swallow once, telling myself not to be stupid. "Terrible stuff, Jade, of course, but what about it?"

"Look where she was found."

The remainder of the article tells me the name of the pharmacy and quotes a brief, sympathetic statement from its manager. I put the paper down and give my assistant a questioning glance.

She sighs. "It's exactly opposite DG Allen Enterprises. Don't you think that's odd?"

"You think Dominic killed her and is using me as an alibi?" I can't help but laugh at the idea. "He wasn't covered with blood and sporting a wild look in his eyes when I saw him. Far from it."

"Yes, you go ahead and laugh. But I still think it's strange that on the same night this poor woman is killed, Mr. Allen arranges to meet you again."

"It's a coincidence, sure. Look, I know Dominic isn't your favorite person, and he's a businessman with a killer instinct—excuse the pun—but you don't really believe he'd actually murder someone, do you?"

I'm still laughing as she frowns and stalks back to her desk.

"No," she says. "Not directly anyway, but there are other ways to kill, you know. Just be careful, will you?"

I stop laughing. "Okay, okay. Listen. I've got an appointment with him on Monday. I'll mention it then. See if he confesses, though he won't as he's got nothing to do with it. You're too hard on him."

"Only because—"

"I know." I hold up my hand, and Jade falls silent. "Only because you're being loyal. And I'm grateful…you know that. It seems to me there's nothing we can do until Monday anyway, so I may as well get on with other work. Where's that number you gave me? The foreign caller?"

Jade hands me the information, and I perch myself on the edge of my desk. Putting the phone on speaker mode, I dial the number she's written down in her large, open handwriting. When the line is answered, a young female voice trills something incomprehensible into the air, followed by a pause and then:

"Good afternoon. Delta Egypt. May I help you?"

I share a quick glance with Jade, then explain I've been given this number to ring. There's a pause, then the sound of an internal connection being made. It's picked up. There's a silence, but I know someone is there on the other end of the line, waiting. Waiting. Without even knowing why, I hit the disconnect button, push myself off the desk, and head to the window. It feels cool against my forehead. Outside, the traffic is caught nose to tail in the beginnings of the rush hour.

"Any thoughts?" Jade asks at my shoulder. I hadn't heard her get up.

"Not yet. I expect I'll have some soon, though. Still, at least there's one good thing to say."

"And that is?"

"I don't have to decide whether or not I take Dominic's case. Someone else has already assumed I have."

CHAPTER 2

The first thing I notice is Dominic has changed the colors of his office suite. Even though it doesn't matter how I look, I'm wearing my best suit—bought with my father's money when I first started out in this business—inherited cufflinks, and a pair of shoes I have polished until I could have used them as a shaving mirror. My hair is smoothed down with gel, but I've been twice to the Gents to check it. I don't recognize his PA and wonder what happened to the other woman, but already the new slim brunette is smiling at me and asking if I want coffee.

"No. Water, thanks."

She brings me two bottles of cool water and a glass. "Mr. Allen tells me you won't want ice. Is that right, sir?"

I nod. "Yes. Yes, that's fine. Thanks, again."

"He'll only be a few minutes, Mr. Maloney," she sings out and returns to her typing. She's faster than Jade, but it doesn't matter. There are more important things than keyboard skills. Especially for someone in my business.

I while away the four minutes before my allotted appointment by admiring the new outer office décor. The PA's desk is vast and pale and curved, the computer as thin as a sliver of ice, and the carpet a sea of soft lilac. The leather armchairs are a rich and earthy brown, and I make a mental note to upgrade my own furniture soon, if cash flow allows it. Five minutes and seventeen seconds after two-thirty PM, the internal phone finally buzzes, and the PA picks it up. "Yes, Mr. Allen," she says and smiles at me.

"Please come through now, Mr. Maloney."

She opens the door to an empire of ivory-colored paneled wood, contrasted with two red tapestries. Under my feet is a deeper pile of carpet, this time in champagne, that you could fall into and lose yourself, and straight ahead a desk with nothing on it at all except a slim, black laptop. On my left, a plinth of water falls safely forever in a sparkling sheet of movement. At the other side of the room, there are two red leather sofas, three matching armchairs, a light oak wooden table, and a large drinks cabinet. This is where Dominic is standing, his back to me.

"Thank you, Deborah," he says, without turning around. "You may leave us now. While Mr. Maloney is here, I don't want to be disturbed."

"Yes, Mr. Allen."

The door clicks shut and the two of us are alone. I stroll across the room toward him, my feet soundless, as Dominic finishes pouring drinks and at last swings 'round to face me. For a second, his eyes widen.

"You look good, Paul," he says. "Nice suit."

"You've seen it before, but thanks. I didn't want to look out of place."

"You never have. Please, sit."

It's the first time I've seen him close up in the flesh, in daylight, since we split. An extra three years, four months, and four days have only improved what was, to me, perfect to start with. He's a head taller than I am, and his dark blond hair frames grey eyes, an almost Roman nose, and full lips. I'm sure there's not an inch of fat on his muscular body, not like me right now. Today he's dressed in a charcoal suit from Jermyn Street—Dominic taught me well—matched with a blue silk shirt with gold cufflinks, no tie, and all I want to do—for starters—is ease my fingers down his face, kiss his throat, and begin to undo the buttons of that shirt. I hope he realizes none of this.

Exuding a shimmer of subtle aftershave and seductive power, he gestures me toward a sofa, but, instead, I choose one of the single armchairs and try to get comfortable. A second later, he has placed a jug of water on the coffee table, together with two glasses, taken one for himself, and sat down on the sofa opposite me. The table lies between us, and the sunlight from the window frames him so he can see my face, but I can't see his.

I get up and choose the other chair instead. He turns to follow my movement.

"Sometimes," he says, "a cigar is just a cigar. I would have closed the blinds."

"Eventually."

He shrugs. I take a sip of my water. "You've changed the décor since I was last here."

"Of course. We all have to move on. Do you like it?"

"Sure. What's not to like? And a new PA, too. What happened to…?"

"Jacqueline? She left ten months ago."

"What for? Better prospects? More money?"

He leans back and gives me a cool, assessing gaze. "No. I asked her to leave."

"I thought you always prided yourself on choosing the right staff and keeping them."

"I had no choice. I was sleeping with her, and she became too emotionally involved. I paid her off to keep her quiet."

I gulp down my water and try not to choke. Dominic waits for me to recover, but makes no move to help.

"You never paid me off. Didn't I merit it?"

"Of course, but you would never have taken my money. You always had more pride."

This, I suppose, is true, though I'm surprised he thinks so. Especially after our last encounter. No, make that our last two encounters. "Thanks. So now you have Deborah."

"In a business sense only, thus far. I do intend to put our relationship on a more intimate footing in the near future, however, and, when I do, there's one thing I'm sure about."

"What's that?"

He smiles. "She'll be better in bed."

Than who? I want to ask. Jacqueline? Or me? But already Dominic's mind has filed the conversation and moved to the next point.

"Have you had any thoughts about Delta Egypt?" he asks. "What do you intend to do next?"

"You mean, am I going to take the case?" I say.

His response is a quick smile. "Yes, if you like. Are you going to take the case? I would appreciate it very much if you did."

"How much?"

He names a price. I double it, and after a few minutes, we reach a negotiated figure, not including reasonable expenses, which will keep Jade and me going for a good six months. Dominic won't even miss it.

"So," he says again after we've shaken hands on it, "what do you intend to do next?"

"Ask you again whether you have any practical basis, apart from business gossip, for your suspicions about Delta Egypt. Do you, Dominic?"

For two heartbeats, he doesn't answer. Then he says, "I've hired you only to give me peace of mind and a clear path for takeover. No more. No less."

"Okay," I say. "In that case, what I'll do next is the usual. Carry out what initial investigations I can here, then make contact with Delta, pose as a buyer, fly out, and pretend to do business with them. I've always fancied visiting Cairo anyway, so if it's a wasted trip and they're as clean as you hope they are, then at least I can take in some of the sights."

"Do. It's a unique city."

"You've been before?"

"Of course. I never do business with people I haven't met."

I see another chance and use it. "Any prior knowledge of Delta at all? I don't mean recently, but you IT types must meet up at all sorts of events, conferences, whatever, and if so, any impression you might have got at the time is bound to be useful."

He doesn't even blink. "No, I can't help you there."

The way he's phrased both his answers means he still hasn't broken his record of honesty with me, but even so the glass of water in my hand doesn't seem to taste so good any more. I put it back on the table and spring to my feet.

"Okay, it was worth a shot. If there's nothing else?"

"No. Keep me informed of your progress."

"I will. You're a client now."

I'm almost at the door when my memory clicks in. I turn, and he's still sitting, just watching me. "I almost forgot. There is one thing."

"Which is?"

"Nothing to do with the case, but I see a woman was killed and left in the street outside last week. The night we met up. Turning out to be an unusual week for you."

His expression remains the same. "Rather, an unusual week for the pharmacy."

"Yes. An unfortunate coincidence."

"Indeed so. Paul?"

"Yes?"

"When you fly, I expect to pay for club class tickets, not tourist. And stay at the Mena House Oberoi. The views of the Pyramids are unparalleled."

"Fine by me." Knowing I'll get no more information from him now, I place my fingers on the door handle, my body ready to go.

"And, before you go…"

"Yes?"

"Please believe me when I say I'm sorry for what happened before, for how we ended it."

* * *

"The usual?"

Jade smiles and drops her Lulu Guinness handbag down onto the corner table we always try for at The Bell and Book on a Monday evening. "Please."

I nod and shoulder my way to the bar through groups of mixed Germans and Greeks, shirt buttons undone and sleeves rolled up, all raucous with laughter. What they're doing in Hackney is a real mystery. The dark side of London, maybe. Our work local is more East End pub than wine bar, and there's always a distinct smell of warm beer and the barman's sweat, but it's cheap, friendly, and asks no questions.

Much like my taste in men. Apart from when it comes to Dominic. Damn him for his throwaway comments. I'd been doing well, too, Mr. Professional PI, all business sense and cool assessment, but one mention of our affair from him had kicked my façade away. If only on the inside. I'd started shaking, though, once out on the street.

Now, as I wait to be served, I glance around at the dirty counter, the old beams, the faded carpet, its original pale green long since lost, and wonder what my ex-lover might think if I asked him here. Not that it matters; he'd never come.

"What's it to be then tonight, sir?"

A couple of moments later I'm weaving my way back to Jade, clutching a bottle of Waggledance and one chilled Chardonnay, dry but not too dry. She greets me with a smile that lights up the dusty air.

"Thanks."

"My pleasure."

She sips her drink, crystal half-moon earrings sparkling in the gloom, while I take a longed-for swig of my beer. By the time I wipe my mouth, she's already primed for the kill.

"Pretty boy at the end of the bar's been giving you the eye."

"Sure it's not you? Those earrings would dazzle the angels in heaven."

"Yeah, yeah, that's what you always say."

"But it's true. You keep half the jewelers of Stratford in business. It's obvious I'm paying you too much."

"Dream on." She sighs and takes another sip of her wine. "So, what do you want me to do?"

"What do you mean?"

"If you want me to vanish, I can. There are a million things I could be doing, rather than being a fag-hag for the night."

"Thanks a lot, Jade. Don't you like the boss taking you out for a well-earned drink to celebrate the fact we've broken the back of Monday?"

"I'll drink anything as long as it's free," she says. "But, seriously, why don't you take a look? He's still interested. Even in spite of me. That at least shows determination."

Groaning, I put down my beer and turn 'round. Over the years, I've learnt that when Jade has that look in her eye, it's best to give in with grace. I'll only have to give in with humiliation later on if I don't. At once, I see the bloke she means. He's on his own at the left of the bar, one drink in front of him, so he's not waiting for someone.

And she's right—he's pretty. Young, maybe not even twenty yet, blond hair, willowy, dressed for sex with tight, fuck-me jeans putting everything on view. If I was a couple of years younger, then maybe, but even though he won't be going home alone tonight, it's not going to be me having the pleasure. Even if I was up for it, I don't want a blond; I've had my fill of them. As I'm thinking this, pretty boy catches my eye and smiles, the sort of smile that promises everything and as soon as you want it, sir. Hooker, for sure. Not my scene any more. I frown and turn away.

"So?" Jade asks.

"No, thanks. You'd have to pay for that one, and even if I wanted to, which I don't, I'm not sure I could afford it."

"Oh, well." She shrugs. "It was worth a try. So, as it seems I've got you all evening after all, and don't think I'm complaining because I'm not, why don't you talk me through Mr. Allen's case? Seeing as you appear to be taking it on."

I take a deep breath and tell her everything I know. It isn't much.

"That surprise you?" she asks, her scarlet-and-white stripe fingernails tapping at her glass.

"No, not really. Not after that phone call with the Delta Egypt number attached. Maybe I should've waited for whoever was at the end of that line to speak, but something tells me it wouldn't have been much help."

"What about the meeting with Mr. Allen? Did you glean anything useful?"

"No. He won't tell me why he lied about not knowing Delta Egypt and its managing director, Blake Kenzie, from the past, even though I gave him all the chances to do so. And he won't tell me anything more about his suspicions."

"Sounds like the Mr. Allen we know." Jade shrugs, then adds, "Did you remember to ask him about the woman?"

"Yes, but only just as I was about to go. There wasn't any reaction, and I don't think he's—" I break off as something occurs, something I haven't thought of.

"What? You don't think he's… What?"

"There wasn't any reaction," I say again, this time more slowly. "But maybe there should have been. He didn't ask me why I raised the issue. That's odd. Somehow. Don't ask me how. Tomorrow, I'll do some more research and pull in a few favors, if I still have any left. I'll need your help, too, once I know what we should be looking for. Might be nice to have something to go on when I'm in Cairo. Fourth rule of PI work: never give up hope."

"You're such a dreamer, Paul." Jade takes a sip of her wine. "Is that rule more important than Maloney's Law?"

I haven't thought about Maloney's Law for a while. When I'd first taken her on five years ago, she'd been as keen as a rookie on a stakeout to know all about the business and how I dealt with the exaggerations, prevarications, and simple lies that come my way. Not just from suspects, but from clients, too, God help them.

"How do you know what's true?" she'd asked me. "How do you tell which one's right?"

At the time I'd invented Maloney's Law on the basis that I'd better impress her with some kind of professional expertise and moral standing, but since then, it had stuck and assumed an importance all of its own. And even though—after Dominic, to be honest—it's more or less faded away, I still like the idea of it.

"Hmm, Maloney's Law. Can't remember that one, but, hey, good name. You'd better remind me."

Her answer is a quick and thankfully not too hard punch on the arm from across the table. "Don't be stupid. You know. It's…"

"Sometimes you just have to trust that someone is telling the truth," we chorus in unison and drain our drinks.

Time for another round. And I'm happy to pay again. With the money from Dominic, we could probably afford the pub. Just about. Waiting my turn at the bar, I see pretty boy has gone and think, yes, Maloney's Law is fine as far as it goes, as long as there's no evidence to the contrary. That, as always, is the crucial question.

Right now, of course, some kind of connection between facts is what I need. And I'm not going to find it here.

Neither, it appears later, am I going to find it by ringing 'round the six business and three press contacts I have.

*　　*　　*

Tuesday afternoon finds me, feet on the desk, folding sheets of paper to impossible smallness and arranging them in color-coordinated piles.

"How's it going?" Jade sashays her way in from the kitchen, deposits her chamomile tea on her desk and gives me a shrewd glance. Her earrings seem larger today.

Fierce-looking diamond shapes that almost reach her neck. She must be worried about something. Probably me.

"Fantastic. I can tell you how effective the Delta Egypt marketing department is, as well as show you a public record of their last three years' annual reports. I can also give you a full and detailed account of the personality, lifestyle, and future plans of Mr. Blake Kenzie. He's a man born to an Egyptian mother and an American father, and he seems to have worked his way up from a poor rural Nile background to the dazzling halls of Cairo society purely by dint of his own saintliness. He's earned a fortune from business deals, but makes regular and generous donations to local causes, including, of course, political parties destined to win. That explains his popularity."

"So he's a manipulator and a cheat with something to hide?"

"As always, your gift for summary gets right to the point."

"Thank you. He seems much like our client then. Apart from the background."

"That's unfair. And you know it. By the way, are those new earrings?"

"Sorry." She hesitates. "And don't change the subject. Do you want to hear how I've got on?"

"If it's going to be any help."

I lean back, but not so far that I fall over, and prepare to listen to what snippets of gold Jade may have been able to dig up. She's one of the best computer hackers I know, and I like to think I provide a legal outlet for her skills that otherwise, bearing in mind her moral code, would go to waste.

Nine minutes later, I'm flipping through her comprehensive report. It tells me that, although Blake Kenzie has no known police record, there are periods of time in his business and personal life, sometimes stretching to weeks, that are unaccounted for. Not that he has much of an obvious personal life, with no wife or apparent partner—of either sex—and no known children. Not many friends either, or none who will admit to it. He stands alone. What is Dominic doing with him? All this is good stuff.

However, the information that earns Jade the salary I pay her is the sheet of paper at the end of her report— Blake Kenzie's business schedule. He's in the Cairo office on Thursday. Two days' time. A press call to Delta Egypt in Jade's best journalist voice confirms it, and by the time she puts down the phone, I'm ringing the airline to book the flight.

When I've finished, I give her a thumbs up. "I have no idea how you do it, but thanks. You're a genius."

"I know. And you're a PI. Who are you going as?"

In answer, I unlock my desk drawer and bring out my business cards folder. Not other people's, but mine. Whenever I need to pretend to be someone else for a client, I always have several business cards made up, as you never know when they'll be useful again. The one I choose today is one I used for the first corporate case I ever had, and I'm rather proud of it: matte black background with gold scales logo and lettering, Paul Maloney, Special Investigations, International Monopolies & Markets.

"I never thought we'd see that one again," Jade says. "We must be going posh. Does the patch-through number still work?"

It does, though not before several phone calls and some speedy testing. Not that I think it'll make any difference.

I'm assuming Mr. Kenzie knows my name already and won't be fooled, but there's no harm in making it look good.

When we're done, I smile at my assistant, who coughs and fiddles with something on her desk, something I can't see.

"Yes?" I say.

"What?"

"You're coughing and fiddling with paper. I know the signs by now. What's up?"

"Nothing, I think. It's just..."

"Go on. Tell me."

She sighs, straightens her shoulders, then stands. Clutching a few sheets in her hands, she walks over. I catch a glimpse of what looks like a typewritten report that she lays, face down, in front of me.

"I found this," she says. "I don't know if you want to look at it, and you don't have to, but I thought it might be useful."

That said, she goes back to her desk, sits, and carries on with her work. I turn over the report, and the scent of this morning's roses seems to wash over my face, clinging to my skin. It's a draft report on the dead woman—initial findings, assumed cause of death, and preliminary, if so far abortive, police investigations. Her throat has been cut, and there's some evidence of sexual activity, but it's not conclusive.

Jade hasn't printed off the pictures with the report, although I know there must be some and I also know I won't ask for them. There's no point. The woman here, a slim brunette, is thought to be in her early twenties, so there's no need for me to check any photographs. The body has no identification. The only items recovered, apart from her clothes, are a silver necklace with one small star and a torn-off scrap of paper scrawled with the word Bluesky, the latter found neatly folded in her bra. A plea has already gone out for reports of any missing women, with no results as yet. Good luck to them. It isn't much to go on.

"Bluesky?" I ask.

Jade looks up and shrugs. "Sorry. I don't know what it means. It's just business-speak."

"True. Not much help then."

"You okay?"

Snapping the report shut, I place it on the edge of my desk, as far away as possible. "Sure. Good work, Jade. Doesn't seem much there of use to anyone in terms of identification. They'll have to rely on dental records if no one comes forward to claim her."

She nods, but says no more.

By the end of the day, I'm as ready as I'll ever be. I hope.

"You dancing tonight?" I ask as Jade switches off her computer and reaches for her jacket. Tuesdays are her salsa nights, but sometimes in August, she and the other girls from the class don't bother and just go drinking instead.

"Sure. With these new earrings, why wouldn't I be? You coming?"

"What do you think?"

"Coward. You know you'd love it if you tried."

"Not my scene, no matter how much you ask me. Besides, I need to be my best for tomorrow, assuming your research is right."

"Of course it's right," she starts before realizing I'm joking. "Oh, very funny. Are you sure Cairo is ready for you?"

Cairo may well be ready for me, but I'm not prepared for it. Or the chauffeur.

*   *   *

The moment I step off the plane, the heat wraps around me like another, stickier layer of skin. By the time the customs men are waving me through, hardly glancing at my passport, my shirt is welded to my back and I'd pay a month's salary for water. Not having any change makes water impossible. The smallest of my Egyptian pound notes not only seems to have been processed through the digestive system of a camel, but will probably be the equivalent of two months' wages for the average water seller. The best thing to do is get a taxi to the hotel, where I can have all the water I want, together with some decent beer. Plus points all round.

I'm about to head to the taxi rank when a tall man, dressed in a uniform I don't recognize, steps in front of me. He's holding a silver rectangle with my name emblazoned on it, and it's all I can do to avoid the pull of instinct that makes me want to push him down and run. Not the best idea in an airport full of armed officials.

"Pole Melanie?" the man says, grinning and nodding, and it's another moment before I recognize he's saying my name.

"Yes?"

"Good, good. I know you from photo, sir. You have car, yes?"

"Not yet, no, I'm just on my way—"

"No, no! You not understand. There is a car booked for you. By Mr. Allen. He has booked a car for you, yes? To Mena House, yes? Please, sir, follow me."

He leads me to a dark blue Mercedes gleaming in the sun. Next to the battered old Peugeots and Renaults I've glimpsed steaming for business at the taxi rank, it's a racehorse amongst donkeys. There's just one question.

"Who's paying?" I ask my driver.

"No problem, sir. Mr. Allen, he pays for everything. Even baksheesh, yes?" He gives me a knowing look, eases the hold-all from my fingers, and deposits it in the copious boot. The next thing I know, I'm sitting on grey leather in the back of pure air-conditioned class and facing a drinks cabinet filled with water bottles and whisky. I take the former and wish for the latter, but I'm not at home, and the heat will kill the happiness of it.

The drive to the hotel takes an hour and a half. As I gaze out of the window, it's as if I've not only been transported thousands of miles away from London, but also two thousand years into the past, except for the traffic. The men and women I see wear long, flowing robes in shades of blue, red, orange. Some of the women wear black scarves to hide their hair or carry impossibly tall packages on their heads. Jade would have loved it. For her, it would be like living in Bible times, taking her back to her Baptist roots.

Along the roadside are half-finished houses, children all but naked, donkeys—with visible ribs—grazing on scraps of brown grassland, and broken-down abandoned machinery. Through it all, expensive cars and Western tourists flow into the heart of the city. Rich people. People like me.

I tap on the glass. The driver leans forward, presses an unseen button and the barrier slides across.

"Yes, sir?" he gazes back at me and ignores the stream of battered cars all hooting for supremacy outside us, each one appearing to follow its own set of rules.

"Hey! Watch out."

He swerves 'round a straight-backed woman, dressed in blue, pacing calmly down the middle of the road, and almost collides with a lorry coming the other way. Somehow we survive both encounters, and I look out the rear window to see the woman continuing on her path as if nothing has happened.

"God, and I thought London was bad. Is Cairo always like this?"

Waving one hand in the air, my chauffeur laughs. "No, sir, no, no, no! This is good. Sometimes it is far worse, in the rush hours, yes?"

*   *   *

Arriving at the Mena House Oberoi is like being given the gift of life when you're expecting nothing but the bullet. A lot of this is to do with the Pyramids. My ex-lover is right; they're overwhelming, and Mena House is all but next door to them. Until today, a part of me hasn't believed they really exist, except in films, and certainly not so close to civilization. Aren't they supposed to be in the desert? Or has Hollywood managed to fool me over the years? No more because now I can see. The three great structures dominate the skyline, shimmering in the afternoon heat, and I swear I could almost lean over from where I'm standing and touch them.

"Good, yes, sir?" the chauffeur hands my bag to the eager doorman. "You have not seen them before?"

"Not in real life, no." I tip him anyway, a gesture that doesn't surprise him. My choices aren't going to be constrained by Dominic.

Once in the hotel, I wonder if I'm ever going to be able to leave. The marble lobby floor reflects the lights of at least five glistening chandeliers, and as I check in, I wish I'd shown less business morality—Jade's doing, as always—and not booked myself into the cheapest room available.

"Good afternoon, Mr. Maloney," the man behind the reception desk says. "You had a pleasant flight?"

"Sure. No problems."

"Your room is ready now, sir. And I am pleased to tell you that you have been upgraded. You are in one of our deluxe suites. It is a beautiful room. I trust you will enjoy it."

I raise my eyebrows at him. "Yes, I'm sure I will. But before I do, can I ask who's paying for this?"

"Mr. Allen, sir. He said you are a very important guest. There is a communication for you."

Trying not to think whether all this attention from Dominic is going to make things difficult for me to do the job at all, or whether it might mean something else entirely, I take the letter he hands me and follow my luggage on its journey to my suite. I make no comment as the boy deposits my well-used bag on the bed as if it's designer and shows me 'round the enormous bedroom with its soothing arches and Arabic décor, wooden and ivory furniture, and green silk tapestry. The living room, bathroom, balcony, and dining area all hold to the themes of green and wood and ivory, but each with an individual twist. As his pièce de résistance, the luggage boy flings open the curtains and gestures at the pyramids. Somehow they seem even closer than before. I'm still silent, but when the boy leaves, I tip him double what I'd given my driver.

The first thing I do is ring Jade.

"Hello, Paul. How are you doing?"

"Wonderful. You?"

"Great. What's it like then, the land of the pharaohs?"

"Rich if you're a tourist. Utter poverty if you're not. Come one day. You'll love it."

"Yes, I know. If only my harsh, unfeeling boss allowed me to take leave."

"Oh sure, I forgot. It's my fault. Any updates on Blake's schedule I should know about?"

"No, it's still worth you being there. I checked. The press office confirms he's in all morning tomorrow, though he'll be out at meetings early afternoon."

"Thanks. You're the best. Any other calls I should know about?"

She hesitates. "None of your usual clients; they're all fine. Someone rang earlier, though. Same caller as before, I think. All he said was your name and then he rang off. You will be careful, won't you?"

"You know me, indestructible. Don't worry. I'll be fine. You just look after yourself and try not to leave early while I'm away. I'll ring you tomorrow and let you know how I get on. Who knows, I might even have cracked the case by then. I'm such a genius."

"Of course you are," she says and hangs up.

As I fling myself onto the bed, I can't help hoping I don't find out anything useful too soon.

When I slit open the envelope that Dominic left for me, I find I'm shaking a little.

Paul, the note reads, I hope your journey was a good one and I trust you will find the room acceptable. When I am in Cairo, it is where I always stay. Yours, Nic

Nic. He's signed himself Nic. A name I only ever called him in bed. Or just before it.

CHAPTER 3

I eat breakfast in the Khan El Khalili restaurant and pore over the Egyptian phrasebook I discovered in the bedside cabinet last night. As I memorize what I hope might turn out to be a useful set of words, I admire the brass tables, the marble floor, and the intricate white ceiling. I thank God I don't have to clean it. I glance at my watch for the tenth time this morning and see it's 7:52 A.M., Egyptian time. Already I know it's going to be a hot day, in more ways than one. Breakfast is a feast of bread and butter pudding, fruit, yoghurt, and croissants, plus coffee that could line the stomach in a nuclear attack, if there was one, and I take as much as I can. The day ahead will be long and hard.

Outside, I check my map, get in the taxi I've ordered, and head off to my first meeting with Delta Egypt. In central Cairo, through the press of traffic and the bustle of the streets, I can see the glistening waters of the Nile, taking with them downstream many lifetimes of history and culture. As we drive past the Egyptian Museum, dusky pink and grand, I wonder if there'll be time to visit before I leave. We turn into the heart of the Sharia Qasr el-Nil, the city's financial trading district, and my professional day is about to begin. Time to get into character.

Delta Egypt has the second floor in a four-floor building, situated on the corner of two wide streets packed with shops and bars. The foyer is calm and white, with two statues of eagles on either side of a small water fountain, which provides a soothing background gurgle to the hum of the receptionist's computer. Today, I almost fit into this world, dressed as I am in the suit I chose to visit Dominic's office.

I stride up to the reception desk and showcase one of the two pieces of spoken Arabic I hope I've picked up, at least phonetically. "Sabaah al-khayr. Good morning. I'm here to see Mr. Kenzie of Delta Egypt."

The dark-eyed woman studies my card.

"Certainly, sir," she says in perfect English. "Do you have an appointment?"

"No, but I need to see him urgently."

"I'm afraid, sir, that it may not be possible. Mr. Kenzie is not often here. I'll try his PA for you."

"Trust me"—I lay my hand on hers as she reaches for the switchboard—"if I'd wanted to see Mr. Kenzie's PA, then I would have asked. It's the man himself I'm after, and I think you'll find he's here."

The woman frowns. "But, sir, it's standard practice to contact the PA first and I—"

"No," I cut her off. "Ring him. If he objects, tell him my name. Tell him it's concerning DG Allen Enterprises. He'll see me."

For another second, she stares at me. Then she stabs a number on her keypad and the two of us wait. There's a burst of quick-fire speech I can't understand, and I hear my name, a pause, then she breaks the connection.

She hasn't mentioned Dominic's company, and I just have time to file that as an interesting fact to be mulled over later before she directs me to the lift.

"Second floor, sir," she says.

I step out into sunlight and cool air and find myself face to face with a clean-shaven young man dressed in a dark grey business suit.

"Mr. Maloney?" he asks, and I nod. "Please, come this way."

I walk in his trail past a row of offices, doors all shut, and then out into a communal area filled with low glass tables and easy chairs on one side and a series of work stations on the other. Most are in use, but one or two people are standing, drinking from small white cups. The smell of coffee is overpowering. The windows curve 'round the length of two walls, and I realize I must be facing the intersection between the two streets outside. There's no noise.

"Please," the young man says, "sit."

This doesn't sound like a suggestion, so I obey.

"When can I see Mr. Kenzie?" I ask.

My companion smiles. "Please, wait. I will find out for you. Help yourself to a coffee if you wish, please."

He disappears back the way we've just come and enters an office on the right. At once, I get up, avoiding the coffee machine and the silent workers, and seat myself at one of the empty computer terminals farthest from the corridor. Nobody pays me any attention. The system I'm looking at is a simple one, just a Windows environment with the usual icons on the left. I speed through the more interesting-looking folders, but all that's on there is some company background, at least twenty sparkling PR articles, and a resume of the chief executive that tells me nothing I don't already—

"Ah, Mr. Maloney…"

I glance up as my young escort—or should that be minder?—returns. His brow glistens with sweat, even though the air conditioning is working.

"Yes?"

"If you could…Mr. Kenzie can see you now."

"Good." I take my time bringing the computer back to its home page before standing. "Please, lead the way."

He does, still sweating. Five seconds later, I'm in the office of the Chief Executive of Delta Egypt, and the man himself is striding toward me, hand outstretched in greeting. The décor is stark white, softened only by angular black furniture and the cream-colored orchids on his desk. Blake Kenzie is smaller than I am, clean-shaven, thickset, and swarthy. All these facts I already know, but nothing I have seen has prepared me for his manner. Pale blue eyes look me up and down without expression, judge me, and then move on. I shiver and suppress the urge to run.

"Mr. Maloney," he says, his accent revealing the mix of his American and Egyptian ancestry. As he speaks, he turns away, and I let go of the breath I didn't realize I was holding. "It's good of you to come and see us from such a distance. Tell me, can I offer you anything? Mint tea? Coffee?"

"No. Thank you."

He pauses. "No doubt a wise choice. Here in Cairo, our coffee is best served bitter and is not to the taste of our European friends. However, if I may be so intimate, I question the wisdom of some of your other choices. What can I do for you?"

I don't like his use of the word, intimate, or the way he says it to make it carry a multitude of meanings. Handing him another of my cards, I launch into my spiel, but I've barely reached my third sentence when he takes the card, holds it up in front of me, and tears it into two. I stop talking. With a brief shake of his head, he tosses the fragments into the bin without even looking.

"Please, Paul," he says. "I may call you Paul, of course? I must say I'm disappointed in you."

"Oh. Why?"

"Simple. When I see people in my office, I like them to tell the truth. I don't like to see them lie. I don't like that at all."

I try to understand what's behind his gaze, but it's impossible. "If you already know why I'm here, why ask me to explain myself?"

"Because I like to listen to what people have to say. It's always interesting. You can tell many things from the way they phrase their statements, even the tone of voice. Did you know that, Paul?"

Yes, I do know that. And if I hadn't before, then I'm certainly learning it now. But I say nothing, I just wait.

After a fractional pause, he walks right up to me, so close I can smell the cigars on his breath and his herbal aftershave. He continues, "I am assuming, and I hope rightly, that this conversation is not being recorded in any way. Because if it were, the consequences might be painful. Of course I wouldn't want, even indirectly, to cause your parents any further grief, bearing in mind the unfortunate events involving your…what is that very English word you use? Sibling?"

"No," I say, taking a step back. I try not to blink. Or sweat. Or swallow. "There's no recording."

Another pause. "Good. Those are the first true words you've spoken since you entered the building. Our scanners would have shown if you were lying again, of course, but it pleases me to hear you say it. Now let me tell you the truth also. If I may?"

There's no choice, but I nod anyway, trying to ease the irregular pounding of blood to my ears. Blake Kenzie smiles and saunters away to his desk. Turning his back to me a little and picking up a letter opener, surely for decoration only, he slides it from hand to hand like a toy as he talks.

"The truth," he says. "The truth for me is that I have nothing to fear and little of consequence to hide. It pleases me that your client, Mr. Allen, is interested enough in Delta Egypt to go to the extraordinary lengths of hiring you, a private eye from a part of London I have never been unfortunate enough to visit, to do his dirty work for him. I, too, have people for that kind of business, but I choose not to use them against friends and, I hope, partners. Therefore, I suggest you leave and go back to your home.

And when you do, I trust you'll tell Mr. Allen one important thing."

He pauses, and I see my chance. "And what do you suggest that might be, Blake? I may call you Blake, mayn't I?"

My voice is steadier than I expected, but when he swings 'round, he's clutching the letter opener in his fist, and I flinch. After a heartbeat or two, instead of impaling me with it, he drops it onto the table and rearranges his face into another smile. The unexpected anger is more real, though, and I'm pleased I've managed to rouse it.

"No," he says. "My name, to you, is Mr. Kenzie. Not that it matters, Paul, as I do not think we will need to worry about such niceties again. But, please, be so good as to tell your wage-master two important things instead of one."

"These are?"

"The first is this: if he learns to trust me, then the business we do together will be profitable and he has little to fear. He will find nothing wrong with Delta Egypt."

"And the second, Mr. Kenzie?"

"The second is perhaps more to the point for us today. Tell Mr. Allen that if he uses bad seed, then he cannot expect to harvest good wheat."

*   *   *

Outside, the air clings to every item of clothing and every part of my body. After such a meeting and the realization of how much Blake Kenzie knows about me, I need to regroup. There's no use thinking about it—it won't change anything. So shaking away all thoughts of the past, I flag down a taxi.

"Khan al-Khalili," I say, the name almost identical to where I took breakfast only an hour and forty minutes ago, but the meaning a lifetime of difference away. The old bazaar, Cairo's commercial centre. A good place to get Jade a present. Something normal, something expected. A perfume bottle perhaps or an item of Muski glass, as the blue will go with her eyes. A good place also to shake any tail, if there is one. How does Blake know what he shouldn't? And why?

The taxi deposits me in a square bordered by several cafés and a mosque. I give the driver enough baksheesh to keep his family in stuffed lamb and baklawa for a week, glance 'round to see if I recognize any of the cars now hooting for supremacy around us—I don't—and amble off in the direction of the nearest water seller. Once I've checked the top's not been tampered with, I sit on the small stone wall of the square, open the bottle, and pour half of it over my face and neck. The water runs inside my shirt and over my skin, as cool and refreshing as the first touch of a lover's hand. I shut my eyes for a moment and enjoy the respite, before the blast of city heat rolls back, then I drink the rest of the water and gaze at where I find myself now. Or more vitally who I find myself with.

Several groups of men are drinking at the nearest café, and there are women with young families milling outside the mosque. Donkeys and carts trot through the square and disappear into side streets, their owners shouting and gesticulating as they go. In front of me, a small boy covered with dirt carries a casket of bread twice his size on his head, yelling over and over again in accented English, "Bread! Buy! Bread!"

He looks at me, one small eyebrow raised, but I wave him away and he moves on. As he does so, one of the rolls falls to the ground. He picks it up, spits on it, wipes it on the dust of his robe and replaces it above him. He then makes his way to a group of what look to be Americans on the other side of the square.

My skin is prickling with the sensation of being watched, but nothing around me seems at all out-of-place. One of the men in a nearby café makes me look again, even as I've almost discounted him and moved on. The man is in his thirties, dressed in long, off-white Arabic robes, dark-haired, clean-shaven, nondescript, but something about him draws my eye back. He's not sitting at the same table as the others, but seems to be echoing their conversation in his gestures. They, however, take no notice of him. Have I seen him somewhere before? Today? It eludes me, and as I continue to puzzle over it, the man raises his eyes from the papers in front of him, sees me looking, and at once glances away.

I begin to approach him, striding forward with a confidence I don't feel. He gathers his papers and makes a move to leave, but by now, I'm too close. I notice a twisted scar on his left cheek and realize he's one of the people from the Delta Egypt lounge. As I brush against his table, his right hand flickers near a slit in his robes at chest level, but I keep on walking.

I smile brightly, "Aasef, sorry."

And then I'm gone, weaving my way between the tables and toward the bustle and noise of the Khan Al-Khalili. The streets are narrow and lined on either side by stalls. I push my way through the throng of tourists and traders, donkeys and dealers. When I glance behind me, I don't see the man with the scar, but it's hard to be sure.

The air is laced with pungent spices. With every step, someone smiles, grabs me, tries to sell me waterpipes, carved camels, fridge magnets shaped like pyramids, saffron, or silk. I don't even mind; it's harder for anyone to get as close to me as they might want to if someone else is trying to claim a piece of me first. On the other hand, it's also hard for me to see the enemy, if I'm being pursued at all. Around me, gold, silver, brass, and copper ornaments hang glittering inside the shops like magic curtains concealing a secret cave. Young boys and occasionally women are dyeing cloth, sewing shirts, and carving elephants from stone. Once again, a few paces from the café have taken me back a thousand years.

After five minutes, I've seen nothing that might worry me, and nobody has jostled me with anything more dangerous than a robe called a galabiya or a pair of handcrafted sandals. Maybe I overreacted. Perhaps the innocent man at the café was reaching for a wallet or handkerchief. I turn a corner and see a large sand-colored stone gate covered with intricate carvings. Next to it, a shop selling postcards and a window-full of blue Muski glass catches my eye. The danger, if there was any, is past, and I may as well make the most of my time here. As I reach for my cash, there's a sudden flicker of movement on my left, the impression of tanned flesh and a scarred cheek.

At waist level, the steel of the knife flashes in the morning sun, and there's no time to cry out.

CHAPTER 4

With a speed that comes from instinct rather than thought, I twist my body away from my attacker and grab his knife arm. I slam it back against the stone arch of the gateway.

Scar-cheek lets loose a stream of high-pitched Arabic, and the knife falls to the ground. I punch him in the stomach and yell, "Help! Help me!"

At the same time, both of us leap for the knife, but I get there first. The next second, he kicks me on the side of the head, and I sprawl on my back in the dust, the knife skittering away from my reach. His dark eyes are fixed on mine, and I know if he has the chance, he'll kill me now. But there's shouting, a sense of other people closing in, and then he's gone, through the gate and melting into the crowd. When I glance at the knife, that's gone, too.

"Are you okay?"

"What was that about?"

"Hey, you're bleeding," are the American-twanged phrases I manage to pick out of the medley of foreign sounds and sympathy around my ears.

Someone mentions the Tourist Police, but I wave the suggestion away. I try to get up, but stagger and almost fall again. A short, fat man in an orange robe catches me and all but carries me into the postcard shop. Here, I'm led through cards, kitsch, and toy camels into a small back room with a sink, where the Samaritan turns on the tap, wets a roll of cloth in the stream of light brown water, and holds it onto the side of my head.

I'm not convinced this will help, but I'm too dazed to argue. All the time, he fires off a series of staccato comments I've no hope of understanding. After a minute of this, he's joined by a tall woman who elbows him aside, looks at me, eases the cloth away from his hand, and shakes her head. She smells of lemons.

"Chai, chai!" She gestures to the fat man, and he vanishes back into the shop.

When she places her fingers at the side of my head, I wince. She leans forward and gazes into my eyes, and I wonder if she'll find anything there to her liking. Another torrent of Arabic, but this time the voice is softer. She smiles, then fills the sink with water. She takes a fresh cloth and dabs at the wound with an ointment that makes me flinch. Finally, she stands back, hands on hips and the look of a job well done on her face.

"Shokran, shokran," I say, remembering the phrase at last. "Thank you."

The man reappears, holding a glass. The woman takes it and puts it to my lips, and I can smell mint. It scalds the roof of my mouth, but after three or four sips, the dizziness fades.

When I leave my new friends, I take with me ten postcards, two stuffed camels, a Nefertiti fridge magnet, and a host of good wishes neither side can understand, but they're said with sincerity.

At Mena House, I sleep for five hours and nineteen minutes with no dreams, not even of Dominic. When I wake up, I rebook my flight home with reception, purchase a galabiya at the hotel shop, eat a leisurely early supper, and return to my room where I wait for night to come.

Cairo never sleeps. Darkness never falls, and the shadows shift suspiciously. Men and women seem taller, more confident, and the haze of city heat makes what they do distant and magical. Add in the fact that people out at night are there for a good time and nothing more, even without the alcohol. The mix is just the right strength for undercover work. And, maybe, if I'm lucky, theft.

*   *   *

I'm sitting at a table in a café near the offices of Delta Egypt with a view of the foyer and front desk. I'm wearing the galabiya, but there's a bottle of Stella in my hand. Though I'm not drinking it, the chill from the glass soothes the heat rising from the bodies around me. Somebody has already taken the chair opposite with nothing but an exchange of nods. The air is rich with the smell of grilled lamb and spices. Now and then, I lean back from the window, look at the mass of bodies behind me, and smile. Not enough to trigger conversation, but just enough to make it seem, if anyone is looking, as if I'm part of the laughter and talking.

All the time, I'm looking, too. In just four hours and twenty-one minutes, I've learnt a lot. There are two guards and one monitor in the foyer of the building that houses Delta. Approximately every forty minutes, one of the men will leave and, as far as I can tell, make a tour of the building. This takes between twenty and twenty-three minutes, so they're not being thorough. I suspect some of this time is used for smokes or toilet breaks.

The clock on the wall in front of me looms out of the smoke. I would give half of Dominic's wages, maybe more, for a cigarette, but I gave that up and I won't go back to it. There's a wave of laughter from five elderly men at a side table, and one of them slaps his neighbor's shoulder, squeezing forth another burst of laughter. I signal for the bill, leave money enough for a generous tip on the table, take the parcel I made up in the hotel room, and cross the square to Delta Egypt.

Outside, the air is clearer, but still just as heavy on the skin. The street shimmers with life and people and need, but tonight none of it calls to me. I take a sharp right and jostle my way past chattering businessmen dressed western style and groups of young men still selling their wares. I dodge the old battered Renaults and donkey carts on the street and head to the Delta building, my plan, such as it is, inhabiting my flesh, becoming part of it, with the promise of making it work, making it real.

When I peer through the glass, the smaller guard is on his own. One minute and thirty seconds ago, the taller one left for the routine tour. I have just over twenty-two minutes at best to get what I want from Blake Kenzie's set-up and get out. The package is in my hand, along with a mocked-up signing sheet, and I know the whole idea is crazy, but I'm hoping it will work, as it might be my only chance.

I knock on the window, wave the package and the sheet, and gesticulate down at them both. The guard glances at me, looking so bored I swear he sighs. He can't suspect anything; dressed like this, I look like everyone else, and he can't see the color of my skin from where he's sitting. He gets up, jangling keys at his side I'm sure he won't be needing.

Come on. Come on.

Each second ticks itself by with the beat of my heart. He must take a lifetime, no several, to reach the door.

At last, he opens it. I slam it hard against him, and he staggers back with a low oomph, recovering enough to aim a swift punch at my stomach. Sidestepping, I kick his legs from under him. Once he's down on the floor, I kneel across him, grab his right hand so he can't go for any concealed weapon, and slap a large Band-Aid over his mouth. Ten seconds later, his hands and feet are tied, his mouth still silenced, and I've disarmed him—one handgun, one small knife. I should keep them, but they'll only slow me down and I'm skilled at neither. All I really have to offer are fast reflexes and balls. I just hope tonight they'll be enough.

Five seconds after that, the guard is locked in a cupboard amongst brooms and mops, and I'm feeling grateful there are no signs of curiosity from outside. I climb onto the desk, reach for the CCTV and smash the recording, pocketing the evidence.

I glance at my watch and see three minutes have ticked by. Another quick glance over the system confirms what this morning's visit told me: the alarm is laser and computerized, and there's no way of telling how it connects to each floor. And no time to put Jade's detailed instructions to the test. I'll have to take the lift. Because of the noise and because the guards have been using them, too, this evening, the stairs are too dangerous. I need to move like a cat for as long as I can to give myself all possible chances.

The lift rises upward like a cruise ship drifting out to sea. It takes one minute and ten seconds from the time I call for it to when it stops at the Delta Egypt floor. One second, two seconds. A soft whoosh of air as the doors open, and when I peer out, there's no sign of any guard. I slip through the closing gap and watch as the numbers tick their way up from two to three. It pauses there and then the number changes to four. It stops. Good. That must be where the second guard is. The fourth floor. I hope he's not questioning why he needed to call it up. I hope he'll assume it's his colleague messing with him. Most of all, I hope my luck will hold.

Padding along the corridor, I see nothing's changed from this morning. Same closed doors, same atmosphere of hushed reverence, but this time it's because no one is here, and I'm interested in one door only.

Where does Delta Egypt's alarm system lead to—the local police? Or just internal security? Is it audible or silent, in order to catch the intruder unaware? Whatever, even if I hadn't got the message from Kenzie's behavior, the level of company security tells me there's something in that office I need to see.

From under my robe, I slip out the small tool kit concealed in my belt, unwrap it on the carpet tiles, and decide what to use. Fifty-nine seconds later—twelve seconds worse than my record—I'm in.

I brace myself for the wail of the alarm, eyes skating over the walls for the means to silence it. Nothing. The air is silent. I release my breath and wipe the sweat from my face. The lack of audible response means one of two things: either the alarm, whether linked to an external authority or not, is built to surprise, or Kenzie was lying.

Discarding the second choice, I calculate I have nine minutes thirty seconds at best to get the information Dominic wants and leave. At worst, no more than five minutes.

The list of instructions I've given myself hums through my mind like a mantra. Leave the door ajar so I can hear any movement in the corridor outside…maybe, if I'm lucky, the slight swoosh of the lift. Disable the CCTV, which is well hidden, but not impossible to find. What kind of man has CCTV in his own office? It's easy enough to switch off, then destroy. Next, I make a quick but thorough search of all the cabinets and drawers. Not that a man like that will leave anything there to incriminate himself, but it's foolish to assume he hasn't.

Nothing. As I thought. Because I want him to know I've been here, I leave the drawers unlocked and the cabinets open. I hope before he smiles at what I've done, there'll be a moment or two when he won't.

There are three minutes left, at worst, and, at best, six minutes thirty seconds.

The computer system. It's the only thing left to ransack. I head outside to the computer I'd used this morning. Whatever happens now, this company is hiding something, and Dominic is right. I know it with all my instincts because of the earlier attack. Blake Kenzie is bad news, and I want to know the depths of it.

Outside, there's still no movement and no time to check where the lift is. My fingers slide over the keys, my task made easier by a quick lesson in Jade's IT wizardry. One day soon I'll have to offer her a partnership. As for now, it's switch on, hack in as best I can, search, and plunder. And save, save, save. Behind me, the nightlife of

Cairo pulsates and flickers, and the USB drive chunters away at my side, while I force my eyes up and down the screen, through the file trees Kenzie has allowed to be shown on his public system. In these maybe, just maybe, might lay a clue he's overlooked.

I ignore the folders I saw this morning, concentrating instead on the names that at the moment mean less, but might hide more: the various projects, company reporting, sponsorships. All of it is stored onto the USB drive and, at the same time, I glance through wherever my eye and the mouse take me and…

Come on. Come on. Twenty-eight seconds to my worst-case scenario, twenty-seven, twenty-five—

And something flashes up on the screen that, at the speed I'm going, only hits me two mouse clicks later. DG Allen Enterprises.

Twenty-two seconds, twenty, seventeen. And I'm back, burrowing into the Allen folder, knowing there's no time to read it here, but unable to stop myself, wanting to know, wanting to see. Now.

Fifteen seconds, twelve. A sharp whisper of sound beyond my current enclosed world taps into my consciousness.

The lift.

All my calculations found lacking, I'm out of time too soon. Save the information I have so far, pocket the USB drive, knock the Allen file off screen, and hope I've got it anyway, please God. A brush of rubber sole on carpet and, from along the corridor, words I don't understand are whispered.

There's more than one of them. I'm screwed. Got to get out. Before I've finished the thought, I'm up and running. I don't even pause to see who's after me. Instead, I slam open the nearest window—thank God for old-style Egyptian buildings—pull myself onto the ledge and lower myself down outside, feet searching for a hold. From the silence and emptiness of the building I've just exited, there's a popping noise, then another, and I realize, even though they're not at the window yet, so they can't see me, they're shooting. And using a silencer.

Bloody hell, they're actually shooting at me, the bastards.

Astonishingly, in all my time in this business, that's never happened, though I've been threatened, beaten, and knifed. Perhaps I've just been lucky, or more to the point, perhaps I've just never done my job abroad.

As I hang suspended, scrabbling for safety, my ears are thudding with the beat of my heart, and I realize I've peed myself.

The next second, my hands slip from the ledge, and I'm falling. A scream—mine—shouting—God knows whose—and the popping sound—a third time. A ripe red gash of agony roars through the flesh of my shoulder, and I'm drowning in muck and rustling, a bitter taste in my mouth. Whatever I've landed in with a thud and another scream has broken my fall. As I roll over and out of it, the noise of braying hits me and I see it's a donkey cart, loaded with what might be hay, but at this point I don't care what it is as my pursuers shoot again. Once only. They miss. The old man at the donkey's head cowers and pulls the whole contraption away, yelling and waving a bony fist. I dip and swerve with him alongside the cart, though there's no need as I don't think they'll try anything now, not in full view of the city.

Three seconds later, I'm around the corner of the building and away.

Fifteen seconds after that, I've stopped my wound with cloth torn from the bottom of my robe. There's no bullet, not that I can see and not that my shaking fingers can feel. My second slice of luck tonight. But how long will it last?

CHAPTER 5

"I think you've been lucky, that's all I can say."

"I know." I open my eyes and smile at Jade. We're sitting in the brightness of her living room, a place of flowers and soft corners, cotton and lace. Of course, being Jade, the colors of all these objects are red and green, yellow and blue, but somehow the delicacy hasn't been lost. Just reinterpreted. The armchair, for instance, is shabby, and there's a hint of lavender polish in the air. In the background, the radio is tuned to Classic FM and someone is requesting "The Lark Ascending." Why do they always play that? After the Egyptian experience two days ago, it wouldn't be the piece of music I'd choose, but it's Saturday afternoon, I'm alive, and there's nothing I have to do that can't wait. Here is a good place to be.

"It never used to be like this," she grumbles, collapsing onto the sofa opposite me and readjusting one of her long sapphire earrings. "You know, when I first started working for you, it was much more relaxed. None of these knife attacks, derring-do, and swinging from high-up ledges in the dead of night. Why can't you stick to insurance claims and divorce cases? At least then you wouldn't be shot at, and I know I've said it before, but I'll say it now, I'd feel a lot happier if you had someone look at that arm."

"It's fine. Flesh wound, that's all."

"Yes, but—"

"No. Really. The bullet passed through; there's no danger. I've looked at it, and you've looked at it. I'm grateful you're a genius with the iodine."

"And you're a genius with the clenched teeth and gasping thing. I don't mind if you swear. I'm a lapsed Baptist, remember?"

"No way. Can't have you fainting just when I need you."

The radio hums and soars its rhythm, and the taste of the Rioja we've opened is mellow on my tongue. Not as punchy as whisky or as refreshing as a beer, but it's a reasonable substitute. Jade's lived in Stratford for two years, five months, and two weeks now, and it's not a bad place. Not too far from the main shops and station, and near enough to some essential green space to be desirable.

The area is up and coming. As opposed to where I am in Hackney, which is down and out.

"Paul?"

"Hmm?"

"You haven't told me much about the morning meeting with the CEO. Did you manage to get anything else out of Delta Egypt, apart from a bird's eye view of the Nile? Mr. Kenzie didn't let slip any mentions of Bluesky or anything useful?"

I shift in my seat and put down my wine. "No time to ask. Blake saw through my feeble disguise in less than thirty seconds, made a series of threats, and then bounced me out of the building."

"What sort of threats?"

"The usual…nothing to worry about." Picking up my wine again, I rock it in my hand and watch the liquid undulate 'round the glass. "Any plans for tonight at all?"

Jade shakes her head. "I don't know, all these years we've known each other and you think I can't see through you. Don't bother changing the subject. What threats?"

"Honestly, nothing I didn't anticipate."

"Except?"

"Except he knew about Teresa."

Jade doesn't reply, and when I look at her, she's leaning forward, a frown on her face. "I didn't think you talked to anyone about your sister."

"I don't. Not now."

"So how did he…"

"I don't know. Look, I'm sorry, but I think he was just trying for a reaction. And he got it. Can we talk about something else?"

Reaching across, she pats my hand, her fingers cool, and then smiles, "In answer to your previous question, I don't have any plans. Nothing social, that is, present company excepted. Supper, wine, TV, book, bed. In that order. You?"

"Same."

"Want to join up our action-packed social programs?"

"No, sorry, though it sounds tempting. I want to have at least another spin through the Delta Egypt files this evening. See if anything springs out."

"We can do that together now if you like."

"No, that's okay. I'd like to look at it on my own first. Let's leave any brainstorming session 'til Monday. I'm not planning to ring Dominic 'til then. There is one thing you could do for me, though."

"Name it."

Struggling up from the chair, I pad to the set of hooks I put up for her last year, reach inside my jacket, and find the object I'm looking for. "Could you keep this for me? Don't do any work on it. In fact, I forbid it. Leave it to Monday. But it's just in case—"

"Sure, no problem." Jade takes the USB drive from my fingers and then wrinkles her nose. "Wait a minute. It's not the one you were carrying when you peed yourself, is it?"

"Don't be stupid. Haven't you heard of gravity? It's safe enough. Anyway, it's a copy. The original's with me. I do have some taste and sense of propriety."

"Glad to hear it. Just testing."

"Yeah, sure, don't tell me. I'm easy to tease. And after daring to forbid you to do something, I deserve it." I drain my wine and shrug my jacket over my shoulders. Not that I need it in this weather, but Dominic once told me how good I looked in it. "I'd best go. Thanks for the afternoon break."

"My pleasure." She takes a breath and then stops, as if drawing something back that hasn't yet been spoken.

"What?"

"Nothing."

"No, go on. If there's something else on your mind—apart from warnings about jumping out of Egyptian buildings and not going to the doctor—let's hear it."

There's a silence, then she says, "It wasn't anything special. All I was going to say was I'm having Sunday lunch with my parents tomorrow. Do you want to come? They'd be thrilled to see you."

"A plan to cheer me up by putting me into a family that works?"

"No. It's not like that. I was just—

"Yes, I know. I was trying to be light-hearted, but it failed. Sorry. It sounds like my idea of happiness. I'm up for it, thanks."

At the door, I arrange to pick Jade up in the morning. As I drive home, out of all the factors I can puzzle over, I choose to focus again on why someone with her looks and heart doesn't have a regular partner. Or any kind of partner at all.

In the kitchen, the sunlight is fading. When I get up to turn on the overhead light, my knees creak and my neck aches. Too much time spent peering at the laptop, trying to make sense of the information I've uploaded from the Delta Egypt USB drive. I stretch my muscles in the darkness before heading for the switch. It's part of my business to spend hours going over and over the same facts or following the same person until suddenly the key will fit or the one tiny piece of the jigsaw will cry out to you and you'll see something no one else wanted you to see. That's the kick; that's what keeps me going.

It's not going to happen tonight. Four hours and fifty-two minutes of studying the facts, and I am nowhere near the door, let alone the key. The jigsaw is still just a mass of colors and shapes that make no sense.

Only one thing for it. Time for a whisky. But which one? The glass sparkles in my hand, and I smile. It's not necessary, but I wash and dry the tumbler. Slowly, as if every centimeter of it counts. The traffic outside is thinning, with just one or two groups of teenagers skulking and smoking at the corners where the shadows begin, and two or three women wheeling their prams on the other side of the road to avoid them.

I put the glass on the middle of the table, moving the laptop to one side to allow it room.

I open the kitchen drinks cupboard and study the three choices of whisky currently in the flat, though, from preference, I'd rather have four. First there's the Glenfiddich, as light as water in color, but with a smell to it of barley and honey and the deep taste of malt. A whisky for early summer evenings that promise the full heat of the days to come. It's not for now.

Behind it, the Highland Park glistens amber, and if I open it, I know the smell of medicine and smoke will envelop me, and the taste, once taken, will be full and sweet. It's the drink for when I'm tired or ill. Not too strong and not too weak; it knows where I am and how to reach me. The perfect answer? No, still it's not quite right.

Last of all is the Macallan, rarely opened, its rich toffee glow hinting of secrets not yet understood, not yet known. Yes, this is the one. As I release it, the smell of new leather and dark Spanish sherry settles around me, and I pour a double measure, more, into my waiting glass. The golden liquid swings round, marking its place, waiting for me, calling. I take one deep breath of it, two, and I could already be swimming in its tempting river. My heart beats faster. My skin feels hot.

I savor the first—the best—sip, and the pungent wave of whisky sweeps me away from all lingering thoughts. I could almost be flying.

It's too good for the kitchen with its smell of stale cooking and damp. So, anticipating my next sip, but holding out just a little longer, just a little, I power down my laptop and take the glass and myself into the living room.

The next sip tastes even more powerful. It reminds me of the man who bought it for me. It takes me back to Dominic and the very beginning of it all.

*   *   *

Friday, May 12. I'd been working for one of my regular clients, a local insurance company, and had carried out surveillance on a bloke who was suing their insured for tens of thousands of pounds for alleged injuries caused by non-maintenance of the drills he had to use on the road. Load of old baloney. I'd filmed him at least six times pounding away on the running machines at the gym, the idiot, and the case fell apart. One of my most satisfying moments, work-wise, and one of the most lucrative, too. My client had been grateful enough to wangle me an invite to their posh summer do in the city and, as Jade had been nagging me for ages to get out and meet more people, in the end I'd gone along. Taken her with me, too. I'm not one of those who likes to flaunt his sexuality. What's private is private.

When we arrived, the party was seething with suits and sparkle, canapés and champagne, and Jade's eyes shone in the glow.

"Hey," I whispered, "bet you're glad you're best friends with this old queen now, aren't you?"

She giggled, and the next thing I knew, we were engulfed in a tide of laughter, glasses, and talking to strangers. Jade disappeared, and I didn't see her again to talk to until we both left at one-fifteen A.M. In the glimpses I had, she was laughing or dancing.

After nearly thirty minutes, I'd said the same things to at least twelve people I'd never meet again and spoken twice to my client. Pushing my way through the crowd and seeing a side door marked No Exit, I opened it and slipped out into the clarity of the night air.

At once the heat and brightness of the hotel was cut off, and I breathed in deeply, filling myself with the relative silence you get in the city sometimes. As far as I could tell, I was in a small garden with lavender and rosemary from the faint traces of scent. I've always thought that, at times like that, you needed a smoke, even if you were in the early stages of trying to give the demon up, and so I retrieved my emergency pack from my jacket and started to search for the lighter.

No luck.

"Damn," I muttered.

A rustling sound to my left and one of the shadows detached itself from the hedge, fire flashing at its centre.

"Here," said a voice, male, powerful, older. "Allow me."

I lowered my cigarette to the flame he offered and took a quick first drag. "Thanks. I'm trying to give them up."

"So I see."

He took out a cigarette of his own, lit it, and we both stood for a minute or two in silence. The smoke warmed my throat like a kiss.

"Do you like parties?" he asked.

Peering into the gloom, I tried to make out his face, but it was too dark. "No. Not my scene. I'm Paul, by the way. Paul Maloney."

"I know."

Something inside me jackknifed, and I stubbed out my cigarette on the wall behind me. "Oh. How?"

"I asked around. I have my sources."

"I'm sure you do. Why would you want to know?"

He didn't reply at first, and I fought the urge to get out. Fast. There was something about him that drew me to stay. Besides, I assumed it was business, and, as always, I needed the cash. His problem would be something domestic: divorce or maybe even fraud. When it came, his answer told me nothing.

"That's not important, not yet," he said. "The important thing is that neither of us wants to be in the hotel right now."

"What makes you say that?"

"You're very curious, aren't you?"

"Questions are my business," I said and then added, stupidly, "No, they're my life."

Another silence then, but the quality of it had changed, as if something between us was beginning to ease itself up, out, free, into a form I couldn't comprehend. My heart was beating fast. And still I couldn't see his face.

"There are other ways of communicating, Paul," he said at last. "Questions don't always give people what they want."

"Maybe. Maybe not," I replied, my voice scratchy and strange. "Anyway, Mr. Cigarette Lighter Provider, just what is it you want? And, yes, I know that's a question, but you'll just have to live with it."

"All right," he said. "I'll tell you what I want, although I would have preferred a little more time to lead us there. I want to have sex with you."

I couldn't help it. I laughed. "What, here?"

"Yes, here. It's quiet, it's not cold, and it's dark."

I stopped laughing. "You're serious."

"Indeed."

Okay, I thought. It was one year, seven months and nine days since I'd played the gay clubbing scene—the Saturday before I set up my company—and it had never been in a place as high-class as this. Not only that but, sexually speaking, things had been dead for a while. Maybe this would be the kick start I needed to get living again, and at least no one would find out.

The decision made, I reached out and met the cool flesh of his arm.

"What do you prefer?" I asked, tugging him backward into who knew what, but it would be away from the door. "Hand or mouth?"

"No choice. Mouth," he said and kissed me. It was like opening a door to a room filled with spices, but a second later, one important fact crystallized, and I pushed him away, ignoring the fizz of blood to my head.

"You haven't picked up a bloke this way before, have you?" I said.

"No. Does it matter? Anyway how did you work that out?"

In the darkness I smiled. "Kissing wasn't what I meant by 'mouth,' though I'm not saying I objected."

There was a pause. "I know what you meant, but I wanted to kiss you. I'm not a fool."

"I didn't think you were, but you are straight, aren't you? At least on the whole?"

"If you like to label people in that way, then yes. Perhaps. You see, in my business, you learn two things and you learn them quickly. The first is to be open to the possibility of change and the second is to trust your instincts. When you strolled in with that unnecessary girl in tow, I knew I wanted you."

"Jade's my friend, so leave her out of it. Okay?"

Another pause, then, "Yes. Okay. So what should we do now? You seem to want to take the role of expert here, and, doing what I do, I like to consult the experts. Though I might not always take their advice."

This was the second time he'd mentioned work, and I laughed. "I see. So what is it you do then?"

"That's an interesting question," he said. "Here's my card. When you've worked it out, call me."

And then in a haze of nicotine and seductive menace, he was gone through a narrow, tree-lined exit I hadn't seen before and wrong-footing me for the first of many, many times.

It was only at home later on that I read his card and knew without a second of doubt that, unbelievable though it seemed, what it said was true.

Dominic Allen, owner of DG Allen Enterprises Inc, the biggest IT and software company in the UK, the Attila the Hun of the Western business world and stalwart family man, had propositioned me.

Three days after that, I gave in and rang him. One hour and five minutes after the call, he was in my bed, and I was teaching him things he hadn't experienced before. But in the end, the only lesson learnt had been learnt by me.

Don't fall in love with a mainly straight bloke. You'll never win.

*　　*　　*

Nothing's changed. I'm not winning now. When at last I leave the past and come back to the present, the four walls, the fireplace, the Staffordshire dogs are still with me, but the Macallan is mostly gone. As, of course, is Dominic. I've drained all of the whisky but a few drops at the bottom of the glass and I haven't tasted a thing. A shaming waste. I make the dregs of it last the length of another vital few seconds, the warmth of the malt firing my tongue.

Then I sit back and think.

Dominic wants to buy Delta Egypt. Or so he says. Blake Kenzie isn't the type of man who looks as if he's ready to be bought. Dominic hires me to check out Blake's company, a commission that so far has gained me one near-miss escape with a knife, one amateur circus act, four gunshots, and one flesh wound. Not to mention a dead woman who might or might not be linked to anything and who might or might not be called Bluesky, and Blake's in-depth knowledge of my family life. All of it a barrel of trouble and all this so my ex-lover can find out whether Delta is clean or not. Or so he says, again. The USB drive hasn't helped so far either. Maybe Jade will have more luck on Monday. At the moment, none of the folders tell me anything useful, none of them give me so much as a hint of anything underhand. It's all perfect, maybe too perfect.

Thanks to Jade's and my searches, I now know even more about the history, financial dealings, and planned future of Delta than I ever want to know. There's no mention of DG Allen Enterprises elsewhere than in the name of the downloaded Allen folder, nothing to lay to rest the potential takeover concerns of Blake's staff, so I estimate the talks Dominic mentioned, if any, must be at a very early stage.

The Allen folder itself is a mystery, something for Jade to solve. I hope she's now happily asleep and looking forward to tomorrow. I hope she's not sitting up trying to solve the case I've taken on against her better judgment, or even trying to get into the Allen file. Because it's beaten me back each time. Easy enough to hack into the password encryption it carries in the way Jade showed me, but less easy to work out the significance of what it might contain. It's nonsense—files that appear to have half their contents missing and long lists of names, dates, and numbers mixed up like an unreadable crossword puzzle.

Not only that, but it carries with it some kind of internal virus that causes the whole folder to crash three minutes and forty seconds after I've opened it. Each time I reopen it, the lists are in a different order, and I can't help wondering if Mr. Blake Kenzie, in his rich Cairo residence somewhere, being waited on by his oppressed servants, is laughing at me.

I wouldn't be surprised. That knife attack, not to mention the gun crazies, seemed serious enough. Although the guards worked for the owner of the building, not for Blake himself, I bet he'd been first in line for allowing guards to take potshots at passing burglars. It wouldn't surprise me anyway. Perhaps it's all just a game to someone like him. Maybe the threats and hints he made in his office were a game, too, along with the knife thug and info I downloaded onto the USB drive. After all, if Blake's that good, then why would the knifeman fail? Nobody is that lucky. Especially not me.

But if it's a game, then what are the rules? What are…

A second or two of blankness, then I jump, woken by the soft thud of the empty whisky glass onto the carpet. Leaning over, I rescue it. It's decent quality, and I don't want to buy another. It's gone midnight, so not that late, but, hell, I've had a tough few days and I ought to get some sleep. I need to be bright for Jade and her parents tomorrow.

*   *   *

The morning starts with the knowledge that I've overslept, so when the phone rings, I'm already in the shower and don't hear the message. I just hear the ansaphone click on and off again, but there's no time to respond. Only when I'm dragging on my jacket and grabbing my shades from the hall table do I realize it might have been Jade.

It's not. Neither is it Dominic. Not that I ever thought it might be, of course.

When I pick Jade up in Stratford, she looks like a cool angel in cream linen trousers and a crisp cotton top, navy blue with a thin green stripe. Even her earrings are verging on discreet. Almost. It makes her look professional rather than arty, but by now I'm used to her concept of "parent chic," so I make no comment, pausing only to pat her tied-back hair.

"Very nice…very Miss Moneypenny."

"Oh yes, you do like to live dangerously, don't you?" She slaps my hand away, grins, and sashays into the passenger seat. Her flowery scent fills the car.

Jade's parents live halfway between Colchester and Clacton, in a house built by her grandfather in a time when planning permission was less rigorous. Not that there's anything wrong with it; I just think things must have been simpler then. It's a higgledy-piggledy sort of a place, with rooms curling off from corridors in places you least expect them, and each time I visit, her father seems to have changed something, either in the house, the garden, or the attached allotment. It keeps him busy in his semi-retirement years, Jade once told me, but I think the itch must always have been there.

By the time we arrive, the A12 has gathered the car to its road-maintenance-busy breast and regurgitated us after two hours and twenty-seven minutes of queueing. Mrs. O'Donnell, primed from her enroute conversation with her daughter, sweeps us into the living room where two large glasses of wine are waiting. As I'm the one driving, I'm forced to leave half of it.

"Good journey, dears?" Mrs. O'Donnell—whom I can never quite bring myself to call by her first name—asks with a smile.

Jade launches into a brief and bitter monologue about the state of UK roads which, being the woman she is, soon segues into a bright and gossipy monologue about what she's been up to in the social centre of Stratford. This includes salsa, her reading group currently preparing for discussions on the latest Anne Tyler novel, and whether the late summer sales will be worth investigation. As I know about most of it already, I phase out and sip my wine.

I'm sitting on a plush, deep crimson sofa with Jade to one side and her mother in the chair opposite. The carpet is an old-fashioned, seventies, patterned style, big and bold and bright, or would be if the O'Donnells were the house-proud types, and the walls are a plain sea-green. By all the laws of design, it shouldn't work, but in a room this size, it does. I love it and I hope they never change it.

Leaning back, I close my eyes for a second or two, the background hum of the women's voices acting like a cradle song. The burgeoning smell of roasting lamb and potatoes rocks me into the sort of family comfort zone I never really had. The next thing I know, Jade is leaning over me, shaking my shoulder.

"Hey, Paul, Mum's asked you the same question three times and all you can do is snore."

"I'm not snoring. I wasn't asleep."

"Leave the poor boy alone, darling," Mrs. O'Donnell says. "He's tired; it's a long journey and he's driven all that way."

"No, really, Mrs. O'Donnell, it's fine. I was just listening to you, that's all…what was it you were asking?"

She opens her mouth to reply, but at the same time, the back door clicks open and there's the sound of a grunted hello. Jade's father has returned from his morning viewing of the allotment and this is the cue for her mother to leap up and head for the kitchen to check her husband is all right. There's a lot to be said for rural values, and I'm almost sorry Jade doesn't share them. Might be nice if she leapt up to greet me at the office once in a while. The thought makes me smile.

"What's up with you then?"

"Nothing. I'm just amused by the lies you tell about me snoring."

"I have witnesses. Independent ones." She makes to carry on, but it's too late. The door has already opened and Mr. O'Donnell is standing on the threshold. He's a big man, grey tufts of hair emphasizing his baldness, and whenever I've seen him, he's always dressed as if he's about to step into a tractor and go plowing: baggy, hard-wearing trousers; old striped shirt; and holey jumper, usually green. The opposite in style to his daughter, although their faces are similar, with something about the mouth and nose making my friend a definite O'Donnell.

"How's my favorite daughter then?"

"Dad, I'm your only daughter."

The two of them exchange a quick but sincere hug, and Jade twangs her father's black braces.

"That hurts!"

"Sorry."

She isn't, though, and neither is he. It's part of their ritual of greeting. The sight of it twists my stomach, and I wonder how things might have been if my father had ever been like that, though it's only now I can admit it wasn't all his fault. It took two of us to make my family as it is today; it took two.

Letting his daughter go, Mr. O'Donnell stretches out a gnarled hand, and I shake it with enthusiasm.

"Good to see you again."

"And you, sir. How's the allotment?"

"Can't complain; weather's been kind. The journey?"

"The usual."

We then smile at each other for a second or two before drawing away. This will be the sum total of our direct conversation for the day, but it never feels odd. Mr. O'Donnell is a man of few words, and it only makes me like him better.

Jade's mother calls time for lunch, and the four of us sit down in the small but double-windowed dining room. From where I am, I can see Mr. O'Donnell's garden stretching up to the sheds, and beyond this lays his much-loved allotment. Jade is always proud of the fact that the family has never had to buy their own vegetables, as everything they need is grown on their own land. A world a million miles away from my childhood, where everything came from the most expensive shops possible, and my mother never needed to step into the kitchen if she chose not to. My father hired staff, and the day I finally walked away from it all was, in a sense, one of the best I've ever known. Though, of course, I could never really walk that far away, not then.

Now all four of us munch away on the acres of food prepared by Mrs. O'Donnell. Roast lamb and all the trimmings, and she's added in Yorkshire puddings, too, because she knows I love them.

"Now, Paul, you look like you need feeding up," she says, forking more broccoli onto my plate in spite of feeble objections. "You need to keep your energies going for that dreadful drive back to London, you know, dear. And I imagine that job of yours is quite exhausting, too. Is it going well at the moment? I understand you had to go to Egypt on a case?"

"Yes, Mrs. O'Donnell. It wasn't for long, though; just to ask a couple of people some questions. I was back before Jade had even realized I'd gone."

"That's not true," Jade chipped in. "I knew you were gone. The office was tidy for one thing and—"

"Okay, don't give me a list of everything I do that ruins your day. I know my faults."

"Nonsense," Mrs. O'Donnell says. "Jade is always telling us how easy you are to work for."

"Mum! Don't give away all my trade secrets. If Paul thinks I'm unhappy, he might give me a decent pay rise one day."

I hold up my hands in pretend horror. "Pay rise? I pay you as well? Indeed, I am truly wonderful, and you are lucky to work for me."

"Dream on, buster. You're lucky to employ me."

Her mother laughs and starts to clear the plates, while her father pours his daughter more wine.

During pudding—apple tart and cream—of which I have seconds, I catch up on what's been happening in Jade's parents' village since the last time I visited. It's like something from The Archers, all country walks, fetes, WI meetings, and lunches out by the river. And that's just Mrs. O'Donnell. Outside his home interests, Mr. O'Donnell is kept busy, now he's retired, by county shows and the odd bit of harvesting. I love hearing about it; another kind of a life is always attractive, though whether I could ever move to the country myself is something I've not considered.

PI Rule Number Five: stay where the crime is. And, on the whole, that means cities and people, not villages and fields.

And of course, in the O'Donnell's case, church life. Or rather, chapel life.

"I don't suppose, darling," Mrs. O'Donnell says, as she starts to stack the pudding bowls, "you've had a chance yet to catch up with Steve and Naomi?"

I raise one eyebrow at Jade. "Who?"

"Old friends from chapel," Jade explains. "They've moved into London, Muswell Hill…when was it, Mum?"

"Over the summer. I said you'd pop in and—"

"I know, Mum. I know. I'm dreadful, and I will, honest. It's just that they're so…so Baptist and so pregnant."

Mr. O'Donnell chuckles. "That's not a sin, at least not yet, not even under this government."

"Yes, and you'll tell me they're lovely people, and they are, but all we'll talk about when I go 'round is chapel and babies, and I know zilch about either at the moment."

Jade rests her chin in her hands and looks so disheartened that I give her shoulder a quick squeeze, and her mother hugs her.

"Quite right. You're young yet, darling. There's all the time in the world for whatever you want to do. But there are other subjects apart from religion and babies, and they'd love to see you. Do pop in if you can."

"Yes, I will, I promise."

After lunch, we throw ourselves into the drill of washing-up. There's no dishwasher here, just a strict line of willing helpers organized into military efficiency by Mrs. O'Donnell. Then, all good deeds done, Jade and her mother drift back into the living room for coffee and chat. To give them some mother-daughter privacy, the menfolk, such as we are, take a stroll around the allotment.

I'm not a fan of gardening, but other people's enthusiasms fascinate me. For Jade's father, it's nature and anything to do with growing things. Jade once told me he knows all the Latin names for every vegetable and fruit you can think of, and I don't doubt it. Today, I find myself nodding intelligently when faced with tomatoes, propagation, the greenhouse, how difficult the weather has been for sprouts, and how many potatoes they've grown over the season, whenever that may be.

Halfway 'round the now-familiar stroll, at the farthest point from the house, Mr. O'Donnell pauses.

"Paul?"

"Yes?" I stop, a little ahead of him, and turn 'round. His grey hair is framed by the sun.

"We've been— I mean, Jade's mother and myself—Well, may I ask you a question?"

"Sure." I stuff my hands in my pockets and try to look as if this is a normal part of the tradition. The truth is I've never seen Jade's father look quite so uncomfortable before, and I've never heard him say such a long and jagged sentence either. We're treading on new territory here. I hope we can both navigate it.

"Do you… Are you and my daughter… I mean you both get on so well, do you have intentions?"

Oh, God. Of all the questions running through my head, I've never imagined this one, and, for the first time ever, I regret my decision to ask Jade not to tell her parents about me. If I'd been more honest in the past, this wouldn't be happening now.

"Ah, well, I…" Inspiration dribbles to emptiness, and I look away and then at the ground, rubbing my face. "I'm very fond of Jade, Mr. O'Donnell, of course. I think the world of her."

"Yes, we know that. It was why—"

I push on regardless. "And we're very good friends. We always will be. She's a wonderful person, but I…I don't think we're cut out to be a couple."

"Oh."

When I finally look my best friend's father in the eyes, his frown is as sharp as winter.

"I'm sorry," I say, trying to twist things back to how they were, but knowing, even as I'm saying it, that it might be impossible. "I'm sorry, but then again, Jade's had a lucky escape. She can do a hundred times better then me…more, I expect."

He says nothing in reply. Silent, awkward, all fragile companionship gone, we head back to his home.

"How was the men's talk today then?" Jade says, but, as she looks at the both of us, her smile fades.

I mumble something incomprehensible, whilst behind her halo of blonde hair, Mrs. O'Donnell gives her husband a questioning glance and is rewarded with a small shake of the head in return. The test has been given to me, and I've proved worthless.

The next two hours and nine minutes last a month, maybe more. By the time we leave, I wish I'd managed to learn the gift of honesty before it came to this. The O'Donnells have always been good to me and this is how I repay them.

I can't tell Jade. Maybe she knows more than she lets on, though, as it's only after thirty-four minutes in the car that she throws in the subtle question, after talking for a full five minutes about the latest Big Brother reject.

"What happened in the garden?" she asks, touching up her still perfect mascara in the vanity mirror. "You looked devastated when you came back in after lunch. Both of you."

"What? No, nothing. Nothing happened," I tell her. "I was worrying about the case, that's all."

"Did you talk to Dad about it?"

"No, of course not. You know I wouldn't do that. It's unfair."

Jade puts her mascara back into her green velvet make-up bag and closes it with a snap. "He wouldn't mind; he's very fond of you. You know that. I thought for a second he might have been bringing up religion and children with you, like Mum did with me."

"Come on. She was only asking about those friends of yours. Whom I've never heard of, by the way. Not that I'm accusing you of holding out on me but—"

"I wasn't," she says, not responding to my teasing. "Honest, it's just that Steve and Naomi are people from the past, and I don't know if I've got anything in common with them now. I'm not sure if I can go back."

"Too many Baptists and babies?"

"No." She hesitates, not like the Jade I know. "I suppose I'd love that, too, one day. To go back to chapel and have babies and stuff. All the stuff everyone else ends up with, everyone but you and me, that is. Maybe I'm just jealous, so maybe that's why I'm scared of seeing them."

She stops, and there's nothing I can say to help, but because it's her and I love her, I try anyway.

"Look, don't put yourself down. You're worth more than all of them put together, and you'll get all the stuff you want in the end. Just you wait and see. Babies and husbands and chapels and God knows what else. Steve and Naomi will be jealous as hell of you one day."

"Yeah, I know, maybe." She reaches out and pats me on the knee. "I'm sure it'll be fine. I'll get there in the end, and so will you. We both will. As long as you're not... I mean, and I'm not nagging, I swear it, but you will be careful, won't you? About everything?"

When I glance across at her, for a moment I think she might be about to cry before realizing she's just flicking away a loose eyelash.

"You're right," I say. "We're both going to be fine. As I say, you'll have six husbands and fifty children, at least. Not only that, but I'll finish this case in record time with my top-notch professional skills and be richer than in my wildest dreams. At least for a couple of months. And, yes, I'll be careful. Everything's under control."

*   *   *

At home, I listen to this morning's message again twice and wonder if, no matter what I say, not everything is under control after all.

"Just a warning," the unfamiliar male voice, foreign accent unmissable, says. "Stay away from Delta Egypt."

CHAPTER 6

"You did what?" There's a tremor in Dominic's voice I haven't heard before, and when he places his water glass on the office table, it rocks once before settling.

I repeat my last sentence, the one explaining how I exited the premises of Delta Egypt on my second visit. So far it's been a tale cut short as I haven't yet told him about the USB drive or its copy, or what Blake said to me about Teresa, and I haven't decided whether I will or not.

"Are you all right?"

"Yes, of course. I'm here, aren't I?"

Sitting down opposite me, he says, "So what did you find out while you were there? Anything worth my while?"

A second's hesitation and then I shake my head, relaxing back into my seat and taking care to keep eye contact with him. "No, I'm afraid not. Not so far."

This is true, as it stands. What I'm leaving out, for a variety of reasons, not least because I'm convinced Dominic knows more than he's telling me as well, are the suspicions I have. Most important of these is my instinct about Blake Kenzie himself. The man's a criminal, no doubt of it, and one with something to hide.

Dominic smiles. "You said you met Blake. What did you think?"

"A powerful man, that's easy to see, and someone who knows what he wants and how to get it. You wouldn't want him as your enemy. Intelligent, cunning, dangerous. He didn't like me, but in my business, that's not surprising."

"Very similar to myself then, apart from your last statement."

The palms of my hands grow clammy. For a moment, I have no idea what to say, or even what he might expect me to say, and all I can do is gulp back the ball of confusion lodged in my throat.

Dominic's next question takes us back to our previous course, thank God. "Do you like him?"

"No."

"I see. Perhaps you're right, Paul, perhaps you're right."

There's no time to ask what he means by this as already he's closed the subject and moved on. I wonder what he's running from and why.

"So," he says, tapping his water glass with one fingertip, "I assume you managed to steal at least some of their records while you were at Delta and, if so, which ones?"

"I prefer the phrase 'copied on behalf of a client,' Dominic, if you don't mind."

He just shrugs. "As you wish. But, please, tell me what you've found."

"Nothing, yet. It all looks above board to me," I tell him. "Jade's working hard on getting underneath to anything strange, and I expect to—"

He snorts, and I stop. While he waits, I reach for my water and take one small sip. "Look, Dominic, I know you're paying me good money, and if there's anything to find out—though I doubt it—I'll find it out for you, but I'd appreciate it if you kept your feelings about those I choose to work with to yourself. I've no idea why you've never liked Jade, but she's my friend. Not only that, she's the best computer hacker I know, and I wouldn't have got this far without her. If after this case is finished you're any better off in terms of knowledge, it'll be her you ought to thank."

He nods. "I understand."

I nod back and, after a second, we break eye contact.

"As I was saying," I continue, "I expect to be able to give you a more complete report by the end of the week. This meeting was just to keep you updated."

That's not entirely true. To do that, I could easily have called him, but I wanted to see the look on his face when I told him what had happened in Egypt. I wanted to see if he already knew about it or not. I've done what I came to do, but I'm no better off; he's given nothing away. It's time to leave. Before he begins to think I've called the meeting because I'm suspicious rather than lovesick. Maybe I'm both.

"So, I'll ring you within the next three days and let you know what we've found out. Before I go, I do have one question for you."

"Fine."

"Have you told Blake anything about me, anything personal?"

He pauses.

"No," he says. "What's there to tell, now?"

I head for the door, but once again he doesn't let me go without a final comment for my blood to mull over.

"There is something I believe you're wrong about, Paul."

"What's that?"

"Jade isn't the only one I ought to be thanking. It seems to me you've already done more than enough for the fee I'm paying you. In Egypt alone."

*　　*　　*

I'd given up smoking the day after my birthday, three years, ten months, three weeks, and six days ago, but now, from instinct, I still reach for my pocket outside Dominic's office. There's something about what's been happening to me since meeting up with my ex-lover that's made the years between seem as if they've never existed. It makes me feel as if I've been asleep for too long and woken up not knowing much. About anything.

The sun is hot against my face, although it feels a thousand times lighter than in Cairo. Safer, too. The city, the last full week in August, and the only one not looking forward to the bank holiday is me. I start to walk, hands in pockets, eyes focused on the pavement in front of me, out of habit glancing from side to side now and then, though there's no need. Not here.

I decide to take a bus to hurry back to the familiarity of the office. The urge to be there makes my skin prickle and my legs twitch. This is the moment in a case I love most, the moment where I might be about to discover something, however small and obscure, that will make a difference to the way things turn out. It might be another chance to change an injustice into a justice, a chance I never had with Teresa. It's always been that way, ever since…ever since.

Still, this time it's different, but if Jade and I find something out, where will it take us?

The bus is crowded, the air inside filled with the scent of flesh and flowers. People who work in the city don't take the bus; it's only those passing through who have to do that.

I wouldn't want Dominic's job, even if I had the talent for it or the will. It strikes me how little I know of his past in all the cuttings I've collected of him. He never speaks of it. Even when we were together, it was never a subject for discussion. We never asked about each other's parents, childhood, any of the vast sea of personal history we all carry in our bones. I know why I didn't say anything about my past. Why didn't he? Maybe we both have something to hide. Maybe, when he dumped me, Dominic was right; we never really had the truth of each other.

No, that's not it either. We were caught in the net of his marriage and my obsession, for yes, that's what it was, and still in a sense is. His marriage, a given. My obsession? A factor I've come to terms with now; all that counseling, all Jade's nagging concern must have done something for me in the end. I've lived a kind of a life since Dominic, haven't I? The years have moved past and the seasons come and gone.

But inside I'm still the same. All that professional support wasted. When Dominic rings, I'm there, living, breathing, pulsating for him, no matter what he does. Seeing him after so long has been like waking up from a coma and grasping the chance to live again.

Why did he say there was nothing personal to tell Blake about me? Does he think that? Really?

When will I be free of it, this rock-hard certainty that, even when the book between the two of us seems closed, somehow, somewhere there's another chapter not yet written?

Time goes by that even I make no effort to calculate, and when the waves of memory and desire become too strong and rich for me, I get off the bus, even though it's still several stops away from the one I need. No matter. Any more trips into a history I shouldn't be revisiting will mean I'll never get the job done. The fresh air, or what passes for fresh air in London, will make me sharp again.

As I walk, the buildings around me loom tall and dominant, the people bustling around, in and through them just temporary glitches in the permanent mass of stone and brick. The houses of Hackney, more, of London, will be here long after the small history I bring with me is gone. Everything I feel now is a brief dream only, but a powerful one. At least to me.

It starts to rain, a late summer storm, and I hunch deeper into the collar of my jacket, the droplets easing their way through my hair and onto my neck. At least it's warm, but even so, I quicken my pace as the office comes into view, brushing past one or two groups of young men loitering, out of school and out of luck. At the bottom of the steps to the front door, someone pushes into me. I sidestep away and, with all that's been happening over the last week, raise my hands to defend myself against any fresh attack.

No need, it's just a tramp. He mutters something that could be an apology or a curse. There's a glimpse of bleared eyes and shaggy beard and then he's gone, weaving his way down the wet street, bottle of shop-brand whisky clutched in his fingers.

I smile at my own foolishness, thinking that if the old bloke had waited I would have given him something. Instead, I take a breath of warm, muggy air and make my way inside.

Jade is working, blonde head down and staring at her computer screen as if it holds the secret to the world around us. I hope it does.

She looks up as the door clicks shut behind me and nods. "Hi there. You look happy. Solved the case yet?"

"Yeah, I wish. No, I'm just smiling because I thought some tramp was out to get me. Do you think I'm getting paranoid in my old age?"

"No more than normal." She shrugs, still tapping away.

I hang my jacket up, noting how she hasn't mentioned where I've been. "Thanks for the vote of confidence. How're you getting on? Any luck?"

"We-ll." She hesitates, and I stride across to lean over her shoulder and peer at the list of dates and numbers on the screen.

"What's that? Anything Dominic might want to know?"

"I'm not sure yet. It all seems normal for a business: information about markets; lists of investments; PR plans; all the usual stuff. There is one thing, though."

"What's that?"

"Call me suspicious, but it's all too perfect. Isn't that what you thought when you looked at it over the weekend? It's as if here is a series of files Delta Egypt has had made especially for people who might come along and want to steal their secrets. Every company in the world has secrets, otherwise what's the point of industrial espionage? Not

Delta, though. Their files are squeaky clean. You could put a one-year-old child in the middle of them and there'd be nothing to give its parents a moment's worry."

"So we can mark Blake Kenzie with a clean bill of health when we report to Dominic. And then we can take the money and run, can we?"

Even as I'm saying it, I know it's the best way forward for me and maybe for all of us. Drop the report on Dominic's desk, walk away, and never see him again.

"No, it's not that simple," she says, fingers clicking on the keyboard and taking us both to a screen I haven't seen before. "I also found this. It wasn't obvious, as it was hidden, rather cleverly, too, but I wanted to check everything, so here it is."

I can't see anything different from the list of words and dates she had on the screen before, except that there are more columns of them. Then I look at the new column names: Starlight, Dancer, Bluesky, Aqua.

Bluesky?

I grab my chair and sit down next to her. "Bluesky? The dead woman?"

"Yes. Unless the coincidence is off the scale."

"Unlikely." I'm trying to think, but the connections aren't coming. "Blake knows her? Has information on her in some way?"

Jade shakes her head, "He must do, but…"

"But what?

"But it's not just him. I found this spreadsheet linked from the DG Allen Enterprises folder."

My mouth goes dry. "Meaning if Blake knows something about Bluesky, then Dominic might, too. Or Blake thinks he does. Just what the hell is going on?"

"I don't know, but there's more."

She scrolls down the spreadsheet and halfway down a page with an entry under Aqua, it says: pick-up and.

"And what?" I whisper.

"That's just it, Paul," she begins, her explanation giving me time to catch my breath. "And what? I started doing other stuff, but it kept nagging away, and in the end I came back to it. I went through it all again and something clicked. You see, if you take any of these words or dates, they look just like a jumble of meaningless information: Jan 31, call; when ready, Mar 20; carry on, Jun 0. But I think they're more than that. I think they're half of something else…the end of the date, the beginning of the phrase.

"I wouldn't have spotted it if it hadn't been for that last extra word under Aqua. And then again, maybe I wouldn't have seen it at all, or even bothered with it if it hadn't been for knowing about Bluesky. Where the phrases have been placed, they look like a copy of something else that's been deleted or partially saved in the course of being transferred or downloaded. It can't be that, though. They're too patterned; a partial transfer would be much more random. Still, we were lucky to spot it. I was just being thorough."

"As you always are. Thank you…good work."

She blushes and gives me half a smile. "You're welcome. But we're no better off. Without the other half of the file, we still don't know what it means."

"No, but now we know there's something there, something to find out. No matter what we've been told."

"That's what you like best, Paul, isn't it?"

"What?" The sudden switch in subject matter almost leads to a breach of PI Rule Number Six: never let your staff be more than one step ahead of you, and certainly never show it if they are.

"It's what you like best," Jade says again. "The chance for discovery, bringing a new fact to light. It gets you every time, doesn't it?"

"Is that a bad thing for an investigation agency? If we didn't want to find things out, where would we be?"

"Sure, but what are we going to do about finding the missing half of the file? Maybe I can go to Egypt this time and get the half you left behind in a more civilized and female way, without having to jump out a window?"

"Dream on." The thought of Jade mixed up with Blake's mob makes me shudder. "Anyway, if Blake's anything like the man I imagine him to be, and there's anything else he doesn't want me to find, it'll be somewhere I'd never think of in a thousand years, or he'll have destroyed it."

"So what will you do?"

My sigh is ragged and comes from the gut. "I'll think of something. I'll have to if I'm going to persuade a glimmer of truth out of Dominic, and that seems the only avenue to explore at the moment to get any of the answers. He's not a murderer, but he might know something to implicate Blake."

There's a pause, and Jade folds her arms, skidding her chair back so she all but runs me over.

"Oh yes," she says. "I forgot to ask. How was your meeting?"

"I filled him in as best I could. He's happy to wait for the official report."

I go back to my desk. The rest of the day is spent catching up on paperwork and keeping my other clients at bay. The main subjects occupying my thoughts are what Jade's discovery might mean and how I can make best use of it for my next meeting with Dominic.

Five hours and thirteen minutes later, a calculation that includes the seventeen-minute lunch break I allot myself, we're out of the office. A quick drink at The Bell and Book, which looks as if it could use the custom tonight, and then I'm waving her off on her bike. As she spins her way 'round the corner, I turn my steps in the opposite direction.

It's only then that something occurs to me...something I should have picked up on earlier, if only my head hadn't been full of Dominic and sex. The tramp. When he'd bumped into me at the office, there'd been no smell. And the bottle of whisky he'd been waving was full.

CHAPTER 7

At home, there's no one lurking in the street or the small scraggly bushes, but my muscles only relax when I'm inside with the door double locked behind me. The wait for my first taste of the Highland Park is a long one.

By the second sip, I've checked every room—a mission that doesn't take long—and shut out the world outside behind the comfort of curtains. By the third sip, I'm sprawled on the sofa in the living room staring at the unlit fireplace. I haven't got Dominic what he says he wants. No complete evidence that Kenzie & Co. are crooked and he shouldn't be mixed up with them at any level—not even confirmation of shadiness—just half a document.

Is there a way I can get the information I need to clear my ex-lover's name? And keep myself alive? Haven't I experienced how quick Blake is to act? One meeting, that's all it took, and he wants me dead. I didn't even have anything useful on him when he made that decision. No, I'm wrong. He'd decided what to do about me before I'd even stepped over his threshold. He knew my connection with Dominic and he wanted me dead.

It's as simple as that.

Nothing I've seen or heard proves it for sure, but it's Rule Number Seven in the PI book: in a dangerous situation, if there's a choice between instinct and logic, go with instinct. It won't fail you.

Add to all that a dead woman, threatening phone calls, and one clean, teetotal tramp and I'm spinning somewhere into depths I can't recognize and don't have the skills to handle. I've made my living from people committing adultery, fiddling the books, or cheating on their insurance. All the countless acts of disloyalty that taint a character, take who someone is and alter the color of the person so you can't tell where the white ends and the grey begins, or how one day it may turn to black. Of the three occasions in my life where I've struck out beyond my reach, two of them have involved Dominic: once in our affair and now here when he asks for my help.

It's no good; I can't back out. Wherever this goes, I have to see it through.

My dreams that night are full of memories, but not the ones I expect when I finally crawl under the duvet, four whiskies and one small bowl of pasta later. There's a garden, rich and green, at the height of summer. The sound of laughter, a swing hung between two plum trees, the hushed trickle and flow of water. I'm walking, fingers trailing through roses of yellow, pink, deep orange and the scent of them catches on my skin. I'm a child again, the trees lining my path taller than I will ever be, no matter how much I long to touch their uppermost leaves. Another laugh, this time closer, to my right, and when I turn, I see a young girl skipping toward me, nine years old, her hair held into plaits and her dress and shoes all the colors of the rainbow.

"Dance with me," she sings. "Dance with me," but I can't and already the tears are welling up as the faraway sky darkens. Her eyes are a richer shade of green than mine, and her hair glows ebony against the grass. Behind her stand two figures, their faces obscured, their familiarity a catch in my throat, an accusation. I stumble toward her, and she holds her hand to her mouth as if shutting a secret in a cave. Before I reach her, she turns and runs, her bright dress carving its way through reeds and tall flowers. I chase after her, and branches and leaves cling to my clothes and strike my skin. Behind me, I know the two adults I have seen follow us both. Their presence makes me start to run, but in front of me, the girl runs faster.

Without forming the words in my head, I know I have to reach her before she can disappear or turn in a direction I can't see. My skin is cold and my heart is beating, so loud, so loud it drowns out every other want and need I have ever known. I call her name, but the sound of it is dragged away by the wind and vanishes. Now I stand in a clearing, and the trees above me are dark, thin fingers laced against a threatening sky. Even though I swing 'round the full circle of where I stand, I can't see where the girl has gone. I can't see and I know the adults who follow me will soon be here and the one to be blamed will be me. I should have kept up with her. I should have…

A glimpse of lemon and green and red dress, a flurry of black hair, rich and strong, at the corner of my eye and once again I'm in pursuit. Blood pulsates through my veins, and my breath comes in harsh gasps. Why doesn't she stop? Can't she tell I need her to stop? Please, please, I...

Again we run, through weeds and thistles that snatch and tear at me, though they don't slow her down, and the distance between us remains the same. All I can do is keep her in sight. I can't gain on her, not unless she lets me. She runs like someone whose body is water, flowing over and through any obstacle it faces. I am nothing but flesh. I cannot catch her.

Still I keep trying, trying in a way I don't think I've done before, in a dream I know will lead nowhere. This time it might be different, please God, this time. The girl and I keep running, and behind us, the crashing noise of the adults grows quieter, drifting away at last into memory. When I try to wake, it's impossible. I must keep dreaming, keep running.

After a time I can't count, there's the sound of water, torrential, unforgiving, to our left. The sky darkens again, my heart pounds harder, and the girl swerves toward the river.

"No." My silent voice echoes only in my head, and she doesn't hear me. The sound of water beats faster, louder, as if it could break from its thin banks and overwhelm both of us. "Please."

Above me, the trees vanish, and I'm left standing on wet grass facing a silver river. Somehow, the girl has already crossed the racing flood. I don't know how. She stands, still as a cat, on the other side, sunlight glistening in her hair, and her dress is as bright as roses. For a long moment, she remains there, arms stretched high above her head as if in blessing or a curse. Before I can shout a warning or try to move to help, her slim, white body has plunged into the water, a faint glimmer of yellow, red, green, a swirl of dark hair, and then she's gone.

"Teresa!"

When I wake, I'm crying.

*   *   *

The place is the same as it always is—a wide courtyard leading to a large Victorian house glowing with the colors of earth. I park the car on the gravel, making sure my exit is clear, and when I get out, the smell of grass and clean air almost overwhelms me. For the price of my conscience, I would slip back into my dirty grey Vauxhall and take the road north and home, but if I did that there would be no way back. Something in me still wants that path to be open.

Because here is somewhere I have never invited Jade. I have never found anyone who could take that journey, not even Dominic. My fault. It's something I never told him at the beginning, though I wanted to, and then the moment for it passed.

Before I can knock on the freshly painted, blue front door, it is opened and a tall woman, early sixties, white hair, hazel eyes, gazes at me.

"Hello," she says. "It's good to see you."

Always the same greeting, the two times a year I make this visit, once now on August bank holiday and once just before Christmas. Not Christmas itself, as that would entail too much compromise. Christmas, for me, is a time to be alone.

I smile and wonder if my smile reaches my eyes, as hers almost does.

We drink sherry in a room painted in white and silver. Outside, the lawn is striped as far as the eye can see, and the taste of the sherry is nutmeg on my tongue.

"How is work going?" she asks, putting down her glass and folding both hands onto her lap, as if covering secrets.

"Oh, you know. How is everything here?"

"The same as always."

Always the same. Days of brightness and boredom, the long drift of the countryside, is how Surrey is. Similar in some ways to the life Jade's parents live, but very different, too. Different by means of the parties, the entertaining, the focus on position and appearance, the sense of responsibility and of things being more complex when you dig deeper. I am what I've always been to them: an enigma, an embarrassment.

"And are you okay?" I ask.

"We tick along. How is London?"

"Dark and dreary. Have you been up at all? For a show or anything?"

"No, not recently. I think Jonathan may be planning something soon, perhaps for Christmas? Of course he has his work commitments."

Yes, of course he does. All those times when he has to be up in London without her, and he won't be thinking of me at all. Not that I blame him. Not after what I did.

We lapse into silence. After a while, as we watch five sparrows and a blackbird hop along the patio and peck at the shrubs, she gets up, nods, takes my empty sherry glass, and trots into the kitchen. For lack of anything else to do, I follow her and wonder if it will always be the same. When I enter the kitchen, she's leaning over the oven from which a great grey gust of steam and salt-sea spices fills the air.

"Baked salmon," I say. "Summer food."

She jumps at the sound of my voice, and I take two steps away, but she turns 'round and shakes her head. "I know you like it, Paul."

"Yes, and there'll be plenty left for…later. Can I help?"

A second's tension, then she seems to decide to ignore my gaffe, instead flapping her wrinkled hands as if to flap away the steam. "No. Thank you. I'm happy here, pottering about. You go back to the living room. There are papers to read. If you like, you can help me wash up afterward."

Given my dismissal, I wander back and pat the Staffordshire dogs on the mantelpiece, nearly the twins of mine, before sitting down and rifling through the enormous pile of papers.

I've no idea why they always order all the Sundays; there can't be enough hours in the week to read them before the next supply comes in. Still, it fills my time, so for the next forty-two minutes, I skim-read. It's only when I'm two pages ahead of the phrase I've seen that I realize I've recognized it and have to turn back. The headline from the article, if I can only find it, and the links it makes between something I know and something I don't causes my stomach to lurch in excitement mixed with fear. Eighth rule of PI work: always know which of these two is stronger. This time, I don't.

Sod's Law clicks in, and I can't find what I think I've seen. Is it in this article? Or perhaps it's one I was reading earlier on about crime figures in the country or the one about the falling numbers of policemen. Or were they the same? Feeling my skin prickle, I start flicking back and forth in ever-increasing numbers of pages. From the kitchen, the sound of the pressure cooker being allowed its moment of release whistles a time warning.

Where did I see that phrase, that word? Where?

"Paul! It's ready. Can you open the wine?"

Damn. No time for more searching now; it'll just have to wait. Grabbing the whole of the Sunday Telegraph, I lay it on the arm of my chair and make my way into the kitchen, where I struggle with the cork on the Rapel Valley 2003 Sauvignon Blanc. The wine tastes like honeyed spice.

As we sit at the kitchen table, the salmon, new potatoes, and assorted greens creating an elegant concept on the Wedgwood, there's only one question on my lips.

"May I take one of the papers home? The Telegraph?"

"Today's?"

"Yes."

"But I don't think your… I mean, I don't think it's been read yet."

I say nothing, but start to cut into my food, releasing that salmon-spice pink scent in a fuller wave into the room. She must take pity on me, as her next words come full circle.

"All right, dear. If you're sure you need it?"

"Yes, I do. Thank you." On impulse, I lean over and kiss her paper-thin cheek. Physical contact isn't a journey we've taken in a long time, too long to count, and I can't imagine it will happen again for a while, as she doesn't reciprocate. The knowledge of this burns me, and for the rest of the meal, we remain almost silent.

Afterward, I wash up and gaze at the old clock near the sink as its hands march on to a kind of freedom, however temporary. Then we drink coffee, strong and black enough to cover over the gap between us. We comment on the weather, the situation in Afghanistan, and other major politics, and I smile again at the differences between today and the day spent with Jade's parents.

The conversation runs out a full thirty-nine minutes before I judge it appropriate to leave, and I watch as she dozes, the afternoon light flooding through the window and creating a halo of her hair. I think about searching through the newspaper again, but don't want to wake her. I'll have to buy it later if I can't take it now without a conversation about…him. The house around me huddles closer, bringing with it little flashes of what I've been and what I choose not to remember. When it's time to go, I nudge her arm.

"What? Is everything all right? Is—"

"Yes, it's fine," I interrupt before she can say what can't be said. "Everything's fine. It's just time for me to go."

"Oh. Oh, I see."

She uncurls herself from her chair. Limbs creak and stretch, and skin patterns itself into place, a new shape, a new idea of age. With half a smile, she sees me to the door, but then turns back for the paper.

"Here," she says, taking the Sunday Telegraph from where I'd left it on the arm of the chair and waving it in my direction. "Don't forget this."

"Thanks. I won't."

When I wave goodbye and steer the Vauxhall out of the gravel driveway, the visit isn't quite over; there's still one stop left before I can return home.

The church of St. Peter's glistens in the sunlight, and I notice the weathervane has vanished. Another accident during the course of the year, I imagine, and I wonder if it will ever be replaced.

The churchyard is free of people, and it looks as if the grass has been cut recently. Its fresh green smell wafts the summer along into the approach of autumn. Time passing and the loss of it has been a weight over my head stronger than any sword since that day, though sometimes, if I'm relaxed enough, I can almost remember back to a place in my life when I was free of it. It doesn't matter. It's beyond me now. If I'd been there, maybe she wouldn't have gone. If I hadn't been intent on my own six-year-old interests, sneaking into my father's shed and playing with the child's toolbox he kept for me there, then maybe I would have been in time for her to be safe.

"Come on, Paul. Meet you up the woods in five minutes. See if you can find me!"

I should have gone with her when she called. That day more than any other. But I didn't. By the time I began to look for her, as she'd asked me to, she was gone. My contribution to my sister's kidnapping and assumed murder is something I've never told anyone, not even Jade. It's something I never will. Since then, each beat of the clock has been a small accusation. Each day, each moment I live takes me and all of us away from that moment twenty-four years, ten months and two days ago when our lives changed in a way that could never be un-changed. It's always a part of me.

As is the knowledge I was not the one taken.

Now there's a breeze that lifts my hair a little off my scalp, as I walk around two sides of the small, stone church and into the silence of the memorial area. Not quite a garden as there are no hedges or trees to mark any kind of boundary, but not quite part of the main graveyard either. It's out of the way of the road.

When I'm ready, I brush aside the strands of ivy curving across one edge of the bronze plaque and read the words again:

———

Teresa Anne Maloney,
Lost but always loved

———

Not much to show for a life, however short, and I pray that one day there might be justice, in a place where no mercy was shown. And, as I always do, I think about what her vanishing, the lack of any actual body to grieve over, has meant for all of us, for me. Maybe, without that, I wouldn't be in the business I am today or maybe, without that, I would have already dropped this case. But for Teresa's sake, and for Bluesky's, I want to know the truth.

This time, I stay a little longer than usual; in two months-less-two-days' time it will be a quarter-century since my sister vanished in the yellow and red and green-striped dress she loved so much and that, like her, was never found. If I knew the way to do it, I'd mark my own private anniversary with something more lasting than the twelve minutes I stay here, but I don't know how.

I wonder instead how my parents will make their peace with it and if they have ever wished aloud to each other, or in the secrecy of their own hearts, that it might have been me and not her who was lost.

Back at the car, I lock myself in and run my hands over my face for a long moment. Before setting out from the church, I take the paper my mother gave me and slowly turn the pages, running my eye up and down the columns as I go. That phrase, that word. Where is it? Where is it? Maybe it was only ever something in my head, maybe… But when I least expect it, when I've almost given up hope and marked the incident down to my own imagination, there it is, leaping up from the black print like a message for me alone.

Bluesky. The name on Blake's mysterious file. The woman. I read the article. Then I read it again.

As I drive back home, instead of mulling over the information I've gathered from this unexpected source, I think about the difference between Jade's family and mine. I try to convince myself once again that my father's deliberate absence today doesn't hurt me.

As I ease the car into the only remaining space on the street near my flat, a black BMW, deadly as dark fire, swerves at me from the opposite direction. The next second, it's rammed me at the offside front. As I'm jerked forward with the force of the crash, banging my nose on the steering wheel, the car screeches backward, rubber on tarmac, and takes off with an angry roar.

"Jesus. Jesus Christ."

When I jump out of the driver seat, the BMW is swinging 'round the corner, and I can see there aren't any license plates. I leg it to the end of the street, but it's already disappeared.

By the time I get back to my car, my nose has started to bleed.

Another warning, and this time they haven't kept it verbal.

CHAPTER 8

"Paul? What on earth did you do to your face?"

"Car accident," I grunt out. "Gave me a nosebleed."

"That's not all it's given you, by the look of it." Jade gets up, taps her way over to me in her impossibly high-heeled shoes—red this time I notice, to go with her suit and her matching garnet-and-diamante earrings. She peers at me as if I'm a difficult client whose case might be unsolvable. She may well be right.

PI Rule Number Nine: sometimes your assistant is not wrong. Not a rule I've discussed with Jade much.

"Is that a purple eye, or have you been overdoing the mascara?" she continues, taking a step back and frowning.

"Do you think I'd use something that looks this cheap?"

"Transvestites, so I'm told, spend a fortune to get that effect."

"This comes naturally, or as naturally as one crazed London driver and one dopey PI can make it. Any chance of an ice pack to hold over my fevered brow?"

As I settle into my chair, Jade stops frowning and sashays over to the kitchen. She disappears for a moment and comes back with a small pack of frozen peas I didn't know we possessed, and a tea towel.

"Where did the peas come from?"

"Sainsbury's."

"I didn't know our kitchen could be so useful."

"You never know when an angry client will come in and beat you up. I've been keeping them just in case."

"If an angry client did take a swing at me, I'm sure those earrings would dazzle him into submission."

Jade wraps the pack of peas in the tea towel and presses it against my left eye. "Shut up talking and hold this there for five minutes, would you? It may be the most useful thing we do all day."

In spite of the fact that her breasts are pushing against my face and making me gulp, I obey. Rule Ten in the PI book: sometimes simple obedience is best, especially when handling someone in high heels.

I watch as Jade goes back to her desk, focuses on her screen, and then answers two calls, one from a client I don't want to talk to. I glance at my watch. There are things I need Jade to do. And it has to be this morning.

Because this evening, although she doesn't know it, I plan to see Dominic.

Sliding the ice pack onto the desk, I take the photocopied papers out of my case and glance at them again. "Jade?"

"Hmm?"

"Any chance of you looking something up for me?"

"Go on then, and let's have it."

I show her the papers and, together, we take in the strange connection. As I speak my thoughts aloud, I watch her brush back her hair, fastening it with a clip, and cup her chin on her hand as she listens.

"This changes everything, doesn't it? Shouldn't we go to the police?"

"With what?" I ask. "All we've got at the moment could be just an over-imaginative journalist, some unprovable suppositions, and a leap of faith. Not to mention the fact that some of the information we've come by hasn't been gained by strictly legal means."

"Still, if it's true, it means it's more than just one dead woman. This is serious, Paul."

She's right. It's more serious than anything I've been involved in before. I want to make sure Dominic's in the clear. He has to be. More than that, I need to know the truth.

"I know," I say, as Jade continues to take me in with her big sapphire eyes, "but I need to find out answers. To do that, I first need all the police records you can find. On Bluesky and the rest."

"Sure, but it'll take time. Are you certain this is what you want? Isn't there another way?"

"You mean the legal one? The one that involves walking into the Met, telling the reception officer what I know, and then waiting for them to shine a light in my eyes?"

"The police have more advanced interview techniques these days."

"Nothing like a bright light and a thumbscrew to get the vocal cords working."

"I'll have to try it one day," she says, deadpan. "It might get you telling the real truth to your staff. This is about protecting Dominic, isn't it?"

"Don't be silly. Why should it be?" I turn my back on her, stride over to my desk, and leaf through some papers. "I'm just doing the job I'm paid to do and the one I want to do: giving Dominic the report he asked for and finding my way to the truth."

"I can see that. But you're involved, and not in a professional way either. That's what's worrying me."

There's a pause and I drop the papers down. "I'll be fine. Don't worry about me. Let's just worry about getting the answers and getting out."

When I look at her, she simply nods. "Okay."

"Thanks."

For the rest of the morning, I work on the client accounts I've neglected up until today. I make three phone calls, arrange one initial meeting and a reporting session, and type up a schedule of surveillance for an adultery case. Whenever I glance at Jade, she's either frowning at her screen or tapping away at the keys and juggling with USB drives, in and out of the computer, in and out. The action of playing catch-up makes me realize how much Jade is right in what she hasn't said. I have to raise my game to where it should be in terms of client handling or Maloney Investigations is going to be history. We can't survive on Dominic's fee alone, and there's not just me to consider. There's Jade, too; my failures aren't going to help her.

It's this realization that propels me to my feet and out the door just after Jade and I have split a bacon and avocado ciabatta and a J2O from the corner deli.

"See you later on," I say, wiping the crumbs from my mouth, "by five-thirty for sure, as usual. Do you think you'll have got something by then?"

"I don't know. It's not going well at the moment. Maybe I'm losing my touch?"

She looks so despondent that I can't help giving her a quick, heartfelt hug. Beneath my grip, her shoulders seem small and tense, and I hunker down next to her chair, taking her face between my hands.

"Jade?"

Her eyelashes flutter upward and those earrings glitter in the strip-light.

"Now listen. You're the best there is, and if you can't do it, then what the hell, it can't be done and we'll find another way. You're not losing your touch. I couldn't do this job if it wasn't for you, so please don't say things about yourself that aren't true. Okay?"

She nods, but I'm not convinced she means it.

"Good," I say, "so repeat after me: 'I'm the best.'"

"You're the best, Paul."

"No, no." I groan. "Why don't women ever listen? Say you're the best."

"You're— Sorry. I'm the best."

"Good. Well done." I kiss her on the forehead and get up. "I'm off on surveillance now to try to earn our keep. If you need me, the mobile will be on vibrate."

"Okay." Her sudden smile transforms her face in a moment. "Careful where you put it."

"Watch it." At the door, I give her a wink. "You're getting way too cheeky."

Cheekiness is a good sign, though. I'd hate Jade to be unhappy; I couldn't do without her.

I settle down in the Vauxhall on the corner of one of the not-quite-so-posh Islington roads. The house I've got in my view is a solid, modern red brick construction with a Classical look and two white mock pillars framing a small porch. Even from this distance, I can tell the pillars could do with a fresh coat of paint. I can't decide if it and its owner, whom I've only met once, are on their way up or on their way down. These days it's not always easy to tell.

Today, I'm watching his wife while he slaves away at his medium-level city job. I don't have any doubts she's unfaithful—all I need is the evidence—and I don't have any doubts that I'm happier by far doing what I do and simply being me. No way would I want to be him, for the job or the wife. She lunches, belongs to a tennis club, a reading group, and a Pilates class, gardens and does good deeds. Not enough to fill anyone's week, and as there aren't any children, I can only assume her spare time is spent cheating on her loved one. It shouldn't be too hard to nail her.

And while I'm doing that, I can think about tonight and Dominic.

He phoned me this morning. At home. The shiver of his voice on the line made everything around me glitter, in spite of all my doubts. Even now, I can almost taste his words again.

"Paul," he'd said, "I've noted your report, thank you, and I'd like to talk to you about it. Soon."

Several uncounted seconds passed before I was able to answer.

"Paul?"

"Yes, yes. I'm here."

"Are you all right?"

"Yes, of course. Why shouldn't I be?"

"Good," he said. "In that case, I'd like us to meet today."

"Sure." I'd scrabbled like a child for my Smartphone, but it slipped out of my fingers and glided across the floor. "When? And where? I can be at your office any time."

"No. Not the office. Come to Islington. Come tonight. Cassie's away and the children are on a sleepover at a friend's. Be here by 7."

Before I could take in what he was saying, he'd disconnected. I'd stayed kneeling on the floor for several minutes, phone in one hand. What did he want, and what would I be prepared to give him?

Sitting in my car now and staring at my subject's house, I'm no nearer resolving either question, and it worries me that I haven't told Jade about the conversation. Or about seeing Dominic on his home ground tonight. Rule Eleven of PI work: always keep your colleagues up-to-date with events as they happen.

Today I haven't done that. And because of it, there's going to be trouble.

Don't obsess, Paul, it's never got you anywhere. Look at the house, wait for your client's wife's lover to appear and just do the job.

Where I'm parked isn't too far from where Dominic lives in Islington. I could just drive there and— Stop it, stop it, for God's sake. Concentrate on the task in hand: glance; wait; read two paragraphs of the latest Bosch novel—wish I had some of his luck, though I could do without the action sequences; I have enough of my own— glance again; and so on and so on until my brain pauses and then I'm there. I'm into autopilot when sensation stops and I'm nothing but an eye watching and someone who waits. And waits.

Two hours and forty-seven minutes of nothing creep by, alleviated only by nine minutes of the subject pottering around the garden staring at borders. I've almost given up hope when a maroon four-wheel drive glides to a halt in front of the house. At once, I snap the book shut, shove it into the glove compartment—I hate the thought of Bosch getting messy—and slide down into my seat so no one can see me.

A tall, dark-haired man leaps out of the car, glances once to the left and again to the right, and strides down the pathway to the front door of number fifty-seven. He's good-looking, mid-forties, I'd judge, so younger than my client by at least ten years. What I wouldn't do for an energetic, twenty-year-old bloke eager to learn.

Steady, Paul, keep your mind on the job. The last thing you want is a hard-on.

I wait for twenty-one minutes, then, after taking my Nikon from the floor, I put on my sunglasses and stroll out into sunshine, which holds a hint of autumn in it. Nobody is around to see me; nobody cares.

It doesn't take long to get inside number fifty-seven. When I'm in, I see the walls could do with a spot of decorating and the paper is peeling at the top corners here and there. But there's some pleasant modern artwork, including two watercolor portraits of my client and his wife.

The groaning that greeted me in the hallway when I first sneaked in is reaching a crescendo, and I, like them, need to strike now before the moment is lost.

A quick peek through the half-open living room door shows me a white leather sofa nestling on a beige carpet. Next to the sofa rather than on it, a naked and sinewy back is pumping away in a rhythm all its own on top of what I once heard described as a fine pair of lungs. Straight sex has never turned me on. Still, I can't help but admire the bloke's smooth arse for a second or two.

Then I cough.

As always, it does the trick.

Three seconds later, I have a clear picture of two entwined bodies and two startled expressions, enough of each to aid identity, from whichever angle.

I stay long enough to say thank you on the grounds that politeness is free. Then I scarper before lover boy can blush and reach for his boxers and my client's wife can even think about forming a scream.

Outside, I accelerate away, leaving behind me a cloud of late summer dust and discovered guilt.

Back at the office, Jade glances up at me for a second before returning her gaze to her computer.

"The lover arrived later than I'd thought," I say.

"Whose lover? The subject's or yours?"

"Yeah, yeah. How's your stuff going?"

"Still not as well as I'd like it to be," she says. "I can't seem to get to the level of information we need. The Met must have upgraded their security system, if only for this case, and it'll mean everything will take longer, if I'm going to get in and out of there without leaving footprints."

"Okay, no problem. You can only do what you can, but it's past hours now. Why don't you leave it 'til tomorrow?"

She shakes her head. "No, I'd like to know I can do this first. After this morning's pep talk, I'm not going to let it beat me. After all, I'm the best, aren't I?"

"You certainly are, but don't stay too late. I'd keep you company and get my report on this afternoon done, but

I'm"—I've done well so far in my attempts to seem cool, but the heat on my skin must be affecting my voice— "I'm…out this evening."

"Good for you," she says, still tapping away on the keyboard. "Anywhere nice?"

"Actually…" I pick up the papers on the adultery case, left in a neat pile at the edge of my desk, and begin checking they're in date order. They are. "Actually, I'm meeting Dominic."

The keyboard falls silent, but Jade doesn't move. "At his office?"

"No, not exactly. I'm seeing him at home."

"Your home?"

"His."

"Is that wise?"

I hesitate. The simple answer is I don't know, but I'm going to go anyway. Everything in my body and mind is straining after the fact that tonight at seven, I'll be alone with Dominic again. Anything that might happen after that is nothing but a haze.

"Don't fuss, Jade. It's not going to be a problem. It's a business meeting, that's all."

"Where are his wife and children?"

"All we'll do is discuss the case. I'll give him the latest information and grab the chance to find out what he really knows. After that, I'll head home, pour myself one whisky too many, watch crap TV, and go to bed. So there'll be no difference to what I usually do when I'm not with you, and my private life will carry on in the way it always has done since…since whenever. So please don't go on about it because I'll be fine. Anyway, why do you have to be so Baptist about everything? As your mother reminded us, you're not the best chapel-goer in the world."

By the time I've finished this little speech, I'm standing, fists clenched at my sides. I wouldn't be surprised if Jade up and punches me. I wouldn't blame her if she did, but it's not her style and she just doesn't respond, although her eyes widen as she glares at me.

"God, that was a low jibe, even by my standards. I'm sorry."

She shrugs. "Apology accepted. Would you like a hot chocolate?"

I shake my head, and she returns to her work. For a while, nothing more is said. She's seen the worst of me, both after Dominic and long before. She's seen me drunk, sick, crying, high on drugs, and shaking with frustration and grief. And anger…yes, don't let's forget the anger. She's seen that, too. Not to mention the long haul upward, step by slow step, into something approaching what sanity might be. If it wasn't for Jade, I'd be dead at least twice over. And all I can do is slag her off, putting the knife in at the place it will hurt her most. All I can do is get at the religion I know she still sets such store by, even though I can never understand it. Great move, Paul. What sort of a friend am I?

I ought to get out before I do any more damage.

"Look," I say, dragging one hand through my hair. "I need to go if I'm going to…be ready in time. Sorry again about what I said, and I promise things will seem better tomorrow. Thanks for all your hard work today and don't stay too late, will you?"

She shakes her head, "I won't. See you tomorrow then. Just promise me one thing."

"Sure. What's that?"

"If—no, when—Mr. Allen asks if you'd like to see 'round the house, whatever you do, don't go into his damn bedroom."

"What do you mean? I—"

"Promise me?"

"Okay, okay." I hold up my hands in mock defeat, but by now I'm hardly listening. "I promise, but you're a hard taskmistress. I'll see you in the morning."

And then, head full of the problem of what I should wear tonight and which aftershave to use, and running away from the real problem of my not-quite-over argument with Jade, I'm gone.

CHAPTER 9

I'm exactly four minutes behind schedule. Before leaving for Dominic's city home, I've changed my clothes three times and am still unhappy with the way I look. I decide I don't want to arrive late, but know it will be worse if I arrive early. Much, much worse.

By the time I've found a parking space, I'm struggling to remember the reasons for being here. The case, I think, the case. I have to focus. There are facts I should tell him and facts I have to find out. If only Jade had managed to hack into the records I'd wanted to see, then I might know if I had any evidence at all, rather than speculation, suspicion, and gut instinct. I should run, on two counts: this case and Dominic.

Obstinacy and the need to know make sure I don't.

So instead of taking the sensible course, which would probably involve booking a one-way ticket to Brazil, leaving a cryptic note for Jade to follow me, I get out of the car, clutching a file of papers. The air is heavy and there's a smell of mown grass and late roses. The end of summer.

Dominic's house sparkles in the evening light. There are pillars on either side of an elegant, white stone porch with a set of four steps leading up to a cream front door with an acorn-shaped brass handle. On either side of the façade, the house itself unfolds outward, revealing a richer cream, mock-Georgian piece of pure money. God alone knows what this man was ever doing with someone like me.

Each step nearer the elegant front door brings with it a range of emotions I can't name. Even the thought of Jade slips into free-fall. It's as if there's nobody in this road, or Islington, Hackney, or Stratford; nobody in the whole of London or perhaps for this moment in the world, but me and the man behind the door.

I want to run.

I don't. My feet keep moving onward, and my hand is raised to knock, but before I can, the door is opened.

"Paul." It's a statement. He's had no doubt of me, when all I have for him is uncertainty. And need. Then he makes a slight movement toward me, but cuts it off and says, "What have you done to your eye?"

"Car accident," I reply with a shrug. "It's nothing."

"I see. Come in."

As he stands aside to let me pass, I enter a long hallway carpeted in blue, with a lighter shade of the same color on the walls. There are tall mirrors framed in silver, two Vettrianos, possibly originals, and a dazzle of sunlight from a distant window. As he clicks the door shut behind me, I look at Dominic.

He's opted for smart casual tonight, wearing chinos, something I've never seen him in before, and a silk shirt, white, that sets off his understated tan. His sleeves are rolled up so the light catches the golden hairs on his arms, and as he passes me, there's a hint of spices and lime. His feet are bare.

"Please," he says again, "come through."

I follow him down the hallway and then left into what I imagine is the living room. I've never been here before. He gestures at the nearest chair.

"Sit down. I'll get you a drink. Beer or wine? I assume not being at home you won't want whisky."

"Beer's fine." I want to keep a clear head tonight.

When he's gone, I don't sit down. So far, the interior of Dominic's house is everything I've imagined it to be. But being here tonight is still like something out of time, and I try to tell myself not to be fooled. He's not for me, no matter how much I might want it, and I have to remember what I'm here for.

Standing in the middle of this room, I can't help luxuriating in the deep cream carpet, and I wish my feet, too, were bare. There's more mirror glitter, two Art Nouveau pieces, and on my right, crystal glints in the display cabinet. Not for the first time, I wonder what his wife, Cassandra, is like, not just in appearance, but inside, where it matters.

As if on cue, the photographs catch my eye. Family shots on show on an intricately carved sideboard. Something in me is glad he hasn't removed them. I put down my notes and pick up the first one, admiring the delicate, dark-haired beauty of Dominic's wife and the strength behind her eyes that can't be hidden even at one remove. Cassandra Allen. The echo of her name in my head makes everything blur for a second or two, and for some reason, I think of Jade, so I return Cassandra to the ebony surface, a little back from her original position.

The next photograph I look at shows Dominic's children. From the newspaper articles I've collected, I know his son, Henry, is thirteen and his daughter, Judith, eleven, but apart from those basic facts, anything else is hazy. Dominic works hard to keep his children out of the media, and for that I admire him. Now I find myself looking at a slim, laughing boy with the same cheekbones and dark hair as his mother. He's holding a skateboard and standing near pink roses, with the house suffused in sunlight in the background. By his side is a girl, almost as tall as her brother, but fair-haired and with a face that will one day grow into the likeness of her father's. Even so young, Judith has no need for props. Hands by her sides, open, confident, she smiles at the camera, waiting for the moment of decision when the shutter will click and what she is then will be recorded for all eternity. It's the pinnacle of summer, and the family is basking in its own particular glory.

It strikes me that Dominic has brought up his children well. My ex-lover has a life I have never explored, or wanted to. What am I to him? I half-drop the photograph, and it lands with a thump facedown, and I'm in the process of setting it up again when Dominic re-enters the room.

"Beer, the way you prefer it."

When I spin 'round, he's holding a tray on which are standing a glass of deep red wine, a bottle of Waggledance beer, and another glass. I take the bottle and it's room temperature.

"You remembered," I mutter.

"Of course." Placing the tray on the gilded coffee table, he takes his children's photograph and returns it to the correct position. "What were you doing with these?"

"I was just curious."

He smiles. By now, he's so close to me I could, if I had the courage, reach out and touch him.

"It's a good picture, I think. Of both of them. Do you like it?"

"No."

For a moment, his face spasms as if I've punched him. "Oh? Why not?"

"Why do you think?" When he takes a step back and turns away, I regret my harshness. "Look, they're beautiful children and you're very lucky, but you don't need me to tell you that."

"I love them, Paul."

There's nothing I can say. It's as if he's given me a gift I don't know how to accept…or a warning I can't interpret. After a second or two, he picks up his glass, sips his wine, and sits on the chocolate-brown sofa, stretching out his arms across the back like a lion in control of its prey. I grab my beer, ignore the glass, and swig it straight from the bottle. It helps to ease the dustiness and fear under my skin.

As I take the seat opposite him, something occurs to me.

"Don't you smoke at home? There are no…signs of anything."

"You mean why are there no ashtrays, and why doesn't the house smell of nicotine?" he says with a short laugh. "Simple. I don't smoke inside while my children are here. Let them make that choice when they're old enough. I won't force it on them now."

I nod. If I was a parent, I suppose I wouldn't even have had to ask that, but I've never had the experience to think in those terms. I've never wanted it. The fact of Dominic's fatherhood is being made clear to me for the first time and in a place I never expected it. What am I doing here with him?

The question jolts me out of the slow, sparkling river we are somehow travelling on together, and I remember the reason I have come.

"The case, Dominic. I need to ask you—"

He holds up his hand, and I fall silent, cursing the habit of obedience he can ignite in me even now.

"Please," he says. "It can wait 'til later. There'll be plenty of time for business then. Let's finish our drinks first."

For an answer, I take up the beer, holding Dominic's gaze as I do so, and drain it dry. "Done. Finished."

He smiles. "But I haven't. Not yet. And we have business to discuss."

"For God's sake, Dominic, then let's discuss it. I'm too old to play games any more."

"All right," he says, and I sit back into my chair. "All right. Business it is, but first let's eat."

"I'm not hungry."

"I don't believe you. You've always been hungry. In many ways. But I'm not asking you for anything. I simply want to enjoy your company on an evening when I find myself able to do so. If you want to drink, then drink; if you want to eat, then eat. I don't mind what you do, but I'd like you to stay."

"I don't want to stay."

Something in him seems to fold in on itself, and he waves one hand at me. "All right. Then go. If that's what you want."

Remembering Jade's warning, I get up and stroll toward the living room door, as if I have all the time in the universe and what I'm doing doesn't matter. It does. It means passing where my ex-lover is sitting, as vibrant as a threat and as dangerous. The journey takes a lifetime, and when I'm level with him, he looks up.

"You've forgotten your notes."

His words are quiet, and when I brush my hair back from my forehead, my fingers come away bathed in sweat. "Yes."

"Shall I get them for you?"

"No." A pause. He doesn't fill it, almost as if he knows I have more to say. "You're my client and there are things we need to discuss."

"Yes."

Another pause. I'm held motionless next to him and, this time, I'm waiting.

Then he says, "We'll discuss them, Paul. I promise you. But first I'd like us to have a meal together. It's something we've never done. Not really."

Without replying, I retrace my steps and sit. He takes a gulp of his wine, as if he's been crossing a bleak desert with no hope of water, although he's never moved.

"Thank you," he says.

He cooks, something I never knew he could do. Sitting at the table, I watch him move 'round the vast, airy kitchen like a dancer, adding herbs and a sprinkling of salt to the heady mixture of chicken and ginger, bean sprouts and water chestnuts he's stir-frying. Keeping a watch on the wok, he cuts bread he has warmed in the oven and slides butter onto a dish. When I ask if I can help, he shakes his head, and afterward, we're silent. It feels as if I'm plunging into unknown brightness and if I dare once to open my eyes, then the dazzle might blind me. I can't catch in my thoughts the connection between the reason for coming here and what is happening now.

When the food is ready, Dominic takes the plates into the dining room, its décor cream and gold, wood and silk, and I follow with a fresh beer, the wine, and the bread. As we eat, we talk a little more. We talk of the things that are overwhelming, but which tonight don't matter: Afghanistan, terrorism, America. We also talk about things that are nearer to us, but not too near: the way London is at the end of the tourist season; the latest crime novel I'm reading; the cities Dominic has visited.

And all the time I want to touch him, but I'm afraid.

Finally, he drinks the last of his wine, smiles, and lets the peace and warmth of the evening enfold us both.

"Did you like supper?" he says.

"Yes. It was good, thank you."

"Are you still hungry?"

"No."

"Would you like to see around the house?"

"Yeah, sure," I say without thinking. "I'd like that."

"Come on then." He gets up, indicates the room we're in, and says, "This is the dining room, as you can tell. The living room and kitchen you've seen already, but downstairs there's also a playroom, bathroom, and television room. Upstairs, of course, is breathtaking. It's what made me decide to buy."

I drift in his wake, not listening to his explanations of what I'm seeing and the changes he's made, aware only of his voice and the way he somehow doesn't sound like himself. He could be giving a lecture at one of his many conferences, addressing his executive board rather than being here tonight, letting me see his home for the first time. It's as if he's been switched on by an unknown force and is talking and talking with nothing being said.

When we come to the bottom of the elegant stairway, I hesitate, but the soothing tone of his voice doesn't miss a syllable. Five steps behind, I follow him up. On the landing, he turns left and leads me to two bedrooms. The first belongs to Henry and is filled with all the evidence of boyhood: the skateboard from the photograph; a corner stacked with computer games; a tumble of dirty sweatshirts on the bed. Dominic picks them up with a sigh and drops them into the laundry basket.

"He's never tidy." He shrugs. "No matter what we say."

The second bedroom along is girlhood apricot, but with not a hint of a frill, and I sense that everything here has its place and lives in harmony. There are shelves of books and a pile of hardcover notebooks, all in purple.

"She writes," he says, unable to keep the pride from his voice. "All the time. Of course, we're never allowed to see."

When I look at him, his face is as mellow as I've ever known it, and I wonder, with all the arrogance of non-parental distance, whether Judith is his favorite. I can never ask him this. There are other thoughts, other memories also, that this room stirs in me, but I refuse to face them now.

He shuts Judith's door with a gentle click and leads me farther along to a vast expanse of bathroom, tiled in white with, here and there, a splash of green to refresh the eye. Another few moments to listen and admire, and we are out, heading to the end of the landing where a door with a brass handle beckons us.

"The master bedroom," he says. "With the wonderful views. You can—"

I stop dead, Jade's words at last springing clear into my mind: Whatever you do, don't go into his damn bedroom.

"No," I say.

"What's wrong?" When he turns to look at me, his face is shrouded in shadow, but I cannot explain myself.

Instead, I shake my head and back away. "I don't want to see it, that's all. Don't ask me."

Two steps bring him into the light again, and I see his puzzlement, the mental shrug he uses to deal with something he hasn't understood, but which he counts as too trivial to question. "All right. There are other bedrooms, but I'm sorry you'll miss the view."

When I don't reply, he glides past me, averting his gaze, and again, after a heartbeat or so, I follow him back beyond the stairs and onto a smaller landing. There are three rooms here: the first is a study playing host to another computer, a laptop, and three shelves full of what I recognize as Dominic's collection of netsuke. I've read about this in interviews he's given. I pick one up, an ivory carving of an old man, impossibly small, holding a twisted stick and an artist's palate.

"It's beautiful," I say. "I've never seen one before, not to touch. This isn't all of them, is it?"

"No." Dominic smiles. "The rest are in storage. I rotate them when the mood takes me."

"Why?"

"Lots of reasons: the move from summer to winter and back again; the nature of the work I'm doing here and what I like to focus on when I'm doing it; the different shapes they make in the sunlight. It's hard to explain, Paul."

"I think you explain very well, thanks. But I meant, why do you collect them?"

He answers without hesitation. "The contrast of their intricacy with the broad sweep of the life I find I'm living. It's the chance to contemplate something different and real."

There is no answer to that, or none I can find. I replace the carving, which almost seems alive in my fingers, and we move on.

The second room is a guest bedroom, female and scented in lavender, and the third a smaller spare bedroom, or so he tells me, used only rarely. As I step over the threshold, I wonder if tomorrow Jade will see through my half-promises and lies.

This last room is decorated in pale green wallpaper with a subtle darker green trim and the furnishings are simple: a single bed, pale wood dressing table, and a Victorian mirror. I move to the open window.

"Look," I say. "I haven't missed anything. There's a view from here, too."

It's true. In the pale light of dusk, I can see the outline of a long garden and the smell of roses shimmers 'round my senses. When Dominic moves in behind me and touches me once on the arm, I realize I won't be leaving here for a while.

There's still some fight left in me, though, and I'm proud of the fact.

"We haven't discussed the papers I want to go through and the questions I need to ask," I say. "You promised me that."

"I know I did, but it doesn't matter now. We can"—he has the grace to pause—"look at those in the morning."

I make a sound that's half laughter, half groaning. "Is this why you invited me 'round? Really?"

"What do you think?"

"I think you're someone who knows what he wants and gets it. How long have you been planning this?"

"You won't believe me, but I don't always plan. Ever since I rang you and asked to meet up again that night, I've been hoping," he replies with simplicity. "The hour before we were due to see each other, I chewed my way through two packets of mints. I know you always hated how much I smoke, especially as you were trying so hard to give them up. Couldn't you taste them when you kissed me?"

I don't answer. I'm incapable of it. Instead, I reach for him and begin to twist free the buttons on his shirt. My hands are shaking, and I can't remember what to do.

It doesn't matter because a few seconds later, he's eased me down onto the bed and is running his hand across my stomach. I realize why he's doing it this way and know it will be good for the second or third time, but right now I can't wait that long. I land a fierce kiss on his mouth, but he still doesn't get it, instead pulling away and kissing me more gently in return. I wriggle out of my trousers, turn over, and push myself up on all fours. Grabbing his hand, I wrap it around my cock, already beginning to throb itself home. Finally, I hear the sound of him spitting and feel his wet fingers in my arse.

Even then, there's a moment's hesitation.

"Can I?" he whispers. "Is it…"

"Okay? Yes."

No more words then. He eases my buttocks apart, and I'm stretched wide as his cock enters my body, slowly, carefully, in a way that splits me with a delicious shock of memory. I can tell, even in the net of my own desire, how much he's holding back.

"Paul, Paul." He groans. "God."

A couple of thrusts is all it takes for me and I'm gone, my spunk streaming out over the bed's dark green silk sheets. Behind me, he lurches, cries out again and the two of us collapse in a tangle of sweat and flesh together. His wetness dribbles out between my thighs, and I feel the hammer of his heart against my back.

I close my eyes against what we've done and what it might mean for me and wrap myself up against his legs and chest. We lie there, not speaking, until the pace of his heart—and mine—has slowed. I think to myself, Don't ruin it, Paul. For God's sake, don't ruin it.

"Sorry," he says at last. "I didn't think to use a condom. But I don't have anything, I swear it. I get my health regularly checked. I'm clean."

Dominic's love life apart from me isn't something I want to talk about, but his openness deserves a response.

"I don't have anything either. You don't have to worry." I pause and then move on a little further than planned. "I'm celibate."

He nibbles the back of my neck, his teeth grazing my skin.

"Really?" he says, and I can hear the smile in his voice. "It's nice of you to say it, but you don't have to. I don't believe it for a moment, of course, of someone as sexy as you."

I shuffle myself away from him, as much as I can in a single bed. "It doesn't matter if you believe it or not. It's true. Or was until just now."

"Oh yes, right." He pulls me 'round until I'm facing him and can see every grey speckle in his blue-grey eyes. "This must be a new thing then. When we were together, you could never get enough. So tell me. Make it accurate, as I know how good you are with dates, and make it the truth. When did you last have sex?"

Not even blinking, I hold his gaze. "Three years, four months, and four weeks ago. As it was one of the long months."

For a moment I see him wondering whether to believe me or not, and I see him doing the sums. Then he gets it.

He swallows and looks away. "Well, I've broken your run now."

When he makes as if to get up, I grab his arm and pull him back down next to me. "It's okay. I know this isn't going anywhere; it's just for tonight. I'm not imagining a fantasy future for us, not like last time. I won't try to mess up your life again, stalk you, whatever."

"I didn't think you would. I know it was difficult for you before, for both of us."

I'm not sure about this, as I'd thought that, for him, cutting me adrift had been easy, but I'm not going to argue the point. Not now when we're both half-naked and on a comfortable bed in a house with no one else inside it. I may have been a monk for a long time, but I've never been a saint.

*   *   *

In the morning, when I wake up, my skin is humming, and the air around me is heavy. I'm lying sprawled on my stomach, legs apart. It's how I've spent most of the night, though not all. Dominic and I always liked to have a little variety, even against our natural preferences, and this time has been no different. Thinking of him makes me smile, and I wonder how I've managed without sex, without him, for so long.

"Dominic?"

There's no answer, but from downstairs I hear faint noises of someone moving about. Turning over and letting the sun drift over my body, I feel alive. I wish he was here, but he's never liked just being still after lovemaking. He'd want to be up and on to the next thing, and I suppose in three years, four months, and twenty-nine days he hasn't changed.

I wonder what the etiquette is of being seduced by a client and then having sex with him from dusk to dawn until both of you are electric with long-delayed satisfaction. How do you work yourselves back into some kind of business relationship then? I'm still wondering about it when the door opens and Dominic reappears.

He's wearing a short navy-blue dressing gown and carrying a tray on which I can see a steaming French press, cups, plates, milk, a basket of rolls, butter, and a pot of marmalade. I can't help it. I laugh.

"God, Nic, what's this? Keeping the mistress sweet before packing her off in the morning?"

"Something like that." With a brief smile, he turns his attention to breakfast, and I watch him, realizing as I do that this is a side of the man I haven't seen before, even last night at supper. It's like witnessing a ritual, as if I've come upon him engaged in prayer. He arranges the rolls on the plates, allocating two to each, and then slices off a generous helping of butter from the dish, followed by a spoonful of marmalade. Both these he transfers to the sides of the plates and leaves a knife with them. Next he frowns at the French press and holds it up to the light before, seemingly satisfied, he plunges the filter down to the bottom of the glass jug and pours the coffee into the cups. To these he adds a dash of milk, a little more in mine. He's remembered. Again.

Then he comes to sit next to me on the bed, and I can smell the smoke on him. Still not speaking, he hands me the coffee, and the rich dark scent of it kicks me into a new wakefulness. His grey gaze hooks onto mine, and then, still holding my eyes, he clicks my cup with his before taking a sip. For some reason, and in spite of the depths and heights of our recent physical intimacy, this feels like the closest we have ever been.

"Good morning," he says.

I'm unable to reply as the strangeness of it all is too powerful for me to find any words, but he doesn't seem to mind. Instead, he puts his cup on the bedside cabinet, removes mine from my grasp, and places it next to his. Then he pulls the duvet down a little and runs one careful finger across my right arm so he touches the scar.

"What's this?" he asks. "It's new, isn't it? Since we were last together. Another accident?"

I tell him. He listens to the story without exclamation or question until I'm finished—something that nobody in my life up 'til now has ever done, not even Jade. When I'm through and all the words are silent, he bends down, takes hold of my arm, and brushes the long, twisted line with his lips. He goes on doing this, taking his time until he has kissed the whole length of it. It feels like butterflies on my skin.

When he looks up at me, his eyes are dark, and I do not know what he might be thinking.

"I swear, Paul," he says. "Whatever has happened before and whatever happens now, I swear if I had the gift of it, I would kill whoever did this to you."

There's nothing I can think of to say. So instead of talking, I reach for his hand where it still rests on my arm, bring it to my mouth, and kiss the inside of his palm. Just once, just enough.

Then we eat.

Later in the shower together, we wash each other clean. There's no laughter or talking, and no more sex of any sort, although once or twice we kiss. Gently, as if taking care not to cause pain, though I can't see why either of us would imagine there might be any.

It's only when I'm getting out of my car at home that I see he's placed my file of papers in the back and realize neither of us has mentioned the case.

I'll do it later. There'll be plenty of time. I might even ring him this evening, see if there's any chance of a rerun of last night. No, I'd better not. The family will be back by then, and he hadn't said anything about wanting to see me again. Not for sex anyway. Those days are over. I can't afford to live in my dreams. Maybe last night was just a proper goodbye, something we never had before. Whatever, it'll become clear soon enough, and, until it does, I can't go chasing him like a bee after honey. Those days are gone, too; I'm older now. And obsessive about too many other things to be able to add Dominic to the list again. Besides, he'll have to talk to me about the case at some point, so it isn't as if I won't be seeing him in the future.

At home, sunlight catches the motes of dust floating in air and I make a mental note to do some cleaning. It's already 9:16 A.M. Jade will be wondering where I am.

She'll be in the office dealing with the post, checking the ansaphone, and, with a bit of luck, finishing keying in some of my outstanding reports. And she might even have some good news about the Bluesky connection. I change my shirt and grab a pair of sneakers. I know, as I knew last night when Dominic opened the spare room door, that I'll have to try to find some kind of reason as to why I'm humming and can't keep the smile from my face. I promised her I wouldn't go near his bedroom, but it was his bed she meant, and she'll know just by looking at me that I've had sex at last. Good sex, too. She'll assume Dominic, she'll assume right and I'll be left with an angry assistant. Twelfth rule of PI work: whatever you do, don't upset the staff or you'll never get your typing done.

The sky promises more sunshine as I step outside for the ten-minute walk to Maloney Investigations. Even the air seems brighter, the dry grass greener, and everyone I meet is smiling—unusual for Hackney at the best of times. It's the sort of day that can't help but hold good things ahead, and everyone is picking up on it. One of the rare London days where work will be simple, I'll get one step closer to some good Delta Egypt evidence, I'll discover

Dominic's innocence, I'll take on a lucrative new client, Jade will forgive me, and, even though it's a Wednesday rather than a Monday, it will be an evening for sitting outside drinking beer and talking. Hey, maybe I'll even take her up to the West End, treat her to a show or something…one of those musicals she loves and I can't stand, but what does it matter because I'll be making a friend happy. I'll have a couple of beers inside me and the delicious memory of Dominic to relive. Again and again.

Yes, it's going to be a great day. The best. Or one of them. Nothing can be as good as yesterday.

Turning down the narrow path to the office, I can see Jade's bike chained up to the railings as I take the steps two at a time, marshalling my excuses for lateness. Key in the door, I yell out, "Hi, Jade, it's me. Sorry I'm late. I was just…"

Once inside, my voice trails away. The place is a mess. Drawers and cabinets lie open, their files and papers scattered across the carpet. One of the computers has been torn from the wall, its cables wilting like long fingers over the desk, the hard drive buckled and bent. My table lamp has been smashed, as has one window. As I take a step forward, fragments of glass crackle under my feet. There's an acrid smell I can't quite place, but all the time my mind is working; don't disturb anything, you'll have to call the police on this one, I'll need to see if anything's been taken first, find out what they know, when Jade comes I'll… Jade.

"Ja-ade?" My voice echoes off the walls, and there's no response. And already I'm racing across the office, feet scrabbling on paper and glass, legs knocking against the upturned table, and I'm punching in 999 on my mobile, the vision of her bicycle outside tearing through my heart. "Jade?"

When I slam open the kitchen door, she's lying across the tiles. She's dressed in the ruby suit and cream shirt she'd been wearing last night, an oversize ruby earring hanging forlornly across her pale cheek. Almost the same color as the ugly red gash across her throat. Her blue eyes are staring blankly and have no light in them.

"Jade!" I'm on the floor next to her, knees collapsing, no way of keeping upright or knowing how to any more. There's the sound of my own ragged breath, and from nowhere, the voice of authority in my ear and I'm sobbing, gulping out words I can't make sense of, "Yes, ambulance, police, please, now."

Then I drop the phone as if it's on fire. With no care or understanding for the rules of the profession I've counted as mine, I bend down, gather her into my arms and rock her against my chest, crooning, murmuring endearments as if somehow I could wake her up and bring her back to me again.

This is how the police find us.

CHAPTER 10

Time stops. It hangs like dark clouds over the earth and blocks out the movement of the sun. The stars are unhooked from their moorings, and the sky floats down. There are questions, so many questions, from men with hardness in their eyes and from men with pity, and there's blood on my hands I can never cleanse, even though I didn't wield the knife.

If only I'd been there. I should have been there. I might have been able to help.

I should have been there. This is a phrase I repeat over and over again, sitting at tables, drinking harsh coffee, standing up and leaning against chill white tiles as I piss the coffee away, while outside a policeman waits.

I don't know how long the questions continue or how long the police go on thinking that the murderer might be me or that I know something more they can't get me to say. What I know is outside my capability of telling. Even if that were untrue, I still would remain silent about the things that don't matter now, for a reason I can no longer handle the reaching after. My grip on passing time, which has sustained me for so long, tumbles away, and I'm left spinning.

The thought of Jade fills me with memories so sharp they are almost real, almost happening in the now. I see her smiling up at me from behind her computer, the warmth of her eyes, her laughter, even her disapproval, each subtle change of her face mirroring who she is.

Who she was.

Pictures of her mingle with dreams of Teresa so that instead of the office, the pub, the flat, I remember the garden, the swings, the way my sister loved the roses my father grew. Other memories too: the two of us blowing bubbles from a tube in the living room and laughing when they burst; the time I ran away with her favorite doll and she bit my arm to make me give it back; the time she sneaked me squares of chocolate when I caught chicken pox and then caught it herself from me. I'll never see Teresa again, but it seems impossible I won't see Jade, that I'm left without her, like before.

I know these feelings are selfish, that there are others whose loss is far greater, but I can't summon the strength to glance outside the fragile boundaries of my own existence. As much ask a drowning man to save himself. Besides, knowing the facts has never helped the truth of a thing. It's never been enough to save me. The facts have nothing to do with the truth, and they are powerless to make a difference.

So, during the dark days of September, in the first tides of autumn, I fall down the lines to the dark.

The hours mesh into one. The only things I see are the knowledge of my own failure to act on any of my promises and the terrifying impossibility of a future I can live by. I wonder about killing myself and imagine a multitude of ways to do this: lying in the bath until the water trembles cold against my body and then drifting down until it covers my chin, my mouth, my nose, my eyes, my hair. It will be hard not to try to hold my breath as I go underneath, but it will be quicker if I take that step, trust myself to breathe in the liquid, let it fill my throat and lungs until the pounding of my heart is stilled. For all time.

Or perhaps, it will be easier to use drugs, aspirin for instance, something that will not involve me in meetings with people I no longer know and transactions I cannot remember how to perform. Something simpler than the hard drugs hidden away in the dark corners of the city. The thought of it grips me. It won't let me go.

One evening on a day whose place in the order of the week I can't tell, this is what I do. I take the jar from the bathroom cabinet and pad to the kitchen. In my hand, the small white deadliness glows and seems to sing. I sit down. For a long time, I do nothing. When I'm ready to act, I unscrew the jar and tap out, one by one, the roundness of poison onto the table. It takes so little time. I line them up in rows of nine, the perfect number after which there are no new shapes, no new patterns, and when there are five of these, I stop and wonder how death will taste. Will it be heavy with the knowledge of finality? Or will it soothe me like a child into oblivion? Nothing but a small, apparent sleep, a cutting off from which there is no return?

I take a line of these and, eased into a new but brief routine, am reaching out to take another when, from nowhere, a wave of nausea swoops up from within me. My stomach spasms into freefall, and I barely make the sink before I'm retching up pale powder and liquid and death. I retch and retch again until there's nothing left but exhaustion.

When I wake, I'm huddled and shivering on the kitchen floor, one arm jammed against the table leg, and the remaining pills are scattered around me like confetti. I want to cry, but can't find the tears.

The days pass by, each second carved on my skin. I don't know how to run from them. There is nothing I can do to bring Jade back. I think about starting to smoke again, if only to calm the tremble in my fingers I can't control, and wonder why the energy to plunge back into the comfort of old addictions is no longer there.

Another day, and again I can't remember the name of it, not even whether it's a weekday or a weekend, I stand at the window of my flat and gaze at the street outside. It must be evening or morning as it's dark and the people I see are nothing but more solid shapes in haze. They head purposeful and unsmiling into the narrow boundaries of the view I have. I wish I could have that sense of journey, but it's out of reach. As if I am watching my own falling, a leaf torn by wind from the tree and swinging downwards, I know my own foolishness and these feelings for what they are. Haven't I walked this path before, after Dominic? I should know it for what it is. I should be able to control it, but all my limbs are weighed down, and I can't act to save myself. As I couldn't act to save Teresa, and as I couldn't act, or acted too late, to save Jade.

I should have been there.

Instead, I am here. Watching an unfamiliar world and knowing, though I can't overpower it, that most of all I am afraid. Afraid enough to smash the glass in front of me with my bare fists, the shattered fragments of window slashing my wrists and arms, and step out into naked air. Wondering if I do so, whether the end will be quick and whether, once I have done what I can't undo, I will see my sister and friend again, or whether all beliefs in a life beyond the one we know here are nothing more than fantasy and fairytale. If anyone knew, Jade would, and for a moment, I see her. In my dreams or in the reality I am living in, I don't know. But it's real. I can see her fair hair, the sparkle of her deep blue eyes, the way her lips crinkled a little at the edges when she smiled, the dazzle of jewelry, and the perfume she wore. One step, one step only, would take me beyond the frame and into the deep unknown.

No way back. No forgiveness. The fault, the foolishness is mine, though those I love must bear it.

Still, I breathe, and only due to my own cowardice. Suicide will take courage and the easier choice is to live. As I think these things, the shape of her face in front of me shimmers and shrinks and changes to another much younger face, and again I cry out. The echo of my voice ravages my heart.

My last encounter with the seduction of death comes, I think, in the second week of my self-imprisonment.

It's morning and I'm sitting at the kitchen table when I hear the soft thump of the post landing on the hall floor. The thought of getting up, fetching, and reading any letters passes my mind, an idea that I dismiss at once for being irrelevant. My skin smells sour, and my face itches with bristles. My mouth tastes empty and bitter; I haven't eaten for a while.

Outside there's the sound of cars and people and laughter, and an expansive feeling of calm nestles over me. My eyes are closed, and I know that whatever happens now, whatever I decide, will be lasting. Maybe even irrevocable.

This thought makes me smile. It's been a long journey 'til now and soon, for good or bad, it will be over.

I take up the knife I've been playing with. It's cold, a relief to the stifling warmth of my forehead. It's as if the day will never be cool again, and the only comfort is the sense of icy steel on skin. It's the one good kitchen knife I own. Something Dominic once told me comes to my memory. If you want anything in life, consider the best you can afford, and then pay a little more for what is better than the best.

This I have done. He will be proud of me.

Running the knife across my closed eyes, I feel its strength down my cheek, over the greater softness of my lips and onto the fragility of my neck. The blade nicks the skin there, and the sudden swell and iron scent of blood makes me gasp.

Not here, not now; it will be too hard.

My heart pounds its way to closure. Still bearing the knife, I draw it over my chest and across the tenderness of my upper left arm. There's no hurry. Halfway down, I twist it in my fingers and force the blade into my flesh. There is a bubble of crimson and, yes, I would do it, I would do it now—keep going, keep going, Paul—but the pain is shocking, more shocking than I have reckoned on, and I hear someone—is it me?—gasp while the knife spins to the floor.

I did not reach my wrist. I didn't reach it. But it doesn't matter; it can't matter because there is blood and pain driving me to my feet. For a long moment, I am outside my body, watching myself as I stumble to the bathroom, struggling to stem the flow of blood on my arm, opening the cabinet, and bringing out a length of bandage. I curse myself over and over, as if the words might fly up and rain down on me as a judgment, a retribution.

Now, here, where I have no more answers, no more plans, I begin to find the slow path upward. Still shaking, still unable to stand properly or for long, I lurch back to the kitchen where I left my mobile. It sits next to the knife on the floor where it must have fallen.

The sight of the knife makes me start to sweat, and I hear someone saying, though I don't recognize it as me, "No. No, Paul, it's over. Leave it. Just leave it."

And then, thank God, the phone is in my hand, and I'm dialing a number I still remember. When he answers, I recognize his voice and am taken back to the time when Jade first made me call him.

He says his name and his profession, counselor, and then waits, but all I can say at first is, "Please, please, Andrew, help me."

For a long while, he lets me talk, and here and there, when I most need it, talks to me in turn. While he does this, I am slumped at the table and have taken a pencil and am doodling on a shredded section of newspaper. I can hardly tell what I'm writing.

It's only when my phone call is over and an appointment made for this afternoon that I look at the word I've written. The fact of it makes me struggle for a second or so for breath, and there is a roaring like the sea in my head.

Because the word I have written is Bluesky.

I should have been there.

Bluesky. It's the one thought that makes me get up, counting myself lucky if the night before has held more than an hour or two of sleep. The dead woman and the puzzle of her make me leave the flat, now weary with dust, and pad like a beaten dog through the color and noise of people until I reach the supermarket. There I buy groceries and go home, where I eat, not caring what it is or what it tastes like. It's not much either, and I realize with a grimace that I don't need to worry about my weight any more. If I had any excess, it's gone now.

*   *   *

Twice a week I take the bus to Leyton, sit on a smooth chair in a light grey office, talk for an hour, and also listen to the questions Andrew sees fit to ask me.

Sometimes what he says or asks makes sense and sometimes it doesn't. I give the answers or explore the possibilities in the language I soon pick up again, as if my last extended session with him hadn't been over two years ago. I gaze around at the bright but peaceful prints from the Scottish colorists he displays on his walls. While the words weigh down the air, my fingers touch, hold, and circle, one by one and always in the same order, each of the seven stones he keeps in a blue basin on the table, itself set just to one side of the two of us so there's no barrier. The table always bears a small box of tissues.

I talk about Jade, my failure to keep her safe, the plans she had for the future, marriage, children, a house of her own, all the clichés I know she meant. When I say her name, though, the face I see is sometimes that of Teresa, the two of them blending into one, both running from me so I can save neither. Sometimes I don't know which of them I'm talking about. Each session of soul baring, each tide of words brings me closer to the shore I have drifted so far away from.

Of course, I never talk about Dominic.

Between my conversations with Andrew, I stay at home as much as possible. I see no one else, I speak to no one else, as far as this can be done in the world I live in. I write, once only, to her parents, but the letter is written and rewritten so many times that I never send it. During this month of mist and memory, I don't have the courage. At night, all I do is read books I've read before, as I can't sleep. Andrew suggests tablets that I buy, but never take. One thing I've learnt and learnt well from my past is that some situations just have to be endured.

I don't visit the office. Jade's blood, the shape and feel of her fallen body, lies like a trap in my mind, so I do no work and pay no bills. This I do not tell Andrew. He doesn't need to know.

And so the month passes. Somewhere at the end of it, I turn thirty-one. I don't celebrate my birthday, and neither do I open either of the cards I receive, one postmarked Surrey and one London.

All the time, there are only two questions in my head. Why has this happened again? And why wasn't it me?

Above all, the knowledge I must somehow learn to live with is if I hadn't slept that night with Dominic, then Jade would surely not be dead.

Nowhere, in all this time, do I learn how to weep. The one thing that keeps me going is thinking about Bluesky.

And wondering what I can do to find the truth.

CHAPTER 11

The police release Jade's body on Thursday, September 30. This seems almost too soon for them to have decided there's no hope of an arrest, but I don't question it.

Her funeral takes place on Tuesday, October 5. I only know this as a small plain postcard arrives on the hall floor the day before, postmarked from Essex. When I turn it over, it gives me the reason, the date, and the time and then a simple message, handwritten: We thought you'd like to know.

Tuesday morning, I spend a long time sitting next to the door, back against the wall, knees bent, gazing at the long crack from floor to ceiling opposite me. It's so familiar by now that I hardly register it. Instead I think of other people's kindness and how far my own falls short.

Maybe, now, it's time to move on.

In the bedroom, I pull on a pair of jeans and a jumper. There's no point looking smart, as there's no one to see. For the first time in weeks, I shave, first trimming my unwanted new beard down to the skin so the razor won't cut.

At the door, when the sharpness of the air hits me, I hesitate for a heartbeat or two. It's as if I'm breathing in the knowledge of the place where I live once again, even though every day I've been out to the shop to buy food. All that doesn't matter. Now, I close my eyes and smell dust and the dying heat drifting to autumn and winter. I smell petrol exhaust, sweat, and smoke. All the hooks that tie me to the earth.

I open my eyes. This hasn't changed. Nothing I see or smell or hear is different.

Ten minutes later, by the time I reach the office, I'm sweating, even though it's not hot. I could do with a whisky, but there's no chance of that. As I climb the outside steps, taking them one by one, I can't help glancing to the right where Jade's bike was usually chained to the railings.

Don't think like that. Keep focused. Keep calm.

There's no bicycle, and I wonder who has it now. Jade's parents? Some thief? I don't know and it's not important, so instead, I swallow and make my way inside.

The door is hard to open due to the mound of post piled up on the mat. I throw away the junk mail unopened and finish with five letters that might need attention. One day. As far as I can tell, I have, in the course of one month and four days, gained what seems to be three demands for money and two official envelopes, one coming from the largest of my insurance clients and one that has no stamp and must have been delivered by hand. Someone in one of the other shared offices here must have brought it up. I'll open them all later.

In the meantime, there's work to be done and actions to be faced.

I begin with what is simple. Looking around, I can see the police have done their best to leave the premises tidy, but there's a layer of dust almost as thick as the one at home. This is no place to see potential clients, should I have any left. I take duster and polish from one of the cupboards and start to clean. After taking the rough off the main office, I go through the stacks of papers the forensic officers have piled up on the floor in one corner and try to put them in order. From it, I create three smaller stacks:

filing, actionable, important. I abandon these and start to search through the drawers.

As I work, it's as if Jade is working next to me, as if, should I glance up quickly enough or cunningly enough, I might catch a glimpse of her, tapping at the keyboard, frowning at the screen, sashaying in with hot chocolate. Today, if such a thing happened, I would drink the offering with joy and not bear within me one whisper of criticism. Each time I look, without thinking, the image vanishes.

At last one room is done. There is no Delta Egypt USB drive, but I anticipated that. Neither do I think the police have it or they would have asked me about it. Next, I tackle the bathroom, and when I finish, it's as clean as it's ever been.

I haven't entered the kitchen yet.

I will have to…soon. For now, I am, as Andrew tells me, in the stage of avoidance. Damn him, so would he be if this had happened to him. I can't do it. I'm human and no hero. I shouldn't have to do this. Jade should still be here. Jade… God, I wish, I wish…too much, but none of it will help. Too late I wonder if I should have brought someone else with me for this first visit back, but there's no one else I can ask. Not Dominic, not my parents, not anyone.

I have to do it now; if I don't go into the kitchen today, then I never will. I tell myself there's no need to clean it after all and that just being there, opening the door is enough. Then I go in.

There's a rush of bile to my throat, but no tears. The door swings shut behind me as I stand at the sink spitting out the bitter yellow fluid from my mouth. Finally, I turn, lean against the sink, and look around the room.

There's nothing different; nothing in the air that holds the memory of what happened here. I gaze for a long time at the place on the floor where Jade's body lay. Then I wipe my hands over my face, swallow once, and return to the main office.

Before I leave, I remember the correspondence I've saved. As I thought, three are bills. One is framed in red, so I'll pay it first. One month and four days ago, I would have just handed it over to… Another wave of sickness grips me, and I have to sit down, leaning forward and breathing slowly until it passes. There's nothing inside to bring up anyway.

God, Paul, don't think, I tell myself. Don't make these treacherous connections of thought; it's not going to help you. There'll be enough to face later on. I have to stay calm, let the fact that I'm on my own now mesh in enough to tackle the backlog. I have to get back to my abandoned working life.

There are two envelopes left. The first is just routine correspondence from my insurance contact. He has nothing specific for me at the moment, but thinks something might arise by Christmas with a case they're handling. Thank God for that. If something had come up while I've been out of action, then it might have been a source of income gone forever.

I open the last letter. There's no date on it, and its contents make me tremble. My mouth goes dry as I read the brief message: Take this as a warning.

*   *   *

It's raining. As if it will never stop. Jade's parents haven't looked at me or tried to talk to me since I arrived, slipping in at the back where I might remain unnoticed. There was no time to do the polite, human thing. In place of the greeting I should have given to Mr. and Mrs.

O'Donnell come all the tortured thoughts. It should have been me. If I hadn't been screwing with Dominic, Jade would be here now. It would be me lying silent in the dark coffin, and Jade would be crying. That would be okay. She'd cry for a while, then walk away; get another job. She'd forget about this, meet someone fantastic, marry him, be happy, and have all the children she wanted.

That's what should have happened. But because of me, it never will.

Jade is dead.

I should be out there, finding out who did this to her, getting evidence, finding the connection with Delta Egypt. I should be doing everything I can to salvage something from the mess of unfinished business. Instead, I'm standing in a chapel overflowing with people in the rain-soaked, wind-driven Essex countryside saying goodbye to someone I loved. It's a day that shouldn't exist, but it does.

The words of the service mean nothing to me, but they set up a faint echo of a past funeral, another day, another life. Then, of course, there was no body—something from which my family has never recovered—but now the evidence of what the O'Donnells might call "sin" and that

I call crime is all too real. Around me, people start to cry. Gazing at the simple white walls, the bare wooden cross, the cream lilies and roses that crown the coffin at the front, and breathing in the sharp herbal scent of polish, I envy them their release.

The elder in his formal black suit starts to talk about Jade in a way that tells me the information he's conveying is second-hand. He describes a woman he hasn't known for at least ten years, telling us about her school days, her time at university, and then, in vaguer terms, her short-lived career in what he calls "investigative services."

I want to stand, cut across his bland words, and shout aloud about the woman I knew. I want to tell the congregation about the way she smiled, the wildness and glitter of the jewelry she wore, her love of exotic clothes. I want to tell them how she always drank Chardonnay and how she would groan when I teased her about it. I want to let them know her genius with the computer, her love of salsa and all types of dance, and most of all the warmth, wit, and wisdom I have relied on ever since I met her. I want to say all these things and hold the truth of them in my mouth, but already the moment is passing. There is no space for it here. This service is not for me. It's for Jade. For her family.

After the service, we troop quietly out of the chapel, back into the driving rain, following the slow progress of the coffin. Turning up my collar and stuffing my hands in my pockets, I'm careful to look at no one.

We drive to the crematorium in a convoy. I have glanced at the map once and it made no sense to me, but it doesn't matter as we slot into place behind each other. In the rain, there is somehow no dignity to this. We cram ourselves into seats set too close together in a sparse room built for half the number. We listen again to more words of comfort that have either already been said or are pointless for the saying. As we wait, the coffin slides through a thick black curtain and is gone.

A sudden movement at the front catches my eye and I can see Mr. O'Donnell has half-risen in his seat, as if trying to object to the way things are, even now. As he turns, he stares full at me, but there's no quiver of recognition. His face is gaunt and pale, and he looks as if he might fall. A second later, Jade's mother pulls him back down beside her and hugs him close. I can see his shoulders are shaking, and I close my eyes to block out the image.

When the ceremony is over, we file outside into the rain and make our way along a pathway lined with lilies, roses, and carnations. As I begin to wonder when I can leave without causing hurt, there's a light touch on my arm. I turn and look into the eyes of Mrs. O'Donnell. Behind her, Jade's father hovers, but his glance does not stay on me.

"Paul," she says, and it sounds like an affirmation. Of what I don't know. "I'm glad you've come. Thank you."

Her kindness is so unexpected it hurts.

"I'm sorry," I say, and my voice sounds as if it's travelling from a thousand miles away. "I'm sorry about…"

I can't finish the sentence, but she doesn't seem to mind and doesn't at once reply, instead squeezing my arm. We stay in that position for a long time, and I notice strands of grey in her hair I never noticed before and lines at the corner of her mouth. She grips my arm a little tighter and sighs.

"Will you come back with us afterward?" she says. "Perhaps we can talk?"

I'm within a heartbeat of making that step, but when I glance beyond her, I can see the refusal and the pain on her husband's face. If I go with them, there'll only be half a welcome, and I'll be treading his grief down harder.

So I shake my head and free my arm gently from her fingers. "No, I'm sorry. I can't, I—"

"All right," she cuts through me, as if she's heard all she can bear to hear. "I understand. But, please, keep in touch. I don't want to lose the people who have known my daughter best."

I back away from her. I don't know what else to do. Whatever decision I make, I hurt someone.

When the family and all the mourners have left, I go on my own to the place where my best friend is lying. The rain continues to trickle through my hair and down into my jacket, drenching my skin, and the sky is growing darker. It's as if all the words I ever wanted to say to Jade are fighting for escape, but I don't understand what order they should be in or whether they're making sense. In any case, Jade can't hear me, not now, so what the fuck does it matter? I should have said thank you to her, so many times, just for being who she is—was—and for all the times she helped me. The talks in the pub, the meals we shared, the way I could tell her anything—anything—and she would take it all in without judging me. The concern in her lovely, open face when I was unhappy and her joy in the times I wasn't. The way she looked out for me, worried about me, where no one else has done.

Hunkering down, I slick my soaked hair back out of my eyes and blink away the rain. My fingers trace the outline of the words on the plaque her parents have made for her.

———

Jade O'Donnell, beloved daughter and friend
Taken too soon, may you rest in the love of God.

———

And then, at last and from nowhere, I'm weeping great gulps of tears I can't hold in. My body convulses, and I can't seem to breathe, but it doesn't matter. I just keep crying and crying, until there is nothing left but quietness and a sense of something done that can't be undone.

"I'll find them, Jade," I whisper. "Wherever they are, I'll find them. I swear it to you."

When I struggle to my feet and turn around, he is there, and the shock of it sends a wave of panic through my body.

I don't know how long he's been there, what he's seen or how he knew about it all. I don't care much either. He's not wearing a coat, and his posh-git shirt is sticking to his flesh in the rain. I look at him for a long time. Where he's standing means I have to pass him on the way out of the crematorium garden. As I start to walk and draw level with him, he reaches out and touches me. I shake off his hand as if it's fire, but the breaking of the impasse brings me to a halt.

"I'm sorry about Jade," he says. "Please, if there's anything I can do—"

Without even knowing this is what is going to happen, I whip my arm out and I lash him over the face with the back of my hand. I'm glad of it because it's been waiting a long time. He staggers back with a small moan, and I can see the blood on his lips. He makes no move to retaliate.

"You bastard," I say, realizing so many things as I say it. His actions, his words on the night I slept with him crystallize into sudden knowledge. "You knew. You bloody, bloody bastard. Don't you think you've done enough?"

And then, not looking behind me once, I stride over the soaking, sinking grass into the car and start the long drive home.

Where I pour myself a Glenfiddich and down it straight off. Fuck the six P.M. rule. Flame sears my throat and takes away some of the pain. I switch on the TV, get up, prowl like an injured wolf into the kitchen, plug in the kettle, decide I don't want anything that isn't whisky, look into the freezer, but there's nothing there and I'm not hungry anyway.

Back in the living room, the TV is an irritation, so I switch it off, and the silence plunges in like water. The onslaught of tears in the cemetery has cleansed and rewired my mind.

Dominic isn't a client any more. That much is obvious, but there's no way I can give up the investigation. Whoever killed Jade took that USB drive, and I wonder if they know I have the original. The idea I might be in danger myself seems mere objective fact, not something that should give me pause. All I need to know is why the information is so important. No, more to the point, I need to have evidence of what I suspect and I need it quickly.

Without Jade, I don't know the way forward. I have to find one. I need to think laterally. Let all the facts shake down and become part of the way I live. I have to come up with something to take me to the next stage of whatever Delta Egypt is doing.

So for a while, I sit and let the things that have happened and the things that I know slide by without snatching at them. When I'm ready, I call Dominic.

CHAPTER 12

I get his PA and wonder at the hours she works. I'm not complaining; this is what I should have done in the first place. I keep the conversation brief. She recognizes my name, gives me the information I need, and I ring off.

What she's told me will make life easier. The next time Dominic is seeing Blake Kenzie is Thursday this week…better than I'd hoped for. Something I've done, or they think I've done, is worrying them. The best thing about it is that Blake is coming to London for "discussions," and I won't have to fly to Egypt. Cairo can wait. Will Blake's arrival here increase the danger? I think the answer is yes, but it doesn't worry me. There's way too much other stuff to focus on.

Jade is dead and someone has to pay. What I want to know is how much Dominic knows and how involved he is in Jade's murder.

One item I need is the second half of the hidden folders Jade found. If I can get hold of them and interpret them, then I'll be sure. What I don't know and can't begin to work out is what I'm going to do with the information.

There's no point obsessing now or upping my whisky intake while I wait. Whatever happens, I need to be sharp. It strikes me that, when I act, there'll be no room for error. I have forty-four hours and thirty-two minutes before I can see Blake and Dominic together. It will be interesting to see how they react. Until then, all I can do is wait and work.

And how I work.

I re-read the article from my mother's paper. I look at every single item on my USB drive, still wondering exactly who has Jade's copy now. Last of all, I turn to the reports on Bluesky's death again. I have to swallow down bile as I read about the body's cruel bruising, the sexual violence, the blotting out of one unknown woman's life. No mercy, no justice. As I work, the phrases my friend showed me and noted as being important echo through my mind, a background canvas to the slotting in of facts and supposition: Jan 31, call; when ready, Starlight, Dancer, Mar 20; carry on, Jun 0, Aqua and always, always, Bluesky. I wonder if I'll ever be rid of them.

The hours flicker by, and I carry on reading. The air grows ever colder until, at last, I get up and switch on the boiler, not yet set to its winter program.

In the bedroom, I don't bother with the light. A flicker of movement outside the window on the street, dark outline into darker shadow, makes me look and look again. From instinct, I step away from the glass, my eye retaining an image of a man, tall and still. My muscles tense, ready for action. I can feel my heart thudding blood around my body. Three seconds pace by, but when I peer back into the night, there's no one there. Am I overreacting, seeing a threat in every passing stranger? If I keep on doing that, then I'll be lost. I check the doors and windows are locked anyway.

After that, it's back to work to draw as much from the time I have as I can, and when at last I drag myself into bed at almost three A.M., I fall asleep at once.

*   *   *

When the light through the windows wakes me up in the morning, for a second or two, it's as if everything is as it should be. Jade is alive and I'm seven-eighths of the way home on solving a major case in which Dominic has no involvement. Even now, I'm terrified to think he has. Then the great, slow cloud of realization rolls upon me, and I lie, immobile, staring upward at the cracks in the ceiling. I've overslept. It's after nine and it's time to get up.

The hot shower feels good on my skin, invigorating me. I make coffee, black and strong, and sip it as the laptop hums back to life. The hours race by, but the fact that a second reading of everything on the USB drive gives me nothing more than a headache makes me wonder why I'm even bothering. I should be out there trying to get the information that will make the file complete, but the truth is there's no point doing this until Blake gets here. Not that I have any clue yet as to how I'm going to get that information. I'll have to rely on either inspiration or luck. I hope I'm not out of either. For now, I need to ignore the throbbing behind my eyes and take in as much as I can, on the grounds that you can never know too much: PI Rule Number Thirteen. It's not true though, is it? Jade's death tells me that. I rub my eyes, take a swig of water, and concentrate on the screen.

I hear the post arrive and catch the noises of the city: laughter, shouts, the background hum of cars. It crosses my mind that there might be someone out there, watching my flat, waiting for me to appear. They'll have a long wait then. All locks are secured and I'm going nowhere. Lunchtime comes and goes, with the sounds beyond my walls changing in tone and emphasis: more laughter now and more traffic. My stomach protests at the lack of food. I answer it with more of the coffee I make double-strength in the French press. I reheat and refill it five times during the course of the afternoon.

When I've typed up all the notes I can make and the combined knowledge of Jade and myself is saved on three USBs, I'm no further forward. But at least my understanding of the business is greater.

I can do no more. Slamming the laptop shut, I spring up, wipe both hands across my face, and stretch the muscles in my legs and arms. I need a drink. What time is it?

8:32 P.M. I've worked all day. In the kitchen, I pour myself a well-earned Highland Park and feel the fire of it warming the back of my tongue. The first glass I gulp down, wanting the comfort of it more than the savor, but the second I take my time over. I'm only on the third sip when I remember the post.

It's still on the hall floor. As I pick it up, I notice a thick, oblong package with familiar handwriting on the address label. For a ridiculous moment, my mind says bomb: danger, before I recognize who's sent it and give a short laugh. God, I must stop reading all those crime novels. I must stop imagining I'm in a Tarantino film. Yes, I think, I may be a small-time investigator, but I've been knifed and shot at in Cairo, and my best friend has been murdered. I'm in deeper than I've ever been and I'm mixed up with a man who might, if my instincts are correct, be playing a very dangerous game. I have to be careful.

The handwriting on the label reminds me of Jade's. The postmark is Essex.

I tear open the wrapping and then gaze at the tied-up bundles of letters. The covering note is signed by Mrs. O'Donnell. We found these in Jade's private belongings, it says. We think she would have liked you to have them.

I pull the first one out of its green ribbon and read it. Then I find myself crouched on the floor, back resting against the wall, and I read it again. Then I read another and another and another, all from different bundles, and still I don't understand.

I get up, gather the letters to my chest, and abandon any thought of dealing with the other post. In the living room, I spread them on the table gently, as if the slightest movement might tear them.

There are thirty-four letters. Tears slide down my face as I slowly read them all again.

They're love letters, written by Jade and addressed to me. Never posted. She mentions conversations we've had, evenings out at The Bell and Book, meals we've shared or that time when I took her to see Cats, and details of cases only the two of us would know about. All the inner workings of our friendship. And laced between all this are expressions of love, commitment, evidence of a desire I never knew. When I've finished them, I fold the last one up and sit, holding it. My eyelids are hot and prickling, sore with crying. It's as if all the things I've relied on, all the history I thought was mine, has been snatched from my grasp and returned to me in an unfamiliar guise. Why didn't she ever say anything?

What could I have done if she had? God. I bury my face in my hands and groan. I'm sorry, Jade. I'm sorry. Even as the tears continue to fall, the doorbell pierces the still flat and pulls me back into the present. It's late for visitors, too damn late, ten-twenty-three now. I've just decided to ignore it and concentrate on dealing with the aftermath of the package in front of me when it rings again. This time it doesn't stop.

"Okay, okay, for God's sake," I mutter. "Can't you just bloody well leave me alone, whoever you are?"

I peer through the spy hole before opening the door. It's Dominic, and I know from experience that he won't go away until he gets what he wants. The sight of him glowering on the doorstep makes me change my mind, and I try to shut the door again, but he's too quick for me.

"No," he says, sidestepping past me and into the hall. "I want to talk to you, and it has to be now."

I'm pleased to see his lip is a little blue from where I hit it yesterday, but already he's in the living room, shrugging off his coat and laying it across the back of my sofa. He sits without me inviting him, spreading his arms wide and gazing up at me, one eyebrow raised, as if he owns the place. I go to gather up Jade's letters, but there are too many of them. He stands, picks one up, and glances through it before tossing it back onto the table and sitting again.

"How charming. Are they all like that?" he asks.

"Fuck off."

"Rather a purple prose she had. Not the class of love letter I'd send to anyone if I sent any at all."

"Shut the fuck up," I snap back. Then I stare into his eyes. "You don't sound surprised."

"I'm not. But that isn't what I've come to discuss with you."

"Look, what the fuck do you want? Why don't you just say it and go?"

He gives a short laugh. "As you wish. What I've come to discuss with you is the case. I'm taking you off it."

"You don't have to. I'm working for myself now."

"What does that mean?"

"What do you think?" I thump my fist down on the table, scattering Jade's letters onto the floor, and I wish for the second time I'd never let him in.

"Don't do that, Paul. You'll break it. What do you mean you're working for yourself?"

I can't believe he doesn't get it and I can't believe he's behaving this coldly, but when I look at him, there's no deceit in his face. "Jade is dead. You were the indirect cause of her death. I no longer want your dirty money. All I want to find out is the truth and how much you know of it. How much do you know, Dominic?"

I speak slowly so there can be no misunderstanding, and as I do, Dominic gets to his feet, half-turns away from me, picks up one of my mother's Staffordshire dogs from the mantelpiece, and sighs.

"I've never understood your taste," he says. "I'm sorry about Jade, more than you know, but I didn't kill her. It does, though, make it even more imperative that you realize the case is over. Leave it alone."

I shake my head. "You must be out of your mind."

"Please."

"No."

He puts down the dog and swings around to face me. "Then you leave me no choice."

"What do you mean?"

"You're a reasonable man. Or you can be when your heart isn't involved. Or your cock. And, my God, talking of your cock, you've had your share of lovers, haven't you? Not including me. Though my sources reveal you have calmed down since your early twenties, and really I would have thought that would have been a relief to you. Let's see, shall we?"

He reaches into his coat, takes out a sheaf of papers, and unfolds it. Unable to speak, unable to move, I watch him.

"What does this tell me?" he continues. "Hmm, regular use of the physical facilities on offer in the gents' toilets of a Soho nightclub; advertising for a sex partner for pleasure only in the gay press; shagging strangers in the less pleasant areas of Hampstead Heath and—ah, your pièce de résistance, my friend, very impressive, indeed—being questioned and cautioned for underage sexual activity with a minor, the son of one of your parents' neighbors, I believe.

"You've been busy. God, Paul, the boy was only fifteen. Fifteen. A child. What the fuck were you thinking of? You were lucky not to end up in court for that one.

Good job it wasn't—according to the records, though, knowing you as I do, I don't believe it—actual penetration, and that your father's a judge. Oh, and that the lad was said to be willing, of course. That helped. There's more. Shall I go on?"

By now, I'm sitting slumped on the sofa, trying to catch my breath. "How did you know, you bastard? How long have you known about me?"

He waves the papers. "Since we started to fuck each other. All these things that could bring the police down on you, take your livelihood out of your grasp, ruin you even, I've always known. Trust me. I'll do it if I have to. And more. You don't want to be responsible for destroying your father's glittering career, not to mention the distress it will cause your mother. I'm telling you the truth, and you're condemned by your own beliefs. Maloney's Law—you should apply it now."

He waits, while I struggle to breathe and regain control.

"When are you going to destroy me?" I ask him. "And my parents?"

"I won't. On both counts. If you agree to my request. Abandon this case."

"Blackmail then. God, Dominic, is this what you've held against me all this time? Is this what you'd drop me and my family into if—when—this whole case goes down?"

"Of course."

His bloody honesty. It takes away any shaky ground I might have been able to find.

I stand. "And what if, in turn, I tell everyone about our affair? How will your company, your shareholders, your wife, and your children feel when they know the sort of lies you tell?"

He shrugs his broad shoulders. "With your record, who would believe it?"

It's only when he's left me and I have drunk three more shots of the Highland Park, straight off, that I admit he's right.

I walk out into the bleakness of the night. My conscious mind is busy bringing logic to all the things I have experienced in order to survive. In spite of the dullness of autumn, for me there's a clarity in the air that makes everything seem sharper. I mull over tasks while, underneath, at my heart, I am remembering another place, another time when the man I love gave me no choices.

*   *   *

Thursday, April 12…the day Dominic ended our affair. April is the cruelest month, they say, and since then, I've always believed it. He'd promised he'd be with me at nine P.M., though he would have to leave by midnight. Cassie was expecting him. That would give us three hours of lovemaking. Enough, I'd hoped, to get me through another week or two until he decided he could see me again. Please God, let it not be any longer than that, I remember thinking. Please, not this time.

The bedroom was glowing with candlelight, and I'd put a bottle of his favorite Dom Perignon on ice and two glasses next to the bed. Not that we ever needed it. Already I'd showered, shaved with special care, and splashed my face and neck with the aftershave he'd bought me. After several false starts, I'd chosen my newest pair of jeans to wear and a dark green cotton shirt that went with my eyes, or so he'd once told me. I hadn't bothered with briefs; he always liked to see my nakedness under the denim. And now I was waiting. Waiting. Waiting.

8:31P.M. 8:43. 8:52. I combed my hair for the tenth time, smoothing it down to make my face look thinner, more wolfish. The way I think he liked it, though he'd never said.

8:57.P.M. 9:04. God, where was he? Why did he always do this to me? Why did he make me wait? And why did I never learn from it? I should have realized by now he was never on time. I should have been used to it and just tried to be calmer. No point being calm, I was sweating now.

9:12.P.M. 9:22. This was later than he'd ever been before, and my fingers were itching for a cigarette, even though I hadn't smoked for six months, two weeks, and two days by then. Anything to ease the dark, swirling circle in my stomach. What if he didn't come? What if this was it, forever, and I never saw him again? I couldn't... God...I just couldn't think.

9:27 P.M. 9:33. I finished my second cigarette, pacing all the time 'round the flat, touching a picture here, rearranging the mirror so the light from the glasses reflected from it. Please, God, let him come, please.

Should I ring him? No, not yet, he'd be here soon. He wouldn't like me to ring him, not at work.

9:42 P.M. 9:51. I couldn't see how I was going to get through the night. I would have to ring him. I would just have to. I punched the numbers into my mobile, and at the same moment, the doorbell rang and I was there. Letting him in, trying not to touch and keep on touching him, though my fingers fluttered around his skin. They carved the shape, the feel, the scent of him into the air as I took his jacket and tried not to gabble.

"God, Dominic, it's good to see you. I thought you might have forgotten, or worse. I'm glad you're okay. I was worried. I don't know, something might have happened, you know? Look, don't worry about me. I'll be myself again in a minute. You're here now and that's all that matters. It's all that matters."

I reached to kiss him, but he sidestepped me, heading for the living room. As I followed, still clutching his jacket, something inside me ceased to move, and it was hard to think.

Even before I'd had a chance to say anything else, he was already speaking, all the while staring straight at me.

"Look, Paul, I'm not staying. I think you know what this is about. We have to finish it. It's gone on too long. It can't last. We're burning ourselves out. So I've made a decision, and I believe it to be best for both of us. We're through. Our affair ends here and it ends now."

I couldn't speak. Words were crowding up inside me, pecking at my flesh like crows. None of them made any sense. He continued to stare at me. His mouth was twitching, as if he tasted something rotten, but couldn't spit it out.

After another few seconds, I could still find nothing to say. He shrugged, took his jacket from my lifeless fingers, and strode out into the hall.

Finally, I found my voice.

"What?" I stumbled out after him. "Don't be stupid, Dominic. You don't mean that. You can't. You've only just got here. Why don't you stay? Come into the bedroom. I've got champagne and candles, too. You're tired; it's after work. Come on, love. I can help you relax."

By the time I'd finished, I could see his body was shaking, though he didn't turn to face me. I had no idea what was going on. It was beyond my understanding. Even searching my mind for what might have made him say this, I could find no hint of a problem in all our times together. Yes, of course, a few times when we'd made love, and especially the last time, it was as if something in him hadn't been there with me, but that was just tiredness, wasn't it? He was a busy man. It wasn't anything sinister; it couldn't be.

"Come on, please." I laid my hand on his back and whispered, "Let's just go to bed. It'll be fine this time, you'll see. We can talk afterward."

"No. I have to go now. For God's sake, don't you see it's best?"

No, I didn't see. I didn't see at all. So I just wrapped my fingers around his arm and began pulling him back to the bedroom.

"Paul. I mean it." Without warning, his arm whipped out, and he struck me, hard, across the jaw, so hard my teeth cracked and the sour taste of blood filled my mouth. I went down, scrambling and spitting like a wino on the hall carpet. He swung around and headed for the door. I had to stop him.

"Please, Dominic, please. I'm begging you, stay." I flung myself after him, scrabbling at his feet, his legs, the edge of his jacket. "Please, don't leave me. I can't be without you. I can't."

"God, Paul, please." He grabbed my fingers where they clung to him and tried to pull himself free, but my desperation was too strong. "For God's sake, have some bloody pride, won't you?"

But already I was beyond that and I didn't let go. The next second, I caught a glimpse of his shoe aimed at my stomach. Grabbing it, I pulled him over on top of me.

"Please," I said again, clutching him to me. Through my hazy vision, I saw he was breathing heavily, his face twisted with pain. "Please don't leave me like this. I can't bear it. I love you. Can't you see that? I love you and I'll do anything, anything in the world for you. You only have to ask. Don't we have a future? Don't we? I've thought so much of us being together. You could leave Cassie and be with me. You want to, I know you do. Please, I need you. I'll do whatever you want, whenever you want it. Please, please, Dominic."

"For God's sake, let me go. I can't be with you any more. And you're mad. I'll never leave my wife."

"No! You don't mean that. You can't mean it."

"But I do."

Pushing me down, he slammed my head back against the carpet. The world around me spun wildly. He was looking at me, his eyes unfathomable. Suddenly, there was stillness between us.

"Don't go," I whispered. "Please. Don't leave me with nothing."

Something in his expression switched off, and it was then that the terror began.

"All right," he said. "You asked for it. You'll get it."

Before I could object, he had ripped my shirt open and pulled down my jeans. His action shocked me back into myself.

"Glad to see you've made it simple for me, Paul."

"No." I made a move to punch him, but a wave of nausea overpowered me. He took the opportunity to slap my face again and turn me around as easily as if I'd been a child. As he did so, he imprisoned my arms behind me in my shirt.

"Not much of a fighter, are you? PI work or no PI work." I heard the sound of a zip being undone.

A sudden jerky series of movements told me he was bringing himself to hardness. I didn't have much time. I had to reach him, somehow. For all the months I'd known him, in the bedroom he'd always been tender. Now his cock was jabbing at me, but somehow he couldn't find the entry to my arse. I could feel the blood filling my head, pounding, pounding, I—

Then, just as I knew he'd found me, I whispered his name.

"Nic."

At once, I felt him go limp. His breath burnt my neck and then, a second later, he rolled off me.

"God, God, this whole thing is impossible. You're impossible. Don't you see?"

I said nothing. I just let him talk himself out, listening as he swung between anger and shock and I was careful not to make any sudden movements. Underneath his words, I could hear the dark pulse lurking still and couldn't tell if he might attack me a second time. If he did, I had no more resources to make him stop.

When at last he was quiet, I slowly, so slowly, eased my arms free from the shirtsleeves trapping me and turned over onto my side. Even so, the act made bile fill my throat, and I spat out blood and a thin stream of vomit onto the carpet.

"God, Paul."

He reached for me, and, without thinking, I flinched and kicked him away. As if from nowhere, the rage took hold of him again, but this time it wasn't directed at me.

"For fuck's sake, can't you see this is no good?" He slammed his fist against the wall and the plaster cracked. "It's going nowhere. I'll never leave Cassie or my children. We're finished."

"No, please, Dominic, I can't not see you." My mouth was full of staleness. "Please stay and we can talk. I don't mind about Cassie. Please just stay, just—"

"No." He swung around and crouched next to me. Taking my face in his hands, he drew his thumb across the blood on my lip and stared for a long moment into my eyes. Then he spoke slowly and simply, as if speaking to a child. "I'm going now. We won't see each other again. You won't see me again."

He stood. He took two steps toward the door, away from me, then the door opened, the sharp April air filled the hall, the door shut, and he was gone.

10:21 P.M. 10:28. 10:33. The doorbell didn't ring again. He wasn't coming back. There would be no more of this.

Unable to cry, unable even to feel, and registering only the slow twist of pain in my gut, I staggered to the bedroom. There I opened the champagne and drank it from the bottle. Then, for the first of many, many times, I took out my mobile, switched it on, and, still shaking, dialed his number.

CHAPTER 13

When morning comes, I'm lying in my bed remembering. I spent a long time just walking around the streets last night and am aware, as if from a great distance, that I might be lucky to be here today. Bearing in mind Egypt and, more to the point, Jade. The wash of grief when I remember my friend no longer takes me by surprise, and I let it ride over me for a while, even as I'm still thinking of the past. About Dominic, about Jade, and then, slowly again as if slinking back into my own mind after a long journey, about my dead sister and my family.

All of it is floating in darkness together: Dominic's face and my father's anger; Teresa and Jade; my mother. All my life I have tried not to remember what has led me here, but now there's no choice. Today I should be trying to see Blake and Dominic together later this afternoon. I should be trying to understand what my ex-lover has done and why he is now so angry, angry enough to blackmail me, destroy my family, my business and me.

At heart, I know the answer, but now it's the past that haunts me, not the present. There will be time enough for confrontation and maybe confession.

Now I remember Teresa again, the way she smiled, her rich black hair so like mine. I remember a different moment, played out like a film in my head. I remember how she always cheated in Hide and Seek and would never admit it. It was impossible to count to one hundred in the time she claimed. I never minded, though, not when she was with me. Later, when she was taken away and when I came to understand what might have happened that late October afternoon when I saw her once and then no more, I would have been overjoyed to have her cheat again. Sometimes now there is, in my dreams, a glimpse of an unknown face, shrouded so I can't make out its features, and a sense of a suppressed threat, but I can't grasp the connection of this image with what I remember about Teresa and me. On those occasions when it passes through my mind, I wonder if I've simply imagined it, just for the need for completion, and what good it would do if it were true.

It might, after all, be an echo of the pain my parents went through. After Teresa vanished, I don't remember being told anything concrete, either in the immediate aftermath or when the knowledge of loss was rising. It was as if, when my sister left, a long rope was attached to me that kept me fixed to the day it happened, even as I travelled onward and ever onward. Maybe I've been walking with it wrapped around my flesh for too long. Maybe none of it could have been any different.

My parents' grief, and mine, was, on the whole, something we each handled alone. There were three times only when we tried to talk together, as if a boy of six and his parents can talk together. Each time, it drove us farther apart. Not that I understood then. I was simply aware of the emptiness of the house and the deep gloom I could never break through. It became part of my growing up: my mother's sorrow; my father's anger.

Yes, my father's anger. It's one of the memories overshadowing the whole of my family's life after Teresa had gone. So much so that anything there might have been before that time, what he was like, how he was with us, is lost to me. Just as much as my sister is. My father's black rages cancelled out the grief my mother suffered, and from then, she became almost a ghost in her own home, a vanishing presence in my life. All I fought or moved against in the school years, the teenage years, even today, was the overpowering knowledge of him.

He hardly seemed to notice me. Now I think Teresa was the one he must have lived for and after her loss, everything died for him. Even me. Even my mother. Not his work, though. His career as a barrister and then a judge has never faltered, and neither has his subsidiary career as a radio and TV legal expert. It must have been a constant irritation for him to have a son like me, with so little ambition then and with no career now. If Teresa had lived, I'm sure she would have been the one he could be proud of.

Maybe this was why I did everything I could during my teenage years to get his attention. Smoking, drinking, drugs, and sex with what my father, if he'd known about them, would have seen as unsuitable people, and how much worse that they weren't girls. Whatever…it worked, and some of our arguments were the most memorable I have known and the most unresolved. The king of all these rows had come the day he discovered I'd fallen in love with David.

I'd been nineteen, back from university in the Christmas of my second year, and living in a home that hadn't for a long time welcomed me. My parents had new neighbors, the Cunninghams, if neighbors were what you called them, living as they did out of sight of the house itself and across two vast expanses of lawn, although estate is a more accurate description. The Cunninghams moved on afterward, of course.

I met them and their son, David, for the first time on Tuesday, December 15 at a pre-Christmas drinks party my mother was giving. I say my mother, as my father had no interest in socializing with people who would not be able to advance his career. I wasn't interested in making polite conversation either, but my mother's silent rebuke, together with the fact I'd finished my last illegal smoke only that morning drove me down the wide, curved stairs into the warmth and noise of the living room at gone six P.M.

I was glad I'd made the effort. David was beautiful. He was just fifteen years old, and, as my mother mentioned his birthday had been the previous week, there's no excuse for what I did. He was tall and fragile, with soft fair hair, deep brown eyes and a smile that took hold of my heart and twisted it to a new shape inside me.

There's a world of difference between being fifteen and being nineteen, but in a room full of people whose lives and lifestyles I'd long since left behind, David was the nearest to me in age and experience. It wasn't long before I realized how in awe he was of me, someone grown-up, someone who most of the time lived away from home, someone who lived in London, and I lost no opportunity in pressing my advantage. I wanted him to envy me. So I told him tales only one-quarter true about the people I'd met, the nightclubs I'd been to, the things I'd seen.

At the end of the evening, all we'd done was talk to each other, and all the time I'd been drinking in the smoothness of his skin, the way his eyes sparkled a deeper brown in the candlelight, the curve of his neck and shoulders beneath the crisp white cotton of his shirt. I don't think he noticed. Before he left to go home, and in a second or two of time when there was nobody in the hallway but us, he gave me a sweet, shy grin.

"Would you like to come around tomorrow after lunch or something?" he said, hardly seeming to dare to look at me. "We could just do stuff, you know? If you like?"

I pretended to think about it. I didn't want to lose my "adult" dignity or cool in front of David.

"Sure." I shrugged. "Why not? Might get the parents off our backs, huh?"

He nodded, mouth suppressing another smile, and was gone.

The next day, after a night when David appeared in my dreams and the bed was damp with sweat when I woke up, I waited 'til the afternoon before slipping out of the house and strolling, heart beating fast, across the swathes of grass which divided us. It felt like a no-man's land, a journey almost too hard for the taking. When the door to the neighbors' house swung back, David's eyes lit up his whole face.

"Come in," he said. "My parents are out."

We climbed the stairs up to his room. I don't remember what we talked about there and neither do I remember anything about the work he was showing me on his computer. What I do recall is how, not long after he'd let me in, we had our first touch. I ran my fingers across the back of his neck, feeling, with a shock of delight, how the hairs there brushed against my skin.

He stopped talking. I lifted my fingers a little away, waiting for a response, but there was nothing, so I let them fall again to his neck. He shivered once, but still stayed silent.

A few moments later, we shared our first kiss. He tasted of herbs.

When I drew back, I was shaking. "I'm sorry."

"That's okay," he said, and I noticed his face was reddening. "I didn't mind."

I couldn't believe my luck. "Really? Are you okay if… Can I…"

He nodded, and I didn't need a second concession.

We spent a long time that afternoon kissing and touching and kissing again. Nothing too heavy and, at the end of it, I danced across the glitter of lawn between our homes as if I was walking on stardust. I even congratulated myself on my restraint.

That night, I stood naked at my window, pressed my hand against the coolness of the glass and wondered if he was thinking of me.

By our third meeting, we'd stripped down to our underpants. Mine were red, one of a set my mother had bought me for my birthday. His were white. Cool and pure. Touching the outline of his cock beneath the fabric and squeezing, I watched as he stretched out on the bed and I felt him harden in my grasp. The next day, we went farther.

This time, there was no talking. We simply shut the door on the world outside, stood in the boyish winter crispness of his bedroom, and undressed each other, item by item. I can still remember the bright smell of the deodorant he'd used that morning, the freshness of his skin, its creamy promise. And most of all the feeling of safety and rightness, as if the whole world had been waiting for this moment and nothing in the whole world could hurt us.

Beginning to kiss his neck, I worked my way down to his shoulders, nuzzled the length of both his arms and up again, the heat between us making both of us begin to sweat. I traced a path of kisses across his chest, pulling gently at each of the scattering of fair hairs there. Then at last—at last—I slipped my hand inside the waistband of his pants and ran one curious finger into the crack of his arse.

Glancing up at him to check for signs of any objection, I could see his eyes were closed and there was a slight smile on his lips. I continued to slide my hand over the softness of his buttocks and then out and around to the warmth of his pubic hair. My breath was coming in gasps now, and it seemed a length of time before I found myself easing down his underpants and exposing the nakedness and youth of his cock. Like him, it was so beautiful, so full of promise.

I pushed him into a sitting position on the bed in front of me, spread his legs so I was between his knees, leant forward and took his cock into my mouth.

I felt his hardness with the warmth of my tongue.

A second later and the salt-sea savor of his spunk filled my throat and flooded through every part of my being, my arms and chest, my stomach and legs. I swallowed him down and kept on swallowing, wanting him to fill me up until I was overflowing with the taste of him.

At last he was spent, and I let him go from my mouth, reluctantly, tenderly and with countless kisses and licks and soft murmurings.

"David, David, I love you…thank you…I love you. I love you for this…thank you."

He said nothing, but as I grew silent, I felt his hand touch my hair and begin to stroke down to the back of my neck, making me shiver and sigh again.

Then he did the same for me. To my delight, I found he was a quick and eager learner.

And so Christmas and the start of the New Year passed, with David and me spending long afternoons enjoying each other in either his parents' or my parents' house. It was too cold for venturing outside. Sometimes I allowed myself to think ahead to my Easter holidays or the vast expanse of the summer to come, and dream of what he and I might do then, but it always seemed to be too far away, too perfect to be real. I had no idea what our parents might think.

David told me once his father had joked with him about me and he'd talked about our shared interest in computer games, a lie David's father must have believed. Twice my mother mentioned how delighted she was and how pleased the Cunninghams were that I had befriended their son.

I didn't know what to say in reply, so I just nodded and mumbled something. I could see nothing beyond the next kiss, the next touch, the next lick. My father kept his silence, and I never knew what he thought 'til later. Looking back, I wonder how they missed the dance that must have been in my eyes, the sheen of happiness glittering from my skin. David was like a drug to me; with him, there was no need of other stimulation.

After our first fully naked encounter, I took to carrying condoms in my jeans pocket. Not that I mentioned it to him, telling myself it was "just in case," just a "precaution," but taking pride in the fact I was restrained enough not to penetrate him. I convinced myself I was doing nothing wrong. We were just young blokes, messing around with each other, making each other happy for a while. We were fine as we were, nobody knew anything and there'd be no fall-out from this. It was a matter for David and me alone.

Or so I thought. Until, that is, the last time I saw him, two days before I was due back at university. It was a crisp January afternoon, and we were lying spread-eagled on his bed, the rays of the sun drifting across our bodies through the open curtain. Downstairs, I could hear the faint sounds of his mother watching TV and now and again the opening of the patio door as she wandered into the winter garden. She'd smiled when I'd first come in and offered coffee, but hadn't made any further comments when I'd shrugged and said I wasn't thirsty, adding something about the computer, while David led the way eagerly upstairs.

We'd gone down on each other as soon as the door was shut. There was an urgency in it we hadn't experienced before. It hit me then how stupid it was; he was fifteen, and I was nineteen. When I left to go back to London, I told myself, I would end it.

Beside me, David stirred, turning his head to face me so his breath warmed my neck.

"This is nice," he said. "Isn't it?"

"Hmm, yes, it is. Always."

His bedside clock ticked on like the beat of a heart.

"Paul?"

"Hmm?"

"Do you like me?"

"What?" I half-raised myself to look at him. His face was pale, and I could never be sure, neither then nor afterward, but I think his eyes were wet. "Sure I like you. What's there not to like?"

"No, I mean, are you…are you my friend?"

I laughed and hugged his slim body into the wiry darkness of mine. "Yeah, sure we are. We're mates, aren't we?"

He sighed then, the whole length of his flesh trembling against mine, and I could feel my cock begin to harden again. I didn't think I could ever get enough of him.

"So why don't you—" he said and then stopped.

I waited, but the silence only deepened.

"Why don't I…what?" I said.

"Why don't you…you know…do it with me?"

Shutting my eyes, I hugged him tighter, not bothering to ask him what he meant. "God, I'd love to, David, you know that. But…"

"It's not fair. It's not bloody fair. I can't help being young." With a sudden movement I hadn't anticipated, he jabbed me in the stomach and wrenched himself free. The next moment, he was standing naked next to the window, his whole body shaking as if it would never stop. Unsure of what prying eyes there might be outside, I sprang up and drew him back onto the bed, back into safety, hugging and kissing him until the fit was over.

"I know. I know," I murmured. "It's not fair, but it's just the way it is, Davey. It's just the way it is. I'm sorry, but I swear to you it doesn't matter and it won't ever matter how old we are. I'll always be your friend, I swear."

"Show me then." He drew a little away and gazed up at me, his eyelashes wet with tears. "Show me."

"I do. Every day."

"No. I mean show me. Show me you're my friend, and I can be yours."

I didn't know what to say, how to convince him I was telling the truth. He continued to gaze at me, challenging me, and, not taking my eyes off him, I reached out and found my jeans, crumpled at the bottom of the bed. For a second I panicked, then I made contact with the condoms. I tore at the packet with my teeth.

"What do you want me to do?"

When I looked at him, I saw he was trembling, but the tears had gone. Something in me made a last, desperate attempt for sanity. "David, love, we don't have to…"

"Please, I want to."

After a second, I eased him up onto all fours. The blood was pounding so heavily, so insistently in my ears that there was no room for thought. His buttocks were smooth and tight, like silk, and my cock was fully hard.

I stumbled and cursed under my breath as I tried to put on the condom, all coordination lost, but at last I managed it. I spat onto my hands and eased the wetness of my fingers into his arse. Then, stretching him, I entered him with the tip of my cock.

David gasped.

"Is that okay? Does it hurt?" I panted.

"It's fine. Just feels…strange. But nice."

"Yes, I know it." Murmuring soothing words, words of love, I pushed myself farther inside.

Three distinct happenings then took place. First I realized that, for me, being taken was far more satisfying than taking and, though I didn't know it then, always would be. Second, despite, or perhaps because of, this gem of self-knowledge, I came quicker than I'd hoped and I couldn't help it…my cries pulsated out with the rhythm of my body. Third, the door opened and Mrs Cunningham, fresh and cold from the garden, stood motionless on the threshold.

It was then that the real nightmare began.

I don't remember much about what happened afterward; it's a blur of accusation and guilt, yelling and confusion. All I can remember is how lost David looked, how alone, and how the road between him and me was covered with so many brambles I could never find my way through again. There were warnings and threats of police involvement, then questionings and official cautions, but David swore and kept on swearing I hadn't done it to him because his mother's appearance had meant I hadn't finished what we'd begun, that it was just a one-off incident brought on by drink and curiosity.

I don't know what my mother thought, but my father, at last compelled by circumstances to notice me, shouted and hit me once across the face in the privacy of his office. The force of it knocked me down. When I got up, jaw stinging, he'd gone, caught up in his campaign to keep what I'd done out of the eye of the press.

There was a police report; of course there was. Not even my father is above the law. But it, too, was a shadow of actual events and was hushed up, a lost file in some police archive. Not lost enough though that Dominic was unable to uncover it.

I never saw David again. A week later, the Cunninghams had moved out. I returned to London, taking my belongings with me. Giving up my study of law, I took a series of dead-end jobs in shops and businesses, delivering sandwiches and later filing and running errands for an insurance company. In the hope of dislodging the picture of David from my mind and my conscience, I cut myself off from everyone I'd known before. Instead, I concentrated on getting to the end of each long day and earning enough money to live.

The thought of David took a long time to loosen its grip on my heart, but there was one person from university who wouldn't let herself be cut off from my life.

Jade.

She tracked me down, God knows how, as my parents didn't know then where I was, sweet-talked herself into my tiny, shared flat, took away the bulk of the drugs I was using, and listened when I cried. Without her, I think I would have been dead. Despite long nights of arguing, she never persuaded me to go back to my course; that part of my life was over. When she realized nothing she did would change my mind, she switched the focus of her arguments. So, after six months, I found myself helping out on a casual basis that soon became more formal, for the investigating firm used by the insurers I worked for.

The law, but not the law. Near enough to the path I thought I'd travel on to be interesting, but not so near as to be dangerous. Soon it became obvious I was a natural at finding out what nobody wanted to tell me. Later, I realized I loved it. I'd discovered a way to be involved in other people's lives, but always from a distance, where it wouldn't cause me pain. I'd found a place in the world that couldn't be taken away.

And solving other people's mysteries went a little way toward burying the guilt of not being able to solve Teresa's. Sometimes.

It was Saturday, October 27 when Teresa was taken. If she'd lived, she would have been thirty-four years old now. Thirty-four years, five months, three weeks, and two days old.

Even Jade didn't reach that age. The debt I owe her is still outstanding.

This is why this morning, after I've made things ready in the event that the worst should happen, I'm going to put the case and revenge to one side for a while and at last do what I should have done the day I discovered Jade's body. Delta Egypt and the answers I need can wait.

*　　*　　*

"Thank you."

I take the tea offered to me by Mrs. O'Donnell and lean back into my chair. It's the first words I've said since I arrived here five minutes ago, crumpled from the journey. When Jade's mother opened the door to me, she'd smiled as if she'd been expecting me, stepped aside, and said, "Please, come in, Paul."

I'd followed her, thinking again how thin she looked since her daughter's death. In the hallway, she'd come to an abrupt halt.

"Wait here for a minute, would you?"

There was no reason not to obey. As the man most responsible for what had happened, I was here under sufferance, lucky to be allowed entry at all. She'd opened the door to the living room, keeping her gaze on me as if afraid I might either push past her or vanish, though which was the better or worse option I couldn't have said. As Mrs. O'Donnell had slipped into the living room, I'd glimpsed her husband standing at the window and then the door was shut.

Now I sip my tea as if I'm here to make polite conversation about the weather. I do not know why I'm here at all. I only know I had to come.

Mrs. O'Donnell settles herself onto the sofa opposite me, and the light from the window frames her grey hair. She takes a long time arranging her skirt and picking fluff I can't see from her blouse. At last she speaks.

"I'm sorry," she says. "I'm sorry about my husband. He doesn't mean to be—"

"Please," I cut in, anxious above all things to avoid causing this woman any more pain. "It's okay. I understand, so please don't worry."

"Thank you."

There's a pause, and I know I must fill it. She's already walked one pace nearer me by giving me tea. It's my turn now. Still, it's hard to know what to say or how to begin at all.

I place my cup and saucer on the coffee table between us, lean forward, and focus on a point somewhere between the carpet and Mrs. O'Donnell's knees. Then I talk, slowly, seeking confidence.

"I'm sorry," I say, "for everything I've done. I'm sorry I didn't come to see you after Jade died. I should've come, but I was too afraid."

"Why? Why didn't you come to see us? Why were you so afraid? I would have liked to see you then. We both would, I think."

"I know." For the first time, I look into her face. What I see there encourages me to stop for a moment and think a little deeper about what I've done. "I know that. I was frightened of what you might say."

"What did you think that might be?"

I take a breath, lean back in my chair, and gaze upward at the white swirling ceiling patterns. "I thought you'd say it was my fault. I thought it was my fault. We were working on a case, Jade and I, a difficult one. I knew it was becoming dangerous, but I was stupid. I thought the danger was only for me, not for her. I never thought she'd be… God. Anyway, I should've been there. I shouldn't have left early. I should never have left her on her own. I knew she'd work late, no matter what I said. I should've been there to help her. I should have been, but I wasn't."

"Why did you leave her? If you thought the case might be dangerous?"

Swallowing, I place my hands on my knees and feel the slight shake of my leg muscles quivering under my palms. Then I look at her.

"I left," I say, "I left because I badly wanted to have sex with someone I hadn't seen for a long time. I wanted to be with…him."

The word "him" pulls its slow meaning through silence. She nods, as if it's something she's always known, although it's impossible for that to be true.

"I see," she says. "Thank you for telling me that. I know you're a very private person. It must've been difficult for you to say."

I can't reply. I'm empty, winded, as if I've been running uphill. Never in my life have I had to tell anyone about myself in this way. They, like my parents, have either discovered it or it's been obvious under the circumstances, like later on, with Jade.

Mrs. O'Donnell leans forward and pats my hands, just once, as if bringing me back from where I've been. I realize my shaking has stopped. I realize also, with a shock of something unfamiliar, that for once I don't want to run.

"It also explains something about how you and Jade were together," she says. "Thank you. I think then my daughter knew?"

"Yes." I nod. "She knew."

"From early on?"

"Yes. I didn't know she… I swear it. I had no idea how she felt about…things."

Jade's mother sighs. "The letters then. Did you read them?"

"Yes. Did you?"

"No. They weren't written for me. They were written for you, Paul, but when we found them, I knew what they would say. I knew my daughter. I knew how she felt about you, and I also understood you didn't see that, though I never knew why." She hesitates. "Now, of course, I understand. But it doesn't matter because it's still right that you should have Jade's letters. I know you were very fond of her."

"I loved her, Mrs. O'Donnell. I loved her, in my way. She was my best friend; she knew all about me. Things I've never told anyone else, I've told Jade. She saw me at my worst, but she never judged me. I depended so much on her, in so many ways. I miss her, too. I always will. Not…not in the way you and Mr. O'Donnell will, of course. That would be impossible."

At this point, I can't say any more; the tears are too overpowering. And too out-of-place. It's me who should be giving comfort, not receiving it, but today I'm travelling down roads I haven't been on before.

Jade's mother hands me a tissue that I crumple between my hands as I cry. She waits for me to finish, but she herself is calm. Only when the fit is over does she speak again.

"You did your best, Paul. We wouldn't ask for anything more."

"Maybe you should've done."

"Hush…you shouldn't say such things. They're not true."

Her words remind me of something a woman would say to a young child. Maybe right now that's what I am. It's what I feel like.

"Maybe. Maybe not," I say, my voice not quite itself yet. "Still, I wish I'd known your daughter better than I did, Mrs. O'Donnell."

"Perhaps you can," she says.

For the next two and a half hours, we talk about Jade. For me, the sense of release is almost tangible, a physical unpeeling, and I hope it's the same for her, too. She shows me photographs of my friend as a baby, and, as we flip through the pile of albums, I see Jade as I've never seen her before. I see her as a toddler, running at the camera clutching a biscuit, with that huge smile on her face. I see her in school uniform with her classmates, standing tall and laughing, her fair hair spilling out of its plaits. Then she's on a school exchange trip to France, sitting in a café with foreign signs and sunlight on the street outside. She's eating pommes frites with a dark-haired, elfin girl whose name Mrs. O'Donnell doesn't remember. Later, there are photos of Jade at Colchester Zoo with her first serious boyfriend. Both of them are sixteen, and he's holding her hand as if he wants to be there forever. Behind them, a monkey is caught stretching from the bar up to a tree branch.

Afterward, the pictures become more like the Jade I knew at university. Her hair fluffs out in a riot of curls, then smoothes down for a while before giving up and returning to the curls again. Her earrings get larger and her skirts go up, then down, and up. I see her breasts swell into adulthood, whilst her waistline shrinks. Though never as much as she would have liked, I remember. Mrs. O'Donnell laughs when I say this.

"Yes, she always wanted to be thinner. I don't know why. I thought she was perfect as she was, but then I would say that, I suppose."

"No, it's true. She had a great figure. I just wish she'd believed me when I told her so."

I hear about the things I missed out on, some of which I know only by the telling: Jade's love of horses when she was small, but how she could never stay on long enough to make the lessons worthwhile; her travel-sickness and her fear of flying; the way she never felt properly dressed without her watch.

I hear about how she always asked her mother to make her special chocolate mousse on her birthday; the books she'd loved as a child and how sometimes she would try to stay up all night reading them by flashlight and pretending she was asleep.

And I listen to stories about the friends she'd had and the people she'd known then. The woman I am sitting next to on the sofa lets the memories run rich and free. Afterward, when the albums are shut and Jade's childhood and young adulthood packed away until another time and place, I tell her the little I know.

I talk about the favorite table we had at The Bell and Book for our Monday evenings and how she always liked us to order the same drinks first, just for the pleasure of saying, "The usual, please." I tell Mrs. O'Donnell about how cross my friend could get if I accidentally rang her in the middle of any of the American soaps or if she was just about to go to her salsa class.

Leaning back, I talk about Jade's talent with the computer, how she could get to the sort of information I needed for my job, and how much I'd come to rely on her for it. This, I think, comes as a surprise to Jade's mother, and I'm glad I've filled in a detail she didn't know.

I remember the films Jade and I saw together, the nights we went to a show, and the times we spent just chilling out. I recall how well Jade listened and how she could understand the heart of a story without the fullness of words my counselor has always needed, though that, too, has helped me. I shiver when I hear myself saying these things, but the word "counselor," like the word "him" earlier, is allowed to drift between us without comment.

When at last we both fall silent, the room fills with the glitter of early afternoon sunlight and something like peace. As if from a great distance, I hear the back door from the kitchen open and shut again. There's a pause then, as if someone is waiting to see how things are, before the slow sound of footsteps along the hallway. They pass the living room door, but I can't tell if there's any hesitation. I realize I'm holding my breath and wonder if Mrs. O'Donnell is too. At the end of three heartbeats, the footsteps retrace their path. The kitchen door is opened and closed again, and another silence descends.

He must have seen my car through the glass door. He knows I'm still here.

This fact breaks the spell, and I spring to my feet. "I'd better go, Mrs. O'Donnell. I'm sorry to take up so much of your time. I'm sorry about everything, like I said. Maybe we can… Anyway, I should be going. There are things I need to do in London, but I—"

She stands and takes my face between her hands.

"It's all right. It'll be all right," she whispers. "Thank you for coming, Paul."

Then she stretches up and kisses me on the forehead. On impulse, I hug her once before letting go, feeling the slightness of her frame against my chest. When we break away, I glance through the window to the garden.

"Can I…"

"Yes," she says. "I think you should try."

It's the hardest thing I've ever done.

In the garden, the breeze is cool. I stand on the small patio, tomato shed to my right and washing line to my left. Behind me, I know Jade's mother is watching from the living room.

Mr. O'Donnell is bent over the pond, near to the place of our last abortive conversation.

I say nothing. There's nothing I can say. After a while he must sense my presence because he uncurls himself upright and faces me. His eyes are dark like the sea. It's as if he has gone away somewhere I can't reach him; maybe somewhere no one can reach him.

"We talked, Mr. O'Donnell," I say, and my voice is low, barely audible. "We talked about Jade. I hope…I hope you'll let me come back one day and talk about your daughter again."

After a long moment, Jade's father nods once and crouches again to the pond.

On the journey home, the lightness and memory of Mrs. O'Donnell's kiss on my cheek as I got into my car warms my blood, and I know I will return again.

Right now, though, I have a meeting to attend.

CHAPTER 14

The heavy traffic brings me into the city later than I'd
planned, and it's already dark by the time I reach
Dominic's office. Dominic and Blake will have had plenty
of time together, and as each second ticks by, the chances
of success of any sort grow ever slimmer.

Not that I know what I'm doing and maybe today, now,
isn't the best time to be doing it. At least something has
begun to be resolved between the O'Donnells and me. It's
right that should be so, but it's as if my insides have been
scraped out with a sharp-edged knife. PI Rule Number
Fourteen: don't do more than one difficult act in a day.
Any more than that and you won't be performing at your
best.

Too late. I have to do this now. I'll just have to throw
whatever resources I have left at the problem as best I can.

Once in the reception area, I flash my card at the
brunette on the phone, ignore the lift, swing through the set
of glass doors to the stairs, and start to hot-foot it up to
Dominic's floor. Behind me, I can hear a shout of concern

and know security will be onto me soon. Still, the woman being busy on the switchboard has given me a vital four-second start, and I'll just have to use it. I'm relying, too, on the fact they don't know who I've come to see and, therefore, who to warn.

Dominic's office is on the third floor, and I race upward, knocking unsuspecting people aside, yelling apologies to try to avoid early suspicion, and cursing my own lack of fitness. On the second floor landing, my luck runs out. Turning the corner, I come face to chest with a security guard built like a rugby player. I try to dodge him. He feints in my direction. I go the other way; he follows.

There's only one thing for it. I lunge at him and clamp my teeth down hard on his ear. The man shrieks and strikes at me, trying to ward me off, but I hang on, the taste of blood in my mouth. He shrieks again, and this time I let go, shove him backward, and run for the next flight of stairs.

By the time I punch open the door to Dominic's PA's office, she's already on the phone, and there's another security guard standing ready for action. On the principle that in this kind of situation, it's better to fight than run, I spring at the guard, but he meets me halfway and lands a well-aimed blow to my stomach. Winded, I collapse over the PA's desk, slamming the corner of my mouth on something metal. There's an ominous cracking sound and the taste of more blood, this time my own.

As I struggle for breath, the guard grabs me by the neck and pushes me toward the floor. Somehow, I manage to stay upright and lurch at Dominic's door, and together the two of us crash against it. His PA screams. As the door springs opens, the security guard and I fall sprawling onto the carpet.

In five strides, Dominic is up, around his desk and upon us. When I glance at him, I see he's shaking.

"What the fuck are you doing?" he says.

"I wanted to surprise you," I manage to pant. "Did it work?"

Two seconds after that, I'm shoved against the wall, arms and legs spread, and surrounded by numerous DG Allen Enterprises security professionals. There's a rip in my shirt and shattered enamel in my mouth. I spit it out, an action that earns me a thump from the first guard, whose ear is still bleeding. When, at Dominic's command, they turn me around, the only other person in the office I recognize is Blake. He looks on, glass in hand, faintly amused.

"Big welcome for just one bloke, eh, Dominic?" I say, my words slurring through my broken tooth. "What happens if there's an emergency somewhere else? Boy-band here have to leg it there all together again? What is it, safety in numbers?"

"Shut up," he replies, and I do.

I can tell from the sound of his voice that if I open my mouth again, he'll sling me out now. He won't even think about listening to what I have to say.

"He's clean, sir." The only injured security guard speaks for the first time. "No weapons."

Dominic nods. "All right. Thank you. You can go then, Jackson, and for God's sake, get a first-aider to have a look at you. I don't want clients seeing you in that state. In fact, all of you, go. I'll handle this."

There's a moment's hesitation when Jackson looks like he might be bold enough to argue the case. Then he straightens himself and marches to the door, taking his troops with him. Though not before giving my arm one quick twist that sends a fresh spiral of pain shooting upward.

When there are only the three of us left—Dominic, Blake, and me—Dominic walks up to where I'm still standing against his wall. He's breathing fast, and there's a line of sweat on his forehead. I have no idea what he's going to do.

When he's so close to me that I need lean forward only a little to be able to kiss him, he reaches out with one finger and wipes the side of my mouth. When he withdraws his hand, I can see there's blood on it. For a pulse or two, it's almost as if Blake has vanished and there are only the two of us. He takes a pace back, and I begin to breathe again.

"Go and clean up," he says. "In my bathroom. Then we'll talk."

I obey. After filling the sink from tall, gold taps, I wash out the blood from my mouth and wince at the sting of it. Whisky, I think. I'll have a shot of the Macallan later. That'll numb the bastard. Or at least take my mind off it. If I get that far. Then I splash my face, more to kick-start my head than to make myself clean. When I look up at the mirror, the eyes staring back at me are dull and haunted and my lip is already thickening. This isn't the expression of a man on top of the situation he'll have to confront in a minute or two, but it's the only one I've got. I'll just have to wing it. Again.

Trying to conjure up confident and masterful thoughts, I dry myself off on the towel's deep comfort. I give myself the thumbs-up sign in the mirror and open the door to the office.

At once, the conversation stops. Before it does, I catch Blake's low tones. "You have no option, my friend."

Dominic's response, whatever it might have been, is cut off by my re-entry, but I wish I'd been able to hear it. As it is, it's too late now. Still, no harm in trying.

"What option might that be?" I ask, looking not at the Egyptian, but at my ex-lover. "And, by the way, Dominic, I question your choice of who to call 'friend.'"

He doesn't respond, but his eyes flicker in the office light, and he turns away. Blake, on the other hand, joins me on the battlefield, such as it is. "You, Mr. Maloney, don't have the status to ask questions of anyone. I may be ignorant of the finer points of UK law, but it's my understanding that you forced your way into this meeting. We didn't invite you here, and, therefore, you don't ask questions."

"That depends on what kind of questions I'm asking, doesn't it, Blake?"

He just laughs.

"No," he says. "There's nothing you can ask me that would make a difference to my business. You may be extraordinarily lucky, but you're not a commercial threat."

"Lucky? Why might that be then?"

I stare at him for three or four seconds, but he shakes his head and takes another sip of wine. I wonder what he would do if I strode over to him and knocked the glass from his hands so it shattered against the wall, the fragments scattering over the oh-so-civilized carpet. What would he do if I pushed him to the floor and shoved his face in the splinters? I want to hurt him, badly, and the thought of it makes the room in front of me mist over. My breath is ragged, and I can't catch hold of it.

From the corner of the room, Dominic breaks into the sudden standoff. "Just say what you want to, Paul, and go. I think that would be best."

The moment is stretched tight between Blake and me, though I have no idea if he knows it.

Then I say, "All right. You call the shots."

His eyes darken, and I have no idea what he's thinking, not that I ever really have. In the pause between one word and the next, the realization kicks in that I'm standing here in a room with one man who has tried to have me killed, threatened me, and murdered my best friend and with another who has hired me, fucked me, and is now in the process of blackmailing me.

I now say what I've planned. I hope it might fire up some kind of reaction that will bring this whole bloody and impossible case to an end.

"Yes," I continue. "You both call the shots, but I wonder how long for."

Blake snorts and looks as if he's going to speak, but I cut him off. "No, for once you shut up and listen. I've learnt from the information I gleaned from Delta in Cairo. There are two dead women, two I know of, and somehow, somewhere, you're at the bottom of it, Blake Kenzie. And whatever happens, I'm going to find out what you've done and prove it. Starlight, Dancer, Aqua, Bluesky. It sickens me. You both sicken me, and it's…it's enough."

There's more, but already I'm crying, unable to finish, my voice thick with grief. I wipe the wetness from my face. Blake gives a short laugh, but Dominic looks pale, one hand gripping the edge of his desk and staring at a point somewhere to the left of me. He's not even looking at me. God.

I've blown it. Even if I say anything else, no one will believe me; no one will feel any fear. Why should they? It might as well have been nothing. The response I've hoped for, the small push to send one of them, either of them, over the edge into making a mistake won't come. It won't ever happen. No matter what I say. Stumbling out of Dominic's office, down the stairs and past the receptionist onto the wet city streets, I leave behind me two men, one I love and one I hate, carrying on with their deeds as if nothing has happened. And for them, nothing has.

I've not even been an hour at DG Allen Enterprises, but I can't imagine the effort it would take to claw myself back to where I was emotionally when I first walked into reception. I can't face driving. I'll have to abandon the car.

Setting my face into the wind, I begin the long journey home. The drizzle seeps through the collar of my jacket, sending cool fingers down my neck. I continue to walk, not seeing the tall city buildings I pass, the offices, the clubs, the restaurants.

At the end of Old Street, after a few paces, my feet turn aside from the noise and thunder of the Hackney Road with its hospitals and never-ending movement. Instead, I creep home through Columbia Road and the quiet order of Quilter Street. I pass the vibrant colors of Bethnal Green and then veer northward, at last on Mare Street, like a fox seeking refuge from the hunt.

Car lights glitter in the darkness, sweep over me, and are gone. As happened after Jade's death, I've loosened my grip on time, and I don't even want to know what it might be. As I walk, the headlights sliding, fading, sliding, fading over my skin, I undo my watchstrap and let it slip away. For a pace or two, my stride lengthens. All the while, I can smell the day's dirt being washed away in the rain. And perhaps a hope for tomorrow in the passing of bodies in the street, the sound of their laughter or their grim silence, the purposeful tread of their feet.

I keep walking. As I walk, all the acts and memories I've counted as mine seem to fade away, washed clean in the damp city streets. Each step nearer home and familiarity frees me from the things I cling to. It's as if I'm walking my own history to nothing.

I don't understand what is happening, but the ropes holding me to the past are, for the moment, gone.

The houses around me begin to take on recognizable shapes, their dark outlines hovering through the dampness and gloom like ancient creatures. I'm nearly home. The freedom I can taste like the rain on my tongue, the chill on my flesh, is too precious to relinquish now. But where to go to keep it? I could carry on walking, but the final touch of control still lingers on my skin. It would be beyond me to walk without a purpose. Maybe it's the sense of an endpoint to come that has given me the illusion of freedom.

Without conscious thought, I turn off down the first side street to my left, then right and left again. My home and the call of it vanishes, and in front of me I see only the neutrality of the office. On my journey there, I pass one or two groups, laughing, talking, challenging each other with youth in their voices and their walk, on their way to a night out. They take no notice of me.

It's then that the memory plunges in of how it might have been Jade and me doing the same, on the way to the pub, the cinema, a meal out, and I quicken my pace. The office, at least, will bring her close again.

Once there, I remove my jacket, fling it over my chair and pace between the desks. I touch each item I come to as if committing it to memory: shelf, computer, desk tidy, mouse, cabinet, window, and shelf again.

Here. I'll stay here, I think, for a while until I've reached the end of this waiting time. I'll know when that happens. I'll know it, though I can't think how. Then, when it's over, I'll go home, make one of the thousand possible decisions I have to make, and run with it. Commit to it this time and not be afraid. I can't comprehend yet what that one decision will be: breaking into Dominic's office or even his home to search for the other half of the file; trying Blake again to see if he has it, though it will make no sense if he has; telling what little I know to the police and hoping it might be enough. I have to decide soon. It's all I can do, but later. Later.

Later, but not now. Now my legs are shaking and I can't feel my fingers. In my flesh, there's a sense of anything that's left inside being drained away suddenly. The next thing I know, I'm slumped against the desk.

I'm so bloody tired. I must sleep. When did I get to be this tired? I crawl 'round to my office chair. I fall, rather than sit, curving my arms onto the cool wood, my head feeling the softness of my flesh, nestling into bone.

And there's one beat of my pulse, two, then…nothing but darkness and a dreamless clarity.

I don't know how long I sleep, but when I wake, it's with a sense that something is terribly wrong.

CHAPTER 15

It's dark, and I don't know what it is I've heard that's wakened me. Neither do I remember whether I turned the light off or not before I slept. I don't think so. And if I haven't, then—

Another sound pierces my thought processes. It's the sound of the door handle being turned and turned again. I spring to my feet, the chair scraping along the floor behind me. This is far sooner than I'd ever anticipated. I'm not ready. My head is buzzing and my thoughts are filled with air.

Got to get out. Got to…stop them. Got to hide. But where?

There's no time. A flurry of gunfire, softened through the reinforced oak, and the door swings open. Flinging myself forward, I shove it onto the man behind, who rewards me with a sharp curse. Whatever happens, whether I'm dead meat or not, at least I've managed to cause someone some well-deserved pain. When I've landed on both feet again, I don't stop to see the result. In four quick paces, I'm in the kitchen, my fingers struggling with the window latch. This isn't what I should be doing. It isn't what I thought I'd decided, but, shockingly and irrevocably, more than anything, I want to live.

I get the window free and the gush of cold air stings my throat. Got to jump. Don't care how high up I am. There's no choice. One foot is already on the sink and I'm levering up when a hand grips my shoulder and wrenches me back. I hit the floor with a crack, but kick out, landing a blow on my attacker. He lurches back, muttering in Arabic. I propel myself upright and start to run.

I don't get far. His hands seize my legs, and I take a tumble to the floor again, this time dragging him with me. Together we roll over, smashing limbs and backs against cupboards, the wastepaper bin, an old beer crate. I drag myself to my knees and punch him hard, stabbing my knuckles into his eyes. His scarred face jerks back and there's another wail of pain. I recognize him as the knife attacker from Cairo and keep on jabbing. Just as I feel I've beaten him enough to give myself a chance for escape, there's a movement behind me.

Of course…stupid, stupid. There are two of them.

When I turn, fists raised, there's barely enough time to glimpse the shadow of something narrow and long rushing toward my head before I collapse into blackness.

*   *   *

The spikes of light are dazzling and words are being spoken that I can't hear. It seems important I try, but the sounds are too distant, too fragmented for meaning. The sharp yellow of them pierces my eyes, and there's a sour taste in my mouth, a dull thud in my stomach. From nowhere there are other shapes muffled behind unseen barriers, mysterious, threatening. Around me, the darkness becomes lighter, and I'm gasping for air, for escape. The fire in my gut punches a way through my flesh, and suddenly…suddenly, I'm awake, trying to sit up. I can't move my arms, and I turn my head to one side as my body gives one more heave and a stream of clear vomit hits my shoulder and the hardness beneath me.

"You're awake then?" a gruff, accented voice whispers into my ear. "Good. We've been waiting."

I don't answer. I can't. My head is floating in a sea of swirling impressions, and I don't know if I'm going to be sick again. At the same time, I'm racing to understand where I am and what happened. I don't remember. I don't know anything. All I know is that my arms are stretched out alongside my body, and when I try to move them, pain stabs into my wrists. When I flex my legs, there's more pain. The effort makes me gag, and, as I turn to spit the bile out, somebody hits my face hard enough to slam my head back against the solid object beneath it.

"Disgusting," the voice says. "What do you think you're doing?"

I wait for the wave of pain to dissipate and then open my eyes. When I focus, I can see the clock on the wall says 3:15, and the darkness outside tells me it's night. I'm in the kitchen, laid out like a sacrificial goat across my desk, which they must have pushed in here. Why? There's only just enough room for the two men and me. There's a soft fizzing sound I can't recognize. My wrists and ankles are tied with dark brown cords so tight I can see red weals on my flesh. The skin of my back and buttocks feels chilled against the wood, and at that moment, I realize I'm naked. God.

God help me.

"What are you going to do?" I moan.

"You'll find out."

"Ready," says another voice. At the same time, the skin and hairs on my chest seem to catch fire. I scream and spit out a long stream of cursing. "Jesus, Jesus Christ. Jesus."

When I'm finished, I'm panting for air. My skin crackles with heat, and there's a smell of burning flesh and shit.

"You're disgusting," the first voice says again. "And too loud. Make another noise, any kind of noise, and I'll use the point of the knife in you. Understand?"

I nod, and the haze around me lightens. One of the men has moved back from me. Two heartbeats later I hear the fizzing noise grow louder and, at last, understand what it is. In the stillness, it's as if every sound is magnified: my own ragged breath, the soft rustling of the first man standing over me, the ticking of the clock. The bastard, I think, he's branding me with a knife heated in the flames from the gas oven. God, why doesn't he just kill me and have done with it?

There's a grunt, and I know the second man has finished his job. The shimmer of hot steel at the edge of my vision makes me sweat, then the agony of it is placed down on my right nipple. My head jerks back and my legs go into spasm. Trying not to yell, I grit my teeth, and my breath hisses through them, saliva dribbling down my chin. The knife is removed and replaced on my stomach. My mind collapses and then there's nothing but a merciful blankness.

*　　*　　*

A river of fire, so hot it might burn the valleys it flows through, rages at my feet. I'm drifting, carried on a red sea, my whole body glowing scarlet with the pain of it. Around me, bright lights flash. From somewhere there's the sound of moaning, but I don't recognize the voice, and I can't see who it is. I'm still drifting, drifting. It's hard to get my breath, and a sharp slap explodes in my face and I'm being shaken and the world is suffused with light and wild glitter. The onset of it carries a pain I can't take in any more.

"What? Wha…" I mumble, but another slap shuts my mouth. I can feel blood trickling onto my lips. The stale iron taste makes my body shiver.

"I said keep quiet, if you don't want to feel this."

Something pierces the flesh on my upper left arm, and I gasp, "Jesus, please stop."

"Ah, Mr. Maloney, we've only just begun."

The man with the scarred face is talking to me. Good, good, I can work with that. Even with the wall of pain and horror, I can work with it. This is my job. I can deal with difficult situations. It's what I'm trained for, what I'm used to. But not like this, like this, like this. Stop it. Stop it. I have to talk, to make him listen, to make them both listen. Even a few seconds' respite will be something.

"Why…why do you want to do this?"

"Why? We want to know what you've gained from the duplicate USB drive you stole. Because there must be another."

I have no idea what he's talking about. My thoughts are lost in a fog of pain. Something tells me I should know what he means, but I can't get the sense of it.

"I don't understand," I say. "You'll have to—"

He doesn't give me the chance to finish the sentence. Instead, he rams the point of the knife right into my arm. I scream again and then the darkness closes in on me once more.

This time when I wake, there's a white-hot flow of agony across my gut. I'm gasping for breath, sucking for air. The heat burns its way into the flesh just above my cock and there's the smell of singed hair.

"Please, please." My voice sounds like a boy's low whimpering, and I wonder when they're going to kill me.

There's a sense of someone leaning closer, a deeper shade of darkness within the darkness already surrounding me. Then he speaks.

"You want me to stop?"

"Yes."

"Then talk, Mr. Maloney."

For a life-stretching three pumps of my hearts, I still have no knowledge of what he might mean. Then memory eases back into my control. The case. Dominic. The incomplete file, still at home. Blake. The papers. Jade. God, Jade. And—

And something else clicks in.

"You already know." I pant. "You took the USB drive, you bastard, when you murdered Jade."

I flex myself against the ropes as I speak, and the shaft of pain across my flesh is almost unbearable. When I groan aloud, the only response is laughter.

"You are in no position to accuse, I think." His breath withdraws a little from my cheek and there's a faint flash of silver. "Scald this knife again. I believe the lesson should be learnt well."

A threatening swish as the second man turns makes me swallow, and I tense again. God, God, please help me.

The fizzing noise grows louder, and a small moan escapes my throat. Must think. Must keep him—them— talking; it's the only way to survive.

"I'll tell you whatever you want to know. What do you want me to say?" I don't know if the words reverberating in my mind have actually been spoken, or rather whispered, but there's a darkening in the atmosphere around me as the scarred man leans closer once more. What he says makes me want to cry again.

"Now, as you are asking, Mr. Maloney, I am afraid my friend and I have been playing a game with you. You will forgive us? We would love to hear you talk. We are sure that anything you have to say will be most interesting, but it does not matter."

Mindful of my determination to delay whatever this man has planned, I manage to gasp out, "Why not?"

A movement of air and stale breath against my face. I wonder if he has smiled.

"Because," he says, "we already know everything. And you know too much. This is why, regretfully, you will have to die. But not before…this."

Another wave of pain rocks my lower belly, and fresh tears spurt from my clenched-shut eyes. "Please, please."

"Ah, we can only apologize, Mr. Maloney, but really there is no purpose to begging."

He may say more. I don't know, but I'm unable to listen. I'm not ready. I'm not ready for this. I didn't hear the second man come in earlier. If I'd been ready…but Jesus, Jesus Christ, the crystal sting of red-hot metal on burning flesh comes again and I'm screaming.

"F-fuck you, why don't you just kill me, please?"

"Believe me, we will, the long way 'round. Unfortunately, you are not as lucky as your friend. Now there we were merciful and killed quickly. Then again, she was not a man, and so we did not have the pleasure of doing, my friend, what I am about to do with this knife to your…"

The word he spits at me is a foreign one, but I don't need him to translate it. God.

I grit my teeth, trying not to weep. Before he can continue, there's a banging from somewhere outside the office and the sound of shouting.

My torturer grunts what sounds like a command. At once the other man's footsteps head out of the kitchen. As he goes, I hear the click of the gun. The thought that when I'm gone tonight I'll have been the cause of someone else's death, too, makes the bile rise to my throat again, but there's no shot. Instead, there's a distant voice I think I should know, but I can't place.

"What the hell are you doing?" The last word of this question is much louder as whoever it is comes to the kitchen door. I hear a gasp and a rising tone. Somehow it's that which places the questioner for me.

It's Dominic.

Opening my eyes, I blink in the direction of his voice. I can only make out his shadow, the vague shape of him.

What's he doing here? Why has he come? Can't he see the danger? Can't he…

Too late. The answer threatens to overwhelm what little fight I have left. He knows. About this, too. God, God, Dominic knows. He knows everything I've suspected of happening. He has come here, and these men have not questioned it. They have not shot him or hurt him in any way. He knows these men, these…these killers. This, more than anything I have lost or anything I have felt so far tonight, is the one fact that sends me falling, falling into the unknown. It's a realization that causes a low, wailing moan to break from my lips.

The men are talking, arguing, but I do not know for how long or what they say. All I know, as I continue to spin down and down, is that parts of my life I thought would be mine forever, all the things I thought I knew or understood, are being splintered off and lost. I am nothing but flesh and blood. There is no love, no hate, no comfort. I am, for the first time, truly alone.

My breath slowly steadies. For a while, the continuing pain makes me think I'm floating in a place I don't recognize, but which is no longer in flux. Then, at last, their conversation intrudes into my body again.

"This isn't the plan," I hear Dominic say, his voice low, urgent, with something in it I don't recognize. "You were supposed to get in, cause enough damage to get him off the case for good, and get out. We were supposed to keep this clean and simple. What the hell do you think this is, the Third bloody World?"

"We are carrying out orders."

"Not any orders I recognize. Untie him."

A heartbeat's pause and then the scarred man, the torturer, says, "No."

As I shut my eyes tighter, Dominic speaks again, "What the fuck do you mean, no? Here and now, I'm in charge, and you do what I tell you. No more and no less."

"I only take orders from—"

"Yes, yes, Mr. Kenzie, I know. Same old line; same old bad attitude. Well, perhaps that's why you continue to make the mistakes you do. It's time you learnt to get it into that head of yours that Blake and I are partners. What one of us wants, the other wants also." As he says this, there's the lightest of touches on my leg. When my eyes flicker open, I can see he's standing between me and the two Egyptians. His fingers are on my skin and they're as still as his voice is calm.

The first man snorts. "Prove it."

"Prove it yourself," is Dominic's reply. "Here, my phone."

With one sudden movement, he flings his mobile to the man. As he stretches out in an automatic gesture to grasp it, Dominic launches himself across the floor and brings his opponent crashing down. At the same moment, from the doorway, the second man reaches for his gun.

"Dominic! Watch out."

Dominic twists nearer the desk as the bullet fires, narrowly missing the sprawling men and me. There's another burst of gunfire and a sharp cry of pain, followed by…nothing.

"Dominic."

From where I am, I can't see what's happened. I can't see anything, but the silence is unbearable. Making one hopeless effort to strain against the ropes brings no success, but the squirming of my body dislodges the knife resting next to my leg. It falls with a clatter to the floor.

"Dominic? No, Dominic."

A grunt and then what sounds like Egyptian swearing is followed by two heavy footsteps coming closer. I brace myself for whatever is about to happen. Just as the thickset frame looms into my vision, there's a long, drawn-out, strangled cry, and he disappears. A hand carrying something bright and metallic rises and falls, once, twice, each moment of vanishing corresponding with a thud and soft moaning.

Then, silence.

Then, a voice. "God."

"Dominic?"

"Yes." Suddenly, his face is close to mine, his breath warm on my skin. "Thank you for the knife. We're safe. For now. But we have to get you out of here."

It's not that easy. Of course it isn't. The two men are unconscious or dead. Dominic drags them into the main office, unties me as carefully as he can, and uses the same rope to tie their hands and feet. He then turns off the gas on the oven, lifts me to a sitting position and eases me into his arms. Now and again, no matter how careful he is, I can't help drawing in a harsh and ragged breath. The sound of it makes him swear softly.

Half standing, half leaning against him, I try to walk, but my legs are shaky and useless. Each movement of my muscles sends a dagger of fire through my skin. I can't stop the trembling.

"Paul, your burns are worse than I thought. I can get water for you, but I'll need to put you back on the desk."

"N-no. M-must leave. Go n-now."

"All right, but you can't walk. It'll take time, it—"

"C-carry me."

"I don't think—"

"For f-fuck's sake, I don't c-care about your suit, D-Dominic, just do it."

For a moment, his unfathomable eyes gaze into mine. Then, with a suddenness I don't expect, he steps to my side, puts one hand around my shoulders, another under my knees, and lifts me as simply as if I am feathers. This, for reasons I don't understand, makes me laugh.

"What?" he says. "What is it?"

"Just…just…a p-position I could've enjoyed once, but not n-now."

"Be quiet. You're in shock. I'll take you somewhere safe and then ring for an ambulance. I don't want ano— a death on my hands."

"No." I grip his neck with my free hand and wrench him 'round to face me. "No."

"Don't be so bloody stupid. You need medical attention. Where else can you go?"

"Home. Not hospital. Because, fuck you, but you owe me. You owe me. Take me home."

These are the last words I'm able to say for a while as the pain sweeps me away into blackness and noise.

CHAPTER 16

All around me there is the sea and a sound of humming, though there's no indication where it's coming from. The sea is red, but this doesn't strike me as strange. As I walk along, the sand underneath my feet changes to pebbles burnt by the sun, but if I keep walking, the pain is bearable. I'm the only person on the beach, but I don't feel alone. I keep on walking, but there's no sense of having to arrive anywhere; it's the simplicity of the movement that melts the tension away. If I could just keep walking, with the sun on my back and the wind lifting my hair from my scalp, then there would be no danger. Everything would be okay. I don't know how I know that, but it feels like something close to the truth. My bones, my blood sing with it.

Once, however, the planets make their slow spin, turning, turning, and the morning moves to mid-day, then I will have to take the long journey back. When the sun is on my face, then the truth will burn through me and take me…take me—

A rushing movement and I'm caught in a storm, but more than a storm. The sea has darkened to purple, and all the skies are orange, streaked with a deeper fire. It might be beautiful, but my eyes are burning, and there's no air…nothing…to breathe and…

I'm falling, falling with a jolt in my stomach and…

Suddenly, my eyes are wide open and I can see whiteness and a pattern and shadow on plaster. There's the sound of a gasping cry that's mine.

"It's all right, Paul. You're safe. You're at home."

His hand is resting on my shoulder, and I can see the rapid rise and fall of my chest. There's a tea towel wrapped 'round my left arm and it's stained with blood.

"But what…what about the sea? The storm?"

"There's no storm, no sea. It was just a dream. You're awake now. There's nothing to worry about."

I close my eyes and let that thought slide through my mind. A couple of seconds go by, then Dominic removes his hand and here's the sound of gentle splashing. A heartbeat later, I feel coolness on my damaged skin.

"Water?" I say. "It's good. Thanks."

"You're welcome. I found a bucket and some clean cloths in one of your kitchen cupboards. But you still need to get to hospital and—"

"No, please. I meant it. I'm fine here."

"As you wish."

While my breathing steadies to normal, he continues to sprinkle me with water. I hear him get up.

"I'll get fresh," he says. "If you think it's helping?"

"Yes. Please. And, Dominic?"

"Yes?"

Turning to look at him, I say, "Could you bring me some water to drink, too?"

"Of course."

When he's gone, I prepare for his return in the way I've already planned. The effort of this is almost too much. When he comes back, my instinct is to gulp down the water he's brought, but he stops me.

"No," he says, supporting me with his arm. "Try it little and often. Too much too soon will make you sick."

"Okay, okay, but who made you a b-bloody first aid expert?" I grumble, but obey, having no choice.

What feels like ten minutes later, the glass is empty, and I sink back against the pillows.

"More?" Dominic asks.

"No. Thank you." One breath, then another and another. "Dominic?"

A pause before he answers and his voice is guarded now. "Yes?"

"You know we have to talk, don't you?"

"Yes."

Brushing one powerful hand through his blond hair, he grabs a chair and sits next to the bed. There's no grace in it, and Dominic is someone who's always moved with grace. Up until now.

He doesn't look at me, but stares into the distance. The silence is heavy across both our shoulders.

"Talk to me, Dominic," I whisper. "Please."

"All right." He still doesn't look at me. "All right."

When at last he begins, even his voice sounds different. It's lower, more urgent, less cultured, and I no longer recognize the man. "How much do you know, Paul? I mean really know? Not just guesswork."

Now, for the first time since the case started, I tell him what I've found out. "I know about Blake Kenzie's involvement with human trafficking. No, let's call it by what it is—sex trafficking, plain and simple. And deadly. Jade found some of it out from police records and what they implied, and I got a lucky break from a newspaper article piecing the facts together. At my parents' house, of all places. It linked the dead woman outside your offices, Bluesky, with the suspicions the welfare agencies had. It didn't surprise me. Not about Blake.

"What we had was a partial list of codenames and dates for transfers and meeting points, but they didn't make sense. Not without the other half of the information. But right now I don't care about that. What I need to know from you, and I think you owe me the explanation, is how long you've been involved. And why, for God's sake? I mean why? Don't you have enough?"

At the end of this speech, I'm exhausted. Lying back, I close my eyes, partly to gain strength and partly because I can't bear to look at him as he talks.

"You have to understand something about me," Dominic says, his voice hesitant at first. "I realize you think you know me, but I don't think you do. Apart from how we are when we fuck, of course. But you don't know what I'm like, who I am. I know about you: born rich, with rich parents. No matter what happens to you, you'll always have that easiness. A history, a tradition you can rely on. Things are made smooth for you, however difficult they seem at the time. It's not the same for me. That's not an excuse; it's the truth. It's how the world is."

Here he pauses, but I say nothing, knowing there's more to come. When it does, it's not what I'm expecting.

"I'm not like that," he continues. "I was born poor. Of course, I've told Cassie about my past, but not the children. Never the children. Did you know I was born and brought up in a council house? No, I suppose not. Why should you know that? There's no reason to. The first eighteen years of my life were spent struggling for money and for acceptance. I hated the way we had to live and the attitude of those my mother had to deal with. I swore to myself that once I could leave, I'd never go back and I'd never again be poor.

"My sister, Cathy, and I were the first ones in our family ever to go to university. She went to London, but I worked like the devil and begged my school to let me take the Oxbridge exams. They weren't keen, but in the end, they couldn't say no. And I passed, went for the interview, and got into Cambridge. You can't imagine what it was like. The sense of possibility, the opening of a door that had held me back the whole of my life. I walked out of one existence and into another.

"I changed my accent as soon as I'd learnt how. Not only that, but I changed my name. God, do you know you're the only person I've ever told that to? Not even my wife knows that. Just the family I was born into, though I never see them now. I changed my name from Donald, which I hated, to Dominic. Dominic Gregory Allen. It's who I am now. Dominic. The man I became. The man I am. And I kept my promise; I never went back."

A minute ticks by on the clock, and I'm silent. Then I say, "I never knew you had a sister. Is she alive?"

"Is that all you can say? Cathy, she lives in Norfolk. I have a niece I've never seen. I have two brothers as well, though both our parents are dead. Richard is the oldest, and Thomas the youngest. Cathy and I are in the middle. Though"—he laughs, but there's no humor in it—"though,

I suppose it's the fact of my sister that would matter most to you. I should've known."

"Yes," I look at him for the first time since he began his account, and I see his face is unchanged, as if nothing he has said has affected him. "Yes, you should. I think you've been lucky, but you're too blind to know it. What does it matter about your background or who you really are, what you're really called? What matters is what you do with your life. There's more you need to tell me. Tell me about Blake and what you've done."

He does, and this time there are no interruptions.

"I joined my first company, the one I later came to own, when I was twenty-one years old," he says. "I was Dominic Allen by then, of course, with a classy accent and a classy girlfriend in tow, a girlfriend who, when I was twenty-eight, would become my wife and give me that extra edge I needed. Ten years later, I was Chief Exec and the company became what it is today—DG Allen Enterprises. Not just a change of name, but a change of focus, of ambition, too. And whatever you may think of me, Paul, business and making money are the things I'm good at; they're the things I trust. Nothing else matters.

"DG Allen Enterprises has done well for itself since then. We were riding high; we still are. I first met Blake at a conference in Cairo. I know I haven't told you that before. No doubt you found that out for yourself, but God knows why you didn't challenge me about it. Too late now. We get on well, Blake and I. We have the same ethos and the same ambitions. I can do business with him. With him, I can make good money."

He stops and runs his hands up his face and through his hair.

"And I have made money," he continues. "Though, of course, none of it is good, not if we apply your moral code, such as it is, Paul. I knew from the beginning what Delta Egypt was involved in. As well as the IT business. And it's a fair trade, of a sort. Helping to bring in people cheaply to this country from Moscow, Bucharest, Sofia, all the cities where the opportunity arises, to take up jobs for firms where Delta have contacts—dancing, working in nightclubs, escort work, the sex industry. Yes, I knew it. Why not? The market economy is something I've always believed in. I've never judged people for what they choose to do, so why start now? It's easy money. You wouldn't believe it.

"The fact that Blake works from Cairo is the perfect cover. No prostitutes come here from Cairo, at least not directly. It's so easy, in fact, that later on, I decided to buy out Blake's company. At least that much of what I told you is true. And all the time the cash kept on coming and my investments kept on rising. The sight and smell of money in the balance, money that's mine, is a dream to which nothing else compares. Nothing at all."

"Did you never think about what you were doing, about the lives you were destroying?" I say. "For God's sake, did it never occur to you to think of these people as human?"

"I'm not certain what you mean by that," he answers. "Of course, everyone is human, but what counts is power, not pity. And how you use it. I'm not in the business of destroying lives; when people are helped to come to the West, they earn more money than they'd ever do in their home countries. Economic empowerment is what I'm selling. And, yes, I've met some of them.

"One night, for instance, I was in Prague finishing off some business with Blake and with others. I've never relied on one source of income alone. That would be foolish. We were drinking in a bar in a place with strange music I've never heard before. Halfway through the evening, a couple approached us, a slim black-haired woman hanging on the arm of a dark-eyed man dressed in green and gold and dripping with jewelry. Her clothes were expensive, though she wore only a small necklace. They laughed, the strange man and Blake, and said something in Arabic. While they talked, the woman and I sipped our drinks and chatted. Her English was accented, but good. They didn't stay long.

"After they'd gone, Blake laughed, leant forward, and said, "Good product that one, my friend. Nice and submissive when it's called for, you know what I mean? And still tight, of course. Our customers enjoy that. A small part of the fruit of our collaboration, and I believe she will soon be in your country, yes?" Then he stared at me and smiled. And I smiled back because that woman made me realize, as I did the other times I met some of our people, that what we're doing is only helping them get richer. It's not wrong and it doesn't cause pain. As long as they..."

He stops, but he's not finished yet.

"As long as they…what?" I whisper. "Keep to your rules? Don't get sick or catch diseases? Don't try and escape? Play your game?"

"Don't be stupid. It's not—"

But I'm not listening. Something else he's said has sparked a connection for me, and I interrupt him. "Because it goes wrong sometimes, doesn't it, Dominic? The people you deal with do get hurt. They get killed and then what do you do? Keep quiet and hope for better times? This woman you're talking about, the one with the necklace, is she still alive now? Is she? Do you know for sure?"

He closes his eyes. "There are other women—"

"Never mind the other women. Let's look at this one, the one you mention. Is she first in your mind for a reason? Is she…is she the woman outside your offices? There was a necklace there, too, wasn't there? Something small and silver, with a star. Is she…Bluesky?"

There's a silence. He shakes his head. "Yes, but that was a one-off. A stupid mistake and badly handled. When it happened, Blake and I had a huge row and I threatened to go to the police. Not that I would have done, but still, it angered him, and he retrieved the body and dumped it next to DG Allen Enterprises as a warning. Thank God no one made the connection. Except you, of course. I should have known that would happen, shouldn't I? Anyway, I rang you. I was worried. I wanted to scare Blake so he would see how easily what he was doing might be uncovered so he'd take more care. And I wanted to get more dirt to use as a hold over Blake if anything like this happened again. Equal knowledge gives equal power. It's a good principle—"

"So that's why you hired me?" I interrupt. "To gain power over Blake? A stand-off?"

"Yes," he says. "And it worked, up to a point, didn't it? Not that it matters now. Since then, we've tightened procedures, and nothing like this will happen again."

"But it has happened. Jade is dead."

"That was a mistake, too. Blake and I repaired the cracks in our partnership. I told him if we retrieved the information you'd gained and beat you up, you'd let it go, especially if I lost interest, but when it came right down to it, I couldn't be sure a beating was all you'd get. Not after Bluesky. So I rang you. It was the night the family were away—lucky, or so I thought—and I asked you over for the evening, hoping even then you'd stay the night. It would be safer.

"I thought Blake's men would mess your place up a little, take any evidence they could find, and leave. I never imagined Jade would be there; I never thought about what they would do to her. And for that, Paul, I'm sorry."

He stops speaking, and I gaze at the ceiling.

"And last night?" I ask. "What was last night about?"

He groans. "It was about scaring you off for good. After you came to the office, Blake and I talked about what to do. He suggested a threat, a lesson if you like, and I said nothing to stop him. It was the best plan to neutralize you. Before Blake left, he told me that by morning, there'd be nothing to worry about. I didn't reply. I just carried on working. Late. It was as if I couldn't stop working."

"Then?"

"Then, when it was gone midnight, I left the office, got into the car, and drove to your home. I wanted to make sure there'd be no blood on my hands this time, but you weren't there. I sat outside for a while and waited to see if you'd turn up, but you didn't. And you didn't answer your phone. Then, not knowing what else to do, I drove to your office. The rest you know."

"Yes, the rest I know."

Neither of us says anything more for a while.

Without warning, Dominic gets up and stretches, his muscles flexing in the soft light penetrating the curtains. "So then, you know everything now. What I need to know is what are you going to do?"

"I don't know."

"Don't you?"

As he answers, I realize his voice has changed again. It's harder now, more distant, more cultured once more. I see the time for truth is over. Squatting down, he searches underneath the bed, frowns, and then brings out a recording device, still running. He switches it off. I close my eyes for a second and swallow deeply.

"Did you think I wouldn't know?" he asks.

"Did you think I wouldn't try?"

He smiles a little before crushing the device under his shoe. Then he picks up the pieces and lays them neatly on the bedside table.

"I don't think even you can salvage that," he says.

"No."

"So what will you do now?"

The emphasis he's laid on the now doesn't escape me. "What do you think?"

"I can't imagine."

"It makes no difference," I say. "I have to go to the police, tell them what I know, even if it proves nothing."

"Why?"

I look right at him. "If you don't see why, there's no point in me explaining it to you."

When he nods and takes his mobile from his back pocket, I see that, for him, the conversation is already over.

"What are you doing? Ringing for Blake's men to come and finish me off?"

"No." He smiles. "Don't be more of a fool than you are. I'm ringing for an ambulance. I'll make sure the outside door is open. Before I leave, let me tell you one thing."

"What's that?"

"If you go to the police with any of this, then I'll counter-attack with everything I have against you—your past, your criminal record, everything. Not only that, but

I'll claim all your accusations are lies and that you planted information in Blake's and my offices to discredit our companies. This I will claim is because you have become sexually obsessed with me, in spite of the fact we have only met twice and I have never hired you. Those in my employment who may initially believe they know otherwise will in the end back me up; they have no choice. Whatever happens, it will destroy your business, your future, your family, you. Think about it."

I make no reply. There's none I can think of. At the door, he turns to look at me one last time.

"Let me repeat, Paul, that if you go to the police, even without this recording, I will destroy you."

I hold his gaze for a long moment. It tells me nothing, so I look away.

"You've said a lot of things, Dominic, but none of them are real. Or have ever been real. I think you should leave."

When the door has clicked shut, its echo reverberating through the long chill of morning, I cry for a while. Then I stagger to my feet, lean against the wardrobe and reach up for the second device I'd had the sense to place there. I hope it's recorded enough. When the ambulance arrives, my eyes are dry. And I know what I should do, but can I risk everything to do it?

CHAPTER 17

They keep me in hospital for four days. Apparently, it would have been less if I'd come in earlier and had my burns treated at the proper time, and I've been lucky as they're manageable and not life threatening. As these medical terms are flung at my head like so many pebbles, I toy with the idea of saying that when they were inflicted they seemed life threatening enough to me. In the end, I say nothing.

During those four days, I discover three things. The first is that hospitals have a routine more permanently established than my own, and they live or die by it. Being woken, washed, breakfasted, given medication, then the doctor's rounds, lunch, sleep, tea, more medication, dinner, and then blessed sleep again come and go as if there's nothing else more interesting to do. All too often there isn't.

The second thing I discover is, in spite of this familiar sense of routine, I'm not a good patient. When I hurt, I say so, and when I'm bored, I say so.

And the third fact I discover is that the worst thing in a hospital is to have an opinion.

Also during those four days, I receive three visits, although the last two are linked, much like my three new pieces of hospital information.

The first visitors are Mr. and Mrs. O'Donnell. It's Sunday afternoon when the two of them arrive, Jade's mother bustling in with expressions of concern, shock, and relief on her face and a huge bouquet of cream and orange flowers in her arms. Jade's father lurks like an afterthought in the background.

"Paul, my dear," she says, "I couldn't believe it when we heard. We've only just listened to the message from the hospital and came as soon as we could. We've been away, you see. I'm so sorry, but we would've come sooner if we'd known. What on earth has happened? Are you all right?"

As she speaks, I'm struggling to gain a sitting position in the bed. The sudden influx of questions is almost overpowering. I wonder for a moment how they've managed to find out before remembering one of the scraps of paper in my wallet with their address on. The nurses have been busy. "Yes. Yes, I'm fine, Mrs. O'Donnell, Mr. O'Donnell. Really. Or rather I'll be fine. The hospital have it all under control; it's not as bad as it looks."

"Yes, I'm so glad. But you've been burnt. My dear, how on earth did it happen?"

As she sits herself down on the only nearby visitor's chair and leans forward, Mr. O'Donnell takes his place behind her. For a few seconds, they look much like an old sepia photograph of a Victorian couple before he fetches a second chair from the other side of the ward. Suppressing a smile at the image, I give them a cleaned-up version of what happened. They listen with care to my tale of an unfortunate kitchen accident made all the worse by an explosion and the presence of a bread knife. I'm not sure they believe this any more than the hospital staff did, but there's nothing they can do to make me change my story. Besides, if I told them the truth, they'd never be able to comprehend it.

When I've finished, there's a short silence, and then Mrs. O'Donnell says, "Well, I think you've been very lucky. It's a dreadful thing to have happened. Is there anything we can get you while you're here, anything you might need?"

"No, really. It's kind enough that you're visiting me at all and—"

Mrs. O'Donnell sweeps away my feeble objections with a wave of her hand. Over the next hour, I'm bombarded with gifts of soap, shaving cream, toothpaste, magazines, and a selection of books to cover all tastes. Not only that, but I hear about the weather, the sewing circle, the chapel and how good it's been to Jade's parents, not to mention the garden, the redecorating they're doing, and the much improved state of the village shop. It surprises me how much I relax in their company, one chatty and one so quiet. The time speeds by, and when Mrs. O'Donnell gets up to leave, there's a thud of darkness in my stomach.

While Jade's mother is replacing her husband's chair in the corner of the ward, Mr. O'Donnell speaks for the first time.

"Paul?"

"Yes, Mr. O'Donnell?"

He clears his throat and stares down the long line of beds. "I don't believe any of what you've told us, and neither, I think, does my wife, but thank you for telling us it."

I feel my skin color. "I'm sorry, I—"

"Don't be. You have your job to do, but…"

"Yes, sir?"

"Be careful. My…my daughter would've wanted that."

I nod once. A moment later, Mrs. O'Donnell is kissing me on the cheek and making ready for departure. As I watch their two oh-so-ordinary and comforting backs disappear, my one thought is how grateful I am they came at all. After they've gone, the only other thought that concerns me, and which kicks in during the middle of the following night, is what other scraps of paper the nurses might have retrieved from my belongings.

It doesn't take long to find out.

The next day, the day before I'm discharged, or rather before I escape, my mother arrives.

I'm sleeping. When I wake up, her face is the first thing I see, and I have no idea how long she's been sitting next to my bed. For a further moment, I can't remember where I am.

She touches my forehead with cool fingers. "It's all right. You've been asleep. I've been waiting for you to be awake."

Her hand lingers on my head for a while. Then she shifts and pats me on the cheek before bringing her fingers to rest on my arm. The silence hovers between us.

Then she says, "I'm sorry I didn't come before. I wanted to, but…but…"

"It's okay," I say, and in her trailing off I can imagine all the tale of my father's reluctance. "Don't worry about it. You're here now. I'm glad you are."

And I am, though I haven't expected to be. I'm glad my mother is here, visiting her sick son, as somehow this seems right, in spite of how distant I am now from my family. It's as if I've been transported back to the good moments of being young.

My mother just smiles and holds my hand. Now and again, we talk, filling the silence with trivia, and I think how odd it is that I feel more comfortable with Mrs. O'Donnell than I do with my own mother. After half an hour, she releases my hand and pats her hair. "Darling?"

"Hmm?" I mumble a reply, not noticing then the change in her tone from comfort to question.

"I didn't come on my own today, though I suppose you may have realized that already. Your father brought me. I told him I had to come, no matter what, and he drove me. I—"

"Where is he?"

"He's in the café downstairs." She hesitates. "If you wanted to see him, Paul, I think he'd like that. Today, if you feel able to."

"Why doesn't he tell me himself?"

"I don't know."

"No. Nobody bloody knows, do they? Because nobody in this family has the guts to say it. He's ashamed of me, of the past and what I did once. He threw me out then, and as far as I can see, nothing's changed."

"That's not true."

"Isn't it? Really?"

She doesn't answer and, without looking at her, I know she's trying not to cry. I should turn to her, make things right in the way she would want, but I think the days when that might have happened are gone.

"Isn't it true?" I ask again.

"He's your father, Paul. He loves you, no matter what you think."

I close my eyes. "Maybe. Maybe not. To be honest, I've had enough of love. It doesn't make any damn thing right. It never has and it never will."

"I don't believe that's true," she whispers.

"I do. You're entitled to believe what you like."

After that, nothing is said for a few moments. Then I hear the sound of the scraping of the chair as she stands. When I look up at her, she's paler than I've ever seen her before.

"I'm grateful you came," I say. "Thank you. I know this is difficult for you. I'm sorry I can't make things happen as you'd like."

She nods and then says quickly, as if it's something stored in her mouth that she must set free, "I understand. It's been hard for you, too. And for your father. Listen, Paul, there's…there's a small chapel downstairs. It wasn't being used when I looked and there's not a service 'til next Sunday. I'll ask your father to wait there for half an hour before we go home. I thought it would be neutral ground if you changed your mind. I won't interfere. I'll be in the café. I just thought if you wanted you could talk. Goodbye. I'll speak to you soon. I do love you, you know."

Then, without allowing any kind of response, she kisses me on the forehead, smoothes her hand through my hair, and is gone.

A minute glides by. Then another and another. She must have got there by now, down to the café. She must be talking to him, telling him what she's said to me. It strikes me I have no idea what he will think or what he'll do, how he'll react. Will he be angry? Nervous? Even pleased? Or is this plan something the two of them have concocted together and he'll be expecting it? Before my mother left, I didn't ask her that.

Five minutes go by. I should keep count, but what's the point? I'm not going to go anywhere. I'm not going to see my father for the first time in eleven years, nine months, and one day.

I try to sleep, but I can't. When I close my eyes, all I can see is my mother's face. And behind her, a shadow of someone else.

What time is it now? I wish my mother had never come. No, that's unfair. Fifteenth law of PI work: always be fair. I was enjoying her being here, visiting me. Before she said what she'd come to say.

I should do something. Should concentrate on anything that isn't the image of my father, whose face I can't quite form in my thoughts, sitting in the chapel downstairs. Will he be waiting? Would I be waiting if I were him? At all? Damn it. When I snatch up my book, the latest P.D. James, from the side table, even that doesn't work. The words swim in front of my eyes and make no sense together, and I read the same passage four and a half times before I realize that's what I've done.

Just as I drop it back down, the tea trolley arrives. A welcome diversion. Or would be if it wasn't taking so long to get to me. One more minute glides by like ice as tea is served to those nearest the door…two minutes.

"Tea, Mr. Maloney? Or would you like coffee today?"

Gazing up at the volunteer's smiling old face with its border of short, graying hair, I wonder what her life has been like and whether she's ever had to make the kind of decisions given to me today. On consideration, I don't think so and, besides, there's no time to find out. I have less than five minutes to go before my father leaves the chapel. It might just be worth it. It might. There's no time to find out about someone else's life this afternoon, and no time for a hot drink either.

Without knowing it, I've made a decision.

"No thanks," I say to the tea-lady. "Not today. But please could you do me a favor? Could you help me up?"

She does. Walking and any sort of movement aren't bad now. The hospital, whatever I may think of it, is doing its job. The hot air of the ward through the thin poly-cotton of my dressing gown almost seems to brand my skin again. I thank God it can't press against any burnt patches, as they're still protected. The lift slowly disgorges its occupants as I descend to the ground floor. I'm sweating, and my fingers grip my palms as if I'm about to spin off into space if I should ever let go. I don't even know why I'm doing this, why I'm trying, why I'm here.

It's madness. Whether or not my father has bothered to fit in with my mother's plans, it's madness. Nothing will be resolved, nothing healed. I should go back to my bed and try to get some sleep.

Just as I decide this is what I'll do, the lift opens. I've come this far. I may as well go through the motions. He won't be there anyway and nothing will have been lost. Or gained.

Limping out into the stream of bodies all heading up or down the corridor like a human wall of purpose, I realize there's still one fact I need to know. Reaching out, I grab the first uniform I can see.

"Excuse me?"

"Yes?" The nurse stops and smiles at me. "Can I help?"

"Please. Could you tell me the way to the chapel?"

"Of course." She points behind me. "It's down there, third door on the right. Shall I show you?"

"No, no, that's fine," I reply. "I can find it."

As I turn in the direction she's pointed, I see that the clock in the foyer says it's been over thirty-two minutes since my mother left me. I'm already late.

A few seconds later, I'm outside the chapel door. There are no windows so there's no way of knowing if anyone is inside. It makes sense, I tell myself, for a place of prayer.

It makes sense. The door itself is simple, just the word "Chapel" and a note of the service times.

It would be so easy to leave now.

No. It wouldn't. I can't live with the not knowing. I've never been able to.

I push open the door. It feels heavy against my hands. Inside, it's dark, lit only by five small wall lights and a scattering of candles.

I'm alone. Of course, of course.

I should have known it. I didn't know it.

As the door swings shut behind me, a figure appears from the left side of the room and takes a step into what light there is. A tall man, gaunt, black hair with a shadow of grey, face lined now, and with the look of a wolf on the hunt. I could be gazing into a mirror, one far into the future.

The man takes a second step.

"Hello, Paul."

Without a word, I amble, as if there's all the time in the world, halfway down the aisle, halfway to where he is. I steady myself against one of the wooden chairs on my right and lower myself into it. There's a suggestion of movement, a possibility of help offered, but I flinch away.

"No. I can manage."

He strolls toward me, hands in pockets and his long, black winter coat floating open. Every inch the modern celebrity judge, as always. He sits across the aisle from where I am, thank God. Any nearer and I don't think I could deal with it.

"Thank you for coming," he says at last. "I wasn't sure you would. Hell, I wasn't sure I would."

"Ditto. To both."

"Cigarette?"

"No. I gave them up."

"Wise move. Do you mind if…"

"Go ahead."

After taking out a packet of Dunhills, he removes one, lights it, and flicks the rest of them back inside his coat. Then he takes a long, slow draw, so long I can almost taste the spice and scent of it in my own throat, too.

"Why did you bother then?" I ask. "Waiting for me, I mean?"

"Your mother can be persuasive."

"Don't fuck with me, Jonathan. I get enough of that in my life outside this bloody family. Don't pretend you don't do exactly what you like, whenever you damn well like it."

"I'm not the only one."

"Don't change the bloody subject. Why did you wait for me?"

He takes another drag of his cigarette. "I wanted to see you, surprising though you may find that to be."

"Why?"

"You're my son, Paul, in case you'd forgotten it."

"When has that ever meant anything to you? You cut me out of your life when I was nineteen, and, as far as I'm aware, you've not changed your mind since. For God's sake, it's been eleven years, nine months, and one day since you've thought of me as your son, and you don't have the right to criticize me now. It's not something I like to think of much, either…you being my father. Haven't I had to live, ever since Teresa…died, with the knowledge I'll always be second best, compared to her? I know, in a place too deep for the uprooting, that if you'd had a choice back then, you'd have chosen me to die, instead of her.

How do you think that feels? And don't ever tell me that's a lie because I won't believe you."

By the time I come to the end of what I want to say, I'm amazed I've had the words and the balls to say it all so quickly. And that it sounds so little. Still, my voice is raised and I'm stabbing one accusatory finger in his direction. From outside, the door is pushed open, and this acts as a signal for something in me to be unleashed.

"Get the hell out," I yell. "Can't you see this is private?"

The door pulls shut, and we're alone again.

While I catch my breath, my father finishes his cigarette and stubs the remains out onto the floor tiles. Right at that moment, I'd like to do the same to him.

At last he speaks. "I'd forgotten how good you are with time, Paul. It always was a talent you had. I'm glad to see you still have it."

"For God's sake—"

"No," he holds up one hand. "Let me finish. I've allowed you to have your say; you should do likewise with me. And yes, you're right. Teresa was, and always will be, my favorite. She made my life happier than anyone else ever has, even your mother. I miss her every day with every part of who I am. I'm not a fool. I know that will always be the case. And yes, as you say, if I'd had a choice back then, I would, I believe, have chosen for my daughter to live. You accuse me and I have no defense. Guilty, Paul, guilty.

"But none of this matters, does it? Because, even though I hate what you do with your whole lifestyle and the thought of seeing you here and not Teresa crucifies me, even in spite of these things, you are my son. Still. And if you don't believe me, why don't you ask how your friend's body was released to the O'Donnells for the funeral so early? Yes, I still have influence. Though I don't know how any of this can ever be enough or help either of us. In the way your mother would want."

There's a long silence then. When I look up, it seems darker, and I realize one of the wall lamps has burned out.

"Thank you for helping the O'Donnells," I say. "But you're right. It's not enough. I think you should go."

"All right," he says, standing and buttoning his coat. "Your mother thinks we're too alike, you and I. She'd like us to be friends. If we can't be anything resembling father and son."

I let him walk almost to the door before I reply.

"No matter what you think about me, or I about you, I'm glad you waited," I say. "But I don't think we can ever be friends. Not now."

Between us, the atmosphere is filled with emotion. I watch his back stiffen. I wonder if he'll turn around, but he doesn't, and I'm glad of it. He opens the door, and a tide of noise and normality rushes into the chapel.

"I'm glad, too, that I waited," he says. "But, yes, perhaps you're right."

And then he, too, is gone.

That night, it takes too long to get to sleep.

During the whole of the time I'm in the hospital, no stranger visits me, and there are no unfamiliar tastes in my food or drink, no floating shadows half-glimpsed. Not that the thought of my own death seems to have the power to keep me awake in the night; on the contrary, it's more like a distant concept that has no relationship with what is real. Still, nothing happens, and I wonder then if, as far as Dominic and Blake are concerned, any threat I might have posed is over. Instead, what occupies my mind is the thought of what the women whose lives they've ruined have been through. Starlight, Dancer, Bluesky, Aqua. Where are the other three now? What will happen to them?

What I have found out, and what I tried to tell Dominic, is like nothing so much as a deep darkness in a darker night. Since I have known the truth, I have read reports about women—and yes, some men, too—being tricked by the promise of a better life into working in the sex trade. Anywhere in the world where there's enough wealth, people are sold for sex, beaten, tortured, unable for the most part to escape, and doomed to keep on pleasing their owners under threat of death. I have read about children murdered and about women who have returned to their prisons just to save those they love.

I have swallowed down nausea as I looked at pictures of those who have died, either of disease or by the knife or the gun when their disease makes them unsellable. There is a vast swath of crime and pain and prolonged, agonizing death that is hidden so far beneath the surface of the everyday world that no one pays any attention to it. It has sickened me, both because of what it is and because of who, as I know now, is involved in it. And at the heart of it all are real women dying real deaths or living lives without hope—Starlight, Dancer, Bluesky, Aqua.

For their sakes, I resolve to carry on, to do something.

On the Tuesday I leave, it takes longer to check out of the hospital than it ever did to enter it. There are people to see who must give me the all-clear before I can go, whom I've never seen before. I decide against taking hold of my civil rights and just walking out; even for a PI, there are times when the ideal of being a free agent has to bow before the rules.

When, at last, in the dull grey rain of that October afternoon, I ease myself, with care, into the waiting taxi, clutching the precious recording device I've kept with me all this while, my first port of call isn't home. It's the police station.

CHAPTER 18

When I've handed over the recording, the police ask a lot of questions, but this time I tell them the truth as far as I know it. All of it, except for the sexual relationship between Dominic and me. Let them find that out from another source, if they can. Let my ex-lover's family have some chance for survival in all this. Somebody has to be able to walk away, and, for now, it's his children who haunt me. Henry and Judith. I know how it is to have sudden change blow your family apart. Let them salvage something.

Because I have lied before, the police take twice as long, as I knew they would, to put me through the process. Not that I've any complaints; it's no more than I deserve. When they're not questioning me, they leave me alone—apart from one young PC, who looks as if he's only just joined up straight from school—to listen to the recording. They're away for a long time, and after my third coffee, I lay my head on the desk and doze off.

When they come back, the PC, under supervision, writes down what I say and then, at last, I read it through and sign and date each page. All my burns are aching by the time it's over; the knife wound on my upper arm is worst of all. I want nothing more than to get outside and feel the fresh air on my face. What I've given them must be enough as, before I leave to go home, they ask me if I want protection. I laugh it off. It's not protection I want, but company.

By the time I leave, it's 10:02 P.M. There's a cash machine nearby. After checking there's nobody lurking, I take out as much money as I can. Hailing a taxi, I check the driver's credentials, get in, and lock the door behind me. I toy with the idea of The Bell and Book, but it's too soon and doesn't have what I want. Instead, I ask for Soho. Opening the window, I breathe the night chill down into my throat. As deep as it will go.

"Late shift?" the driver says.

"Something like that," I reply.

When we reach our destination, I pay with a large tip and slip out into the rain. A swift glance satisfies me there's no immediate danger. When the taxi departs with an appreciative hoot of its horn, I run as best I can across the street, dodging the crowds, and clatter down the narrow outside stairs of a club I haven't visited since I was twenty-five years and one week old.

It's not changed much. Red and orange flashing lights over the door, suspicious bouncers, a dirty bar, and beautiful men. I order the house beer at a ridiculous price—no Waggledance here—take a corner seat and swallow enough pain killers to launch a new millennium.

Then I study what's available. The stage show won't be starting for another twenty minutes or so, if they still keep the same hours. Before it begins, I plan to have sex with the first willing, dark-haired young man I can find. I just want to feel alive again.

It takes me two minutes to make eye contact with a suitable participant. From what I can see across the floor of dancing, pirouetting, kissing, and grabbing bodies, he's young enough and his hair is the right color. When I catch his eye the second time, he smiles and doesn't look away.

I gesture with my head to where the toilets are, swig down the last of my beer and get up. He says something to whoever he's with and pushes back his chair. By the time I've turned in the direction I want, I know he'll follow.

The Gents smells of sweat and semen. There's only one cubicle free, and I can tell I'm not the only one who wants his five minutes of fun before the performance begins. It hasn't got a lock, but that doesn't bother me. If someone wants to watch, let him. Just as long as nobody kills me before I'm done.

Without warning, I'm pushed from behind into the cubicle. I'm already raising my hand to ward off any attack when I realize there's no danger; it's the boy.

"Hey." He ducks, his accent more East End than Soho. "Stay cool, mate."

"Sorry," I whisper. "I've had a difficult day."

"'S okay. I can help you relax, can't I? You'll have to pay, though."

"That's fine." I push down the frisson of guilt and try, instead, to revel in the idea of no obligation to call, no threat of a relationship hanging over me.

He wedges the door shut with his jumper, which he strips off in one fluid movement. He exposes a tight, tanned belly that hasn't been created by the sun or from just walking either. Up close, his nose is a little crooked, but that doesn't matter. His mouth is wide, his fingers strong and practical, and his eyes a deep brown. He's as far removed from Dominic as I can get.

"What do you want?" he asks, and I tell him. At once he names a price, and I nod. That's fine, too. There's no time to bargain, and, besides, I'm not in the mood.

Sitting on the toilet seat, I try not to listen to the sounds of sex from the cubicles on either side of me. I'm only interested in my own. He eases off my trousers and briefs and unfastens the last two buttons of my shirt. At the sight of the burns on my stomach, one of them still covered up, he frowns.

"What's this, mate?"

"Kitchen accident," I tell him. "I got burnt. Don't worry. They're not catching. I was just…stupid, that's all. They don't hurt much now, if I'm careful."

He nods. "Poor bastard. Unlucky."

He's right about that. Then, conversation over, he kneels between my legs and kisses me softly.

"Hey, nice prick," he whispers.

My cock stiffens in response. With a groan, I arch my back against the cold porcelain. His lips nibble at me, and I groan again.

"You like that, mate?"

"Yes."

"Good. Because I get better."

Then he sets to work and there's no more talking. He's thorough, too. He keeps me hovering for just the right amount of time between pleasure and fulfillment. His tongue licks me and his mouth travels the whole length of me from base to tip and back, over and over again. His fingers follow suit, sometimes coaxing and, more often, holding me back from the inevitable conclusion, just a little longer and a little longer yet. Then the rising excitement, my heart beating ever faster, the eruption of sweat across my forehead, and suddenly, as if turning a corner into a deepening light, I'm there. I come, right in his mouth, the rhythmic pulse of it driving me into him. My hands bury themselves in his dark, soft hair, and my throat gasps out my own joy to closure.

"Jesus. That's good, so good. Thank you. Thank you, thank you."

I hear the rustle of tissue paper and the sound of him spitting out my spunk. When I look down, still shuddering, he pockets the tissue and smiles.

"Hey, my pleasure, mate."

While I catch my breath, he tears off another piece of tissue and wipes my legs and cock dry.

"Thanks."

"'S okay. Do you want to pay now or do you want more?"

I shake my head. "No. No more sex. Not this evening. I just wanted to see…if I could still do it."

"Been having trouble?"

"Yeah, a little. You could say that."

"Must be the company you keep then, mate." He grins. "Ain't nothing wrong with your equipment."

"Thanks. Maybe you're right. It must be the company I keep." As I say these words, it's as if a weight is lifted from my shoulders, and I start to laugh.

My companion glances up at me. "Hey, did I make a joke?"

"No," I say, still laughing. "Not as such. It just feels good to be here, right now. You can't imagine. That's all."

When I've finished laughing and dressed myself again, with care, I get out my wallet and pay him. I add a twenty percent tip on top of the money he's asked for, as I feel it's the least I can do, and his eyes light up.

"Hey, cool. Thanks, mate."

"You've earned it."

As he pulls on his jumper and opens the cubicle door, I wonder if I can chance my luck further.

"Look," I say, and he turns back, his face polite and expectant. "Do you think… I mean I'd appreciate some company tonight, up there in the bar. Could you see your way to being with me this evening? Not sex, but kissing— if you do that—dancing maybe."

"Sorry." He shrugs. "I don't do escort work, mate. Like to keep it simple, y'know?"

"Okay, sure. I understand." As I swallow down my disappointment, he reaches out and pats my arm once, awkwardly, before going back on the hunt again.

"Anyway," he says, "you don't have to worry. Not a looker like you. If you want to make out on the dance floor or during the show, there'll be plenty of blokes out there willing to let you. Trust me."

To my later surprise, he turns out to be right.

When he's gone, I wash my face and hands in the cleanest looking basin, my flesh still glowing with the warm aftermath. All the time, a steady stream of amorous punters meets at the urinals and cruises in and out of the cubicles. Then I dry myself under the air blower and go out to join the beat and rhythm of the club again, trying to be a part of what I once knew.

The show's already started, and I find myself wolf-whistling at the stripper's glistening muscles. When the music starts again, I swing around, a thud in my gut as men start to pair up around me. I needn't have worried. A platinum blond, dressed neck to ankle in sleek black leather and silver chains, slips up from nowhere, grips my arm, and we start to dance. And more. Groin to groin, legs gliding together, hands exploring, no questions asked. Twice he presses me on one of my burns, but the painkillers are working, and it's easy enough to slide his fingers elsewhere.

"Accident, sorry," I explain over the wall of sound. "Not you."

He shrugs, grins, and three beats of my heart later, his tongue meets mine, lip melding to lip. God, it's been so long since I've done this. I've forgotten how good it feels. All that matters is the need of the flesh, with no tomorrows and no guilt. My blood is swooping and wheeling with the roar in my head.

By the time the show starts once more, I'm onto my fourth partner. The trannie on stage is singing. I see my whore from earlier dancing with someone and try to catch his eye again and smile, but he doesn't notice. Or more likely, chooses not to. I can understand that. I don't like being interrupted when I'm working either.

At a table wet with spilled drink, I squeeze myself next to two young blokes dressed in high campery and make-up, and necking as if they're joined at the mouth. I wonder if it's exclusive. It isn't. I buy each a Bloody Mary and find out the shorter darker one has a tongue stud, and the tall blond, a nipple ring. It never gets serious. They're more into each other than me, but it's a break from the heat and sweat and muscle of the dance floor, and I'm not complaining.

When the music changes to seventies disco, I'm up and working the room like a pro. Thank God for hospital drugs strong enough to keep a dying horse on its feet. The evening goes on into morning. By the early hours, I'm drunk, exhausted, aching, and happy. The end of the night finds me back in the toilets with the blond, black-leathered bloke I first made out with on the dance floor. And I'm thinking I might have been premature in saying earlier that there'd be no more sex, just touching.

Because the leathered bloke is half-sitting, half leaning against one of the basins. We've filled it with cool water, and I'm busy splashing him and kissing him. So far, so good for my assumption. But at the same time, our cocks are ramrod free, though I can't remember that happening. We're both rubbing each other up and down, up and down, faster and faster, not caring about the blokes around us pissing or necking or doing whatever it is they want to. Tonight is magical and nothing can stop it.

I come first, and a second later, he does, too. Collapsing against him, both of us gasping and laughing and wet, I see our spunk oozing together over his leathers, my shirt, our fingers. I can't help but laugh again.

"Sorry," I say, wincing as the pills finally begin to wear off, and my burns grow painful once more. "Your trousers. Didn't mean to mess them up. But, God, you're so cute."

"It's okay; don't stress it." He laughs, eyes glowing in the strip-light. "It's fine. Craig, my name's Craig. And you're cute, too. More than cute."

"Craig." I test out the word and like the way it feels on my tongue. "Hello, Craig."

"Hello…"

"Paul."

"Hello, Paul. Nice to meet you."

Again we kiss, and I help him down from the basin. Taking the sparse remains of the hand tissues, we clean each other up, tidy our clothing, and head back to the bar, now almost deserted.

At the door to the street, he reaches into his pocket and brings out something I can't see. "Do you…"

"What?"

"Do you want my number? Maybe you could ring me sometime, and we could go out for a drink or…"

"Or have sex?"

"Yeah. Or have sex."

Reaching out, I run one hand through his dyed blond hair. Early twenties, I think, maybe on the look-out for something serious for the first time. He's unlikely to find it here. I'd better explain how things are and quickly.

"Look, I was just out for some fun tonight," I say. "I've had a bad few days, and I wanted to forget it for a while. I'm not in the market for anything more than that, not right now."

"Shame." He shrugs and looks down. "I fancy you like crazy. Shame to waste it."

I smile, stroke the back of his neck, and allow myself one long, rich goodbye kiss. As we disentangle ourselves, he slips whatever it is he's been holding into my back pocket.

"What's that?"

He steps away, and his blush rises. "Just my card. I'm not dumb enough to ask for your details now, but you never know, you might change your mind.

"Thanks, Craig," I say. "Now I can see it's time to get going. I make no promises, but whatever, I've enjoyed myself. You're a superb kisser."

He smiles, and I find myself admiring the crinkle around his hazel eyes.

"Thanks, yourself. You give a bloody good hand-job, Paul."

"Glad to hear it."

It's already after six-forty-five. I grab the morning paper from a newsagent just opening on the corner of Old Compton Street and wander down on my own to Leicester Square. I read the news. And read it again.

Dominic's arrest for questioning is on page three. Or rather, not arrest. There's no mention of any charges yet. He's just helping them with their enquiries. The police have moved fast. My recording and statement must have been more successful than I'd hoped. No, it's not just me. They must have been working things to a point of action way before this, and what my contribution has done is speed up the inevitable. The recording was good. I heard it. I know. My statement, too. They've added it to the sum of their findings and they've sprung the trap.

Good luck to them.

I hope Dominic survives.

No. No, I don't. Not after what he's done and the way he's walked away from it. And not after Jade.

I read the item again. The main thrust is suspected human trafficking, which is no surprise. Dominic's family is mentioned, his company, too, but then I expected that. It's part of the story. As is Bluesky and what happened to her. What does make my mouth go dry and my muscles tighten is the mention of Delta Egypt that comes in the penultimate paragraph. It's just a throwaway comment, focusing on Dominic's business dealings with Blake Kenzie, but the fact that this is part of the first tranche of reporting is enough for me to drop the paper onto the bench, sit back, and think.

The police are farther along in their investigations than Jade and I ever supposed. If Blake is mentioned here, then they already know, or suspect, that the two companies are involved in the trafficking together. And have proof beyond what I might have been able to add to the mix. Because, if Dominic has been brought in for questioning, then Blake also must be facing the police in an interview room. Whether here in London or back in Cairo.

All this means the shit has hit the top of the wall and is even now glooping down, muddying everyone who comes into contact with it. I might well be in more danger than I thought. Until now, I've assumed I'll go down when Dominic plays his final cards and makes his counter-accusations. Now, it looks as if the fall-out from Delta might catch me instead. In a much more deadly fashion.

Today, the thought of Blake's henchmen acting out their bloody fantasies with me once more gives me more trouble than it did yesterday. The encounter with the hooker and then with Craig, while not lasting in any sense, has changed things.

I want to be here. Alive, sitting on a bench in the middle of London, feeling the beat of my heart in my chest and the flow of blood through my veins. I want to enjoy the warmth of the air on this mild October morning. I want to hear the sounds of the city moving from sleep into the vibrancy of day: the tramps on the far side of the square from me drinking and squabbling; the early morning workers hurrying along on their way to their offices; the stray clubbers creeping home. All of it, the noise, the shit, the color, the smell is worth hanging onto, no matter what the cost. I don't want to be on the other side. Not even if Jade is there. Not yet.

I want to live.

Because of that and that alone, I'll take my chances with Dominic and his threats against me.

This decision made, the next realization is it'll be safer not to go home. Being at the office is beyond my courage now. I have to think what to do, where to go to wait for the inevitable explosive statement from my ex-lover. I've not been followed from the hospital or the club. I could run.

I could, but I won't. Somewhere, it has to end. I need to be where there's a television or radio tuned to breaking news. Someplace where I'll know when the death blow has landed.

Launching myself upright from the bench, I start to walk and keep on walking. I don't know where I'm going, but I know it has to be deeper into London, to be amongst people as the morning broadens out into day. Not too many people, though, not so as danger might come unseen, unannounced.

All I can sense is my sweat and the sound of my breathing. Though I look behind and around myself once, twice, there's nobody I see to distrust. Nobody is there. Nobody cares.

Keep on walking. Keep focused. That's important. I can't lose my purpose now. I'm looking for one thing and one thing only. Somewhere to step aside for a moment, somewhere with a television and a chance to drink in the news. The news about me maybe. And then a chance to think.

I find the perfect place, a small café in The Strand. It's empty except for one old bloke, dark-skinned and muscular, behind the counter and a couple of young women who look like they've been out all night and plan to spend all morning discussing it. Through the smeared window, it looks bleak, metallic, but clean enough, and it's got what I want—a working television. The colors and lines of it flicker across my eye, and I blink.

When I push open the door and walk in, the rich scent of coffee and warm bread makes my stomach twist and groan. It seems like I haven't eaten in years, and now I'm starving. As I enter, the two women stop talking and turn around to stare at me. They look me up and down once in experienced assessment, find me wanting, and turn back to their conversation, whispering behind manicured hands. Can't say I blame them. I must look like crap, though I've not yet studied myself in a mirror to confirm this diagnosis. Must smell, too, of smoke and sweat and sex.

As I approach the counter, the old bloke picks up a clean white tea towel and steps back, wrinkling his nose, but saying nothing. Behind him, in the mirror, I can see a slight figure, hunted, suspicious, with a frown on his pale face. His hair is unbrushed; his eyes are bleak. He looks as if a change in the wind might make him lash out without warning. He looks like me.

"Sorry," I say with a gesture of appeasement to the old bloke. "I've had a rough night. I'll have a coffee."

"What do you like?" he says, his accent strong Italian. He waves his tea towel at the hand-written menu on the counter.

"Espresso. Double, please."

He deals with the machine and pours out the dark, pungent liquid. When the time comes to pay, my skin goes cold for a second or two as I wonder if I've even got the cash for this, but the coins I scrape together from the depths of my pockets are just enough.

As I take the cup and head to the nearest seat not next to the window, I point at the television. "Do you mind if I watch the news?"

With a shrug, he glances over at the two women. He says something rapidly, in Italian I imagine, and they look up and say something back. It sounds chatty, informal, as if they all know each other. I hadn't realized the women were Italian, too. Their whispers hadn't penetrated that far. Whatever, their answer must be in the affirmative, as he picks up the remote and switches through a couple of channels until he reaches a breakfast news program.

"Thank you," I say, trying to take in all three of them with my smile. I sit down where I have a good view of the screen and also the door. Because you never know.

I swallow down another couple of pills with the coffee and stare at the television as if it's about to bring me my future. I can't seem to understand what it is they're talking about; the images sway back and forth, in and out, and I have to blink and shake myself to bring them back into clarity. News items appear and disappear. The mouths of the people talking make meaningless words that don't reach me, and I realize the volume is too low. Of course. It doesn't matter, though, not yet.

Then, suddenly, there's a picture of Dominic close up, an old one, next to a shot of Scotland Yard. Seeing him there makes my heart beat so loudly, I'm surprised when the women carry on chatting as if they haven't heard it. Seeing him in this context makes everything that's happened real, solid, and not just a nightmare of my own imaginings. God. They're talking, talking, but I can't hear. I have to hear.

From my sitting position, I swing 'round in appeal to the proprietor again, not caring if my voice is too high, too harsh. "Excuse me?"

"Si?" he says, turning to face me.

"The volume? Please?" I make a desperate movement of my hand at my ear, and he sighs.

"Okay." He reaches for the remote, a look of boredom on his lined features.

Still he's too slow, too slow, and I leap up and grab the remote with one hand, still clutching my coffee cup. "Sorry, I just— Sorry."

No time for further apologies. In two strides, I'm at the screen and have put the sound up four notches. The reporter is still talking. Now he's standing outside Dominic's house in Islington. It seems a lifetime since I was there. He nods to the camera, apparently in answer to some question the presenter might have asked and continues:

"Yes, that's true. And since this morning's early encounter with the police, there've been no statements from Mr. Allen and no further clarification from Scotland Yard concerning the reasons for Mr. Allen's apparent arrest. Or, indeed, any confirmation that any formal arrest has been made. We've been advised that it may have something to do with the breaking case of human trafficking the police have been investigating, but the exact nature of Mr. Allen's involvement remains unclear. A gentleman who described himself as Mr. Allen's solicitor arrived at the house here in Islington ten minutes ago. He was admitted by a member of his family, presumably his wife, Cassandra Allen, but has not yet left. As I've said, no indication of the nature of any charges, if there are, in fact, to be any charges, has been made."

Even as the reporter is speaking, there's a flurry of movement behind him, a sense of something about to happen. Dominic's front door opens and then shuts just as quickly. On the threshold stands a lean, bespectacled man in his late fifties, holding a sheet of paper. He begins to walk toward the gathered reporters. I've never seen Dominic's solicitor, but it's obvious who it is.

Here it comes then, I think. Here it comes. Dominic's counter-attack and then everything I've known or worked for will vanish—my business, my life, my family, me.

The reporter glances back and steps to one side, so the camera can zoom in. He keeps on speaking.

"As you can see, the gentleman understood to be Mr. Allen's solicitor has just exited the house and is heading in our direction. He may well have a statement to make to us, at which point we hope to learn more about this mysterious case."

The solicitor comes to a halt on the pavement as the journalists jostle for position around him. He glances into the camera. His eyes are sharp, intelligent. Dominic has chosen his representative well. Dropping the remote, I grip the counter so hard with my free hand that pain shoots through my knuckles. No matter now, as the mouthpiece begins.

"I have a short statement, which Mr. Allen has asked me to read out to you, but I'm afraid I cannot answer any questions at this stage," the solicitor says, unfolding his papers, and I think, Go on. Go on then and let's bloody well get it over with. I'm as prepared as I can be.

"Mr. Allen would like to say this: 'I very much regret the events of this morning and the distress it has caused and will cause my family and colleagues. I have spent many years building up the expertise and reputation of DG Allen Enterprises, and I trust that those currently in charge of proceedings in my absence will continue to act with integrity and professionalism in every challenge and opportunity they face.

"As from this moment, I am stepping down from my position as Chief Executive Officer, and the Board of Directors will, as a result, take over my duties until such time as a replacement can be appointed. I admit that mistakes have been made, and I'm prepared to pay for them as the law decides. That's all I'm able to say at this moment. Thank you.'"

I am wrong. I've not been prepared for this.

I could never have been prepared for this.

Why?

On the screen, the crowd of journalists explodes with questions that will not be answered until much later. In the television studio, the presenter kicks into an improvisation that can tell us nothing we haven't already heard. In a small café in London, meanwhile, my cup drops from my fingers and shatters on the tiles in a combination of whiteness and searing heat.

I think it's over.

And once again I'm wrong.

CHAPTER 19

During the next month and four days, the long, cold haul through the end of autumn and the beginning of winter, I become a news junkie. As, I imagine, do many around the country. I learn about the sudden—but only partial—destruction of Blake Kenzie's human trafficking empire and something about the long hours of police and welfare agencies work that has made this possible. I learn how Blake disappeared just hours before the swoop was due to take place and wonder how he found out and where he is today. I miss the chance of seeing him suffer for Jade's death and wonder if I'll ever be able to let that need go.

I wonder, too, about the fate of my attackers and whether they were already dead when Blake or his messengers got to them. And I wonder if Dominic has thoughts to spare for that in the middle of everything else he must be going through. I learn how several of Blake's closest contacts in Egypt, the UK, and along the smuggling route have been captured and questioned and are now facing imprisonment. For how long, who knows? His empire has suffered a blow, and I'm grateful as, without it, I, no doubt, would be dead. To them, I'm small fry now, unimportant in the grander scheme of their difficulties. I've been forgotten and, I think, because of that and that alone I'm alive.

Most of all, though, I learn more about the people whose lives Dominic and Blake have ruined. Not just facts and figures either. No, millions of others and I hear for the first time the real story: tales of suffering from women forced to work in the sex trade, stories that no one will ever forget. For a while, Bluesky and what happened to her is the main focus for speculation, but the facts are few, and neither Blake nor Dominic is accused of her murder. Or Jade's. Any evidence I could bring to the table is nothing but circumstantial.

The police don't call me. My business isn't ruined, my family is safe, and life eases itself back into a new path that, step by step, becomes a kind of routine. Even my wounds heal, but I will be scarred for life. Dominic has set me free by a silence I can't understand. For as long as he sees fit to keep that silence, I will walk in it.

I clean up the office and, after a while, take on a few new cases. They don't grip me in the same way, but bring in some much-needed money. I stop thinking I'll see Jade each time I look up and notice her empty desk. Sometimes I can even manage half a day without wondering where she is. I miss her. I miss her dazzle and glitter, the sense she always gave me that life was fuller than I'd imagined and there was more to hope for than I could guess. I wish I'd had the chance to tell her this is what I'll remember. Always. Twice I visit her parents. The awkwardness is fading. It helps all three of us to be together, to talk about her, or at least I like to think so, but maybe I'm fooling myself. All I know is they don't turn me away.

Once, on Wednesday, October 27, I think about calling my own parents, but decide not to. Not for a while. On that day, I sit in my office, unplug the phone, and light a candle, watching it flicker as it burns. And I remember Teresa at 3:29 P.M., the last time I saw her, twenty-five years ago. I think also I might cry a little, but I can't be sure.

So the autumn ticks by, the days grow colder and the long nights longer. There's a feeling in the air as if something is changing, but I don't know what. When I get up in the morning and look in the shaving mirror, each time I expect to see something different, and each time I'm disappointed. Same green eyes, same dark hair, same hunted expression. I look a little older. At least I'm alive, I tell myself. I'm alive and others are not.

When I say this to Andrew, he smiles and lets me talk. Not that I'm going as often as before, but when I've got the cash, I find it helps. I'll have my final session one day soon, and I'll walk away and not make another appointment at his front desk. I'll keep his card, though, just in case.

I have a sense of waiting. I don't know what for. It's as if I'm marking time, looking for some kind of permission to be given or a point to be reached to allow my feet to choose a path I can't yet see. The journey into darkness, the chance of a light. This isn't something I talk about at any of my sessions during those autumn weeks, but it's as real as if it's been carved on my skin, as real as the physical scars I carry. I can neither ignore it nor confront it. The rules I've made my life by are vanishing, and I don't know what may be left to replace them.

Most often, that knowledge keeps me awake at night, my skin as cold as loss. But sometimes it gives me a sense of standing in a city square with no borders and all around me a sense of space. Inviting, dangerous, unexplored.

Dominic, of course, doesn't stay in police custody for long. In a matter of days, he's granted bail and released on condition that he reports on a regular basis to the police. This small break in his routine is no balance against the misery caused to Starlight, Dancer, Bluesky, or Aqua or any of the hundreds of others. To him, the two things are not even comparable; he being rich and they being poor. When I think of that and all that he told me the night I nearly died, the nausea lurches up, and I have to stand, panting like a dog, over the sink until the sickness subsides again.

Still, riches can't help every situation. There will be a trial. I wonder how long it will be before he goes to court and how long the sentence will be. He'll have good lawyers, and even though the media have spent countless column inches telling us their outrage at the crime, the punishment will never be enough. I wonder what he thinks when he considers the rapid downhill track that DG Allen

Enterprises is on and when he might be free again to start another business. A man like that won't disappear into obscurity. It's not who he is. Finally, I wonder what this will do to his marriage and how much he might miss his children.

In the middle of November, at the start of one of the coldest nights I have known, he comes to see me.

When I open the door to him, I wonder if this after all is what I've been waiting for. Even so, for a blink of time, I don't recognize him—he's grown older, and his face, almost gaunt, has new lines. Still, despite myself, despite what I know, it's as if my blood is singing.

"Dominic," I say, before I can control myself.

He doesn't answer, and I gaze at him. Without glancing away, I reach out sideways until I feel the shape of the emergency cigarette packet on the hall table. I pull one free, pick up the lighter from the drawer, and offer him the cigarette. He almost drops it, so instead I take it, ease it into his mouth, and light it for him.

"Thank you," he says and stands there, unmoving, apart from the slight shake of his body.

Glancing beyond him, I see no one else. "Did you come on your own?"

"Yes."

"Where are you living now?"

He names a location on the eastern outskirts of the city, the sort of area he hasn't been used to for a long time. Maybe he sees my surprise because he almost smiles. "No money, Paul."

"What about your family?" I ask. "Do you see your children?"

"Yes, sometimes, when Cassie allows it. But not alone, never alone. Are you… Are you all right now? Your injuries, I mean?"

The night air gusts in between us like memory, and I shiver. "Yes, I'm fine. Thanks. Look, what do you want, Dominic?"

He hesitates, drops his cigarette on the step, and crushes it underfoot. "I want to talk to you."

"Don't you think you've said enough?"

"This is different."

I step to one side. "You can have ten minutes. No more."

"Thank you."

In the living room, he paces across the carpet, touching the wall, a chair, the mantelpiece. He runs his fingers along a line of books on the shelf, his movements jerky. I watch him from the doorway and wait until he turns to me.

"You won't believe me," he says, "but I'm sorry for what happened. For using you, threatening you. I didn't realize— No, that's no excuse for anything. There isn't an excuse. I'm sorry."

He's right. I don't believe him, but that isn't what I'm interested in.

"Why didn't you cut me loose?" I ask him. "Why didn't you let me and my family be destroyed? You said you would when that moment came. I was ready. In the end, I was ready. But you didn't do it."

He looks puzzled, as if it's an issue he's worried at himself over many days and weeks, but has been unable to turn up the answer. I can imagine how, in the middle of everything else going on, that must have angered him. He's always prided himself on knowing the answers.

"Why not?" I say.

"It's stupid, isn't it?" he says, almost smiling. "You can work out your life for so long. You can know exactly how you'll react to every situation you have to face, and make strategies to win and win again, until winning is your trade, nothing else. There's no room for mistakes or for pity. Only for success. And then something happens…something you don't expect, and there are no more strategies or action plans. At least, not ones that fit. Something comes free, Paul. It comes free, and it can't be put away again.

"When it came to it, I cut everyone adrift, everyone and everything I'd ever known, in order to try to save myself. My job, my company, my home, my friends—what there are of them—and my life. Even Cassie and…and my children." He passes one hand over his eyes, and I almost want to comfort him, maybe even touch him, but I can't move to do it. "Even my children. Henry, Judith. Everyone. Everyone, except you."

"Why not?" I ask again. "Why not me?"

"I wanted to, very much," he says, and, as always, his capacity for a kind of reality pierces me. "But when it came to it, I couldn't do it. Not to you. The truth is…the truth is I love you, you see. More than anything, more than myself. And I know…I know that nothing I can do will ever be enough for what I've done. Maloney's Law—I crucified it, didn't I? And you. But try to understand now that I love you, and for once in my life, I'm telling you the truth. And because of it, I want to ask you one question."

He stops then, and when he glances at me, his face is wet with tears. I have never seen him cry before.

"What question is that?" I ask.

"Maloney's Law," he whispers. "Please, Paul, do you think, one day, you can trust me again?"

In the silence, when I look at him, the path before me is clear and for the first time I'm not afraid.

"I'm sorry, Dominic," I say. "There are more laws than just one. Though you think what you're telling me is true, it's also true that friendship is more important than love. Jade taught me that. And you and I, we've never been friends."

CHAPTER 20

When the papers are gathered, I place them in the metal bin. It's large enough to take them all if I press them down. Then I lean back against my desk for a moment, wiping both hands upward over my face and through my hair. Four days, nineteen hours, and thirty-seven minutes have passed since Dominic and I parted, for the final time, I think. I hope. I hope. It's enough; it's time.

I remove the battery from the smoke alarm, take up the lighter I've brought from home, and flick the flame over the first layer of paper. It catches more easily than I'd imagined, and I watch the papers and photographs and print blacken and burn. After a minute, the fire is fierce, but it's contained. I'm not afraid.

When it's over, I replace the alarm battery, pour water over the ashes, take the empty folder that has for so long contained everything I have collected about Dominic, and bury it deep in the cabinet. One day I might use it again for some other case, but not yet. Still, I'm glad I've done this in the office. Fire has a cleansing property.

The day is not quite finished yet. I have one more duty to perform.

The Bell and Book is quiet tonight. Soon it will be December and then the end of the year, the beginning of the next. With it comes a chance to start again maybe…I don't know. All I know is the sense of waiting, of marking time, that's haunted me since Dominic was arrested has gone. All I'm left with is the open space and the possibilities of the journey to come.

I shake my head free of its thoughts. No time for philosophy. I'm here for a purpose and I should fulfill it. It's Monday night after all. 6:13 P.M.

At the bar, I order two drinks and pay with a fifty-pound note. It's all I've got. The barman sighs, shrugs, and scrabbles for change. I pocket the coins, but clutch the notes, carrying them and my order across to the table in the corner. Our usual. No…my usual now.

After putting down the drinks, I sit and open my wallet to put the notes in. As I do so, something drops to the floor. Something small. A white rectangle. I pick it up and see it's Craig's card, from my night in Soho one month and ten days ago. It's crumpled, but the print is still clear.

Smiling at the memory, I read it for the first time. Craig Robertson, it tells me. Professional Model and Actor. That makes sense. He was a good-looking bastard. Slim enough for it, too. I believe what it says as he didn't have the style of a hooker. Too straightforward, and he didn't ask for money. Not much of a job, but then again neither is mine.

I turn the card over. On the back is his home address, phone number, and mobile number, and, for a moment or two, I think about calling, but it's probably too late. He won't remember me; the young move on so quickly. Still, I don't throw it away. Instead, for reasons I can't explain, I bring the card briefly to my lips before slipping it into my back pocket and feeling the reassurance of its shape there.

Maybe, I think. Maybe. But not today. Not yet.

Right now, in the glittering, changeable present, I reach over the table, raise the glass of Chardonnay and smile.

"Happy birthday, Jade," I say. "Dazzle them in heaven."

Maloney's Law
Copyright © 2016 by Anne Brooke

Third edition
May 2016
With thanks to Amber Quill Press, where this novel was previously published.

About Anne Brooke

Anne has been writing contemporary fiction and fantasy for over twenty years. She is the bestselling author of gay thrillers *The Bones of Summer (Maloney *2)* and *A Dangerous Man,* both available at Amazon. Her websites can be found at www.annebrooke.com, www.gayreads.co.uk, www.gathandria.com (for fantasy fiction) and www.biblicalfiction.co.uk.

More Books from Anne Brooke

Anne's Amazon page: Author.to/AnneBrooke

Any questions or comments, please email:
annebrooke1993@gmail.com

One Last Thing ...

Reviews, however short, are a lifeline for independent authors such as myself, and so if you've enjoyed *Maloney's Law*, I would be very grateful if you could take a few seconds to let other readers know by leaving a review at Amazon. Thank you!
All the best
Anne Brooke

Printed in Great Britain
by Amazon

19698290R00219